Group Hug

ARIELLA TALIX

Group Hug

Ariella Talix

Copyright © 2024 Ariella Talix, all rights reserved.

Ringmaster Publishing

Cover Design by Dar Albert, Wicked Smart Designs

E-Book ISBN: 979-8-9856766-9-3

Paperback ISBN: 979-8-9895156-0-8

Hardcover ISBN: 9798871658123

You can never have too many books or too many hugs.
—Gina House

Everybody needs a hug. It changes your metabolism.
—Leo Buscaglia

My fashion philosophy is, if you're not covered in dog hair,
your life is empty.
—Elayne Boozler

One

TODAY IS THE DAY I'M GOING TO DO IT. NO MORE procrastination. I need a roommate, or I'll lose this house. And if I lose the house, I'm completely screwed. I've had months to myself to reorganize and heal my crushed heart.

My granddad willed the house to me free and clear, but I was forced to take out a mortgage on it. There are also the HOA dues, utilities, typical repairs, and taxes to pay. I could sell the place and make a killing, but I don't know where I'd go because everything is so damned expensive now. A house like this requires plenty of upkeep, and I sure can't manage it comfortably on my income alone right now. A roommate would be a big help.

"Man up," I mutter to myself as I hit "enter," posting my ad to the roommate finder app. The ad sounded good to my ears—like I'm fun but serious, clean but not obsessive… *Wait!* This isn't a dating app. What have I done? I should have talked more about square footage, bathrooms, a garage—that kind of thing. Instead, I added, "Must like dogs." Who does that? I want to grab the ad back and delete it. I want to restart.

…Actually, I just want to be happy again.

I push that thought to the back of my mind. I can't let myself go down that road again. It's time to shape up and move on.

Within minutes of my dithering about redoing the ad, my phone rings, and I have an appointment with some dude who wants to come to look at the place today. Honestly, he sounds pretty cool, but who knows? Then a minute later, a woman calls, so she's coming over too. I really just need to share the space with one other person, but maybe two would make it even better. I could save some money and not constantly feel like I'm just breaking even. Anyway, I schedule them for half an hour apart, so I'll see what I see. If anyone else contacts me, I'll have some decisions to make. No one else calls right away. Is that good? I dunno. Did I screw up the ad? What's normal? Two calls? Five? I know there are a lot of apartments around here that are for rent, but possibly not so many houses.

Fifteen minutes after the guy is supposed to be here, he knocks on the door. Okay, so punctuality isn't his strong suit. Maybe he needed to get gas on the way, or his grandmother called him, and he didn't want to cut her off. I'll keep an open mind.

"Hey," he says as I open the door. "Callum O'Malley." He extends a large hand that I grasp firmly, noting his excellent handshaking skills. My granddad always said you could tell a lot about a man who shakes hands well.

"Nice to meet you, Callum. I'm West… ah… Weston Alister." I try to keep my handshake firm without squeezing the daylights out of the guy, but I suddenly have the weirdest feeling of… good grief! I'm attracted to him! Where did *that* come from? And I don't even want to let go of his hand. Okay, so there were those couple of times I experimented with messing around in college, but I was a little high, and I thought I'd outgrown that phase. So I try to ignore his sexy blond scruff and thick head of hair. He's wearing a worn leather jacket over a goofy "Kiss the Cook" t-shirt that makes him positively adorable. Did I just think the word "adorable?"

He has a trim, muscular build, and he's a little taller than me. His eyes are soulful hazel and seem to be penetrating right through me. I clear my throat and ask, "Did you ah… have any trouble finding the place? I thought you might since you're a little late…"

He blinks at me like I have an extra head. "Um, no. I wasn't aware that there was a tight schedule for 'dropping by' to look at the house. Sorry. Must be my misunderstanding."

"Oh… ah, no. It's just that you're not the only candidate."

But just then, before I can ask him in, I hear a car door

slam and quick little footsteps coming up the front walkway. We both turn to see a petite woman marching with efficient strides up the bricks to the front door. Good lord. The woman is the most exquisite little creature I've ever seen. Boner alert! What the heck is going on today?

Callum steps closer to me and loudly announces the obvious, "I was here first!"

Geez, buddy. Desperate much?

The woman turns her enormous brown eyes in my direction and flips a lock of wavy auburn hair over her shoulder as she declares, "But I'm *desperate* for a place to live."

I guess there's a lot of that going around today.

"And," she continues, "I love dogs!"

With raised eyebrows, I regard Callum, and he immediately claims, "So do I!"

Shaking my head with a chuckle, I tell them, "Come on in, I'll give you the grand tour, and we can all get acquainted. Callum, I assume this is Petra Feeney. Petra, I'm Weston, and Callum here also needs a place to live."

"I can move right in!" she nearly shouts.

At the same time, he claims, "I'm a really good cook!"

This perks up my interest, so I ask, "How did you learn to cook?"

"My great-grandmother got me interested originally, but then I went to Vincennes University to study culinary arts."

Ah. I thought he might be a guy who'd be close with his granny, but *culinary school*? This could be amazing. "Really?"

My interest piques even more as I think about having someone around who likes to cook delicious meals. Or any meals at all if I'm being honest. I'm so hopeless in the kitchen, I've been known to screw up PB and J sandwiches. Friendly warning… They don't taste too good when made with rye bread, and lettuce doesn't "fancy" them up. I've been sticking to nuking hot dogs and canned soup a lot lately. My dwindling funds haven't encouraged a lot of take-out. Did I mention that I *really* need a roommate?

Bringing me out of my gastronomic reverie, Callum replies, "She did. I just had to be careful with some of the ingredients she tried to use. Nana was known for keeping things around past the expiration date. Part of why I asked her to show me how to cook was so I could investigate her fridge regularly. I'm sure I pissed her off a few times when I threw stuff away." He chuckles fondly. "But we all worried about her when she was left to her own devices too often. She would be proud to have inspired me to study culinary arts, I think. I'd hoped, even though I was just a kid, I could teach her a few things about food safety, but she was pretty set in her ways. Anyway, she's been gone now for several years."

Nodding sympathetically, I usher them in and indicate the living room, dining room, and kitchen on the ground floor. It's an open plan with a spacious hearth room connected to the kitchen. The half bath and laundry room are also off the kitchen. Then I lead them up the stairs. "The basement is finished. There's a large screen TV down there as well as a ping pong table and some other stuff," I tell them. "I'll show you that later."

It's a fairly typical four-bedroom, three-and-a-half-bath with a large sloping backyard that backs up to a shared green-space and a picturesque pond. The patio is a covered brick space off the lower level with a hot tub and an outdoor barbecue setup that I love. Living here in Carmel, Indiana, the climate is great for half the year, but winter can be darn cold. That's Carmel pronounced CAR-mul like the candy, not Car-MELL like the town in California. Tourists always get it wrong, but that's Indiana. We have more odd names, like French Lick and Gnaw Bone, and weird pronunciations of towns in this state than you can believe. My favorites are Versailles—which is pronounced Vur-SAILS—and Russiaville which is pronounced ROO-sha-ville. Those crazy Hoosiers. After the French settlers who founded the state all died off, I guess the residents didn't know how to say the names of the towns and just made up their own goofy shit.

Upstairs, two of the bedrooms are furnished with the basics—a double bed, end tables, a chest of drawers, and a small desk. As soon as he sees the first one, Callum exclaims, "This one would be great for me." It does look masculine, all done in tasteful blues, browns, and grays.

But geez, this guy seems anxious… or desperate.

The second one is roughly the same, but with a lighter color palette that includes some pastels. Petra announces, "I love this one. It's perfect."

Okay then.

The third bedroom across the hall houses my weights at one end and my desk at the other, so it's my gym and home office. Other than that stuff and a lumpy futon, it's pretty empty, though it has a bunch of books on the desk and stacked around on the floor. I explain to them, "I need a private place for video meetings. The desk faces the door so I can have the wall behind me for a backdrop." There is an attractive painting behind the desk that I hope makes people feel calm.

I had been feeling pretty good about the space, but seeing it through my potential roommates' eyes, the books look sloppy. "I guess I could use a bookshelf," I mutter half under my breath.

"What kind of work do you do?" Petra asks, bringing me out of my reverie about bookshelves.

"I'm a psychologist, but instead of office hours, I have video chats with clients." They both give me odd looks. Great. "Don't worry; I'm not in the habit of psychoanalyzing people unless they ask for it and pay me." Changing the subject, I direct them onward down the hall. I don't tell them my client list is far too short, and I need to do something about that. Now.

"If you guys take these rooms, you'd have to furnish your own linens and share the bathroom across the hall. Is that cool with you?" I eye them and see only eagerness on their faces.

They look at each other. Petra smiles and nods. "Fine with me," she assures us.

"Okay with me too as long as you aren't a mess." Callum gives Petra a teasing look.

"I'm not a messy person," she huffs. "I hope *you* can remember to put the toilet seat down."

Great. Are they already on each other's nerves, or was that his weak attempt at flirting? Did he just wink at her? I look closely, and she seems to be blushing faintly. This could get interesting.

I show them my bedroom and ensuite bath for good measure. It's definitely bigger and nicer by far, but hey—it's my house. I have room for my large king bed, a spacious sitting area, and a walk-in closet. I've always liked this room, especially now that I have my own stuff in it. I used to live in my office/gym room. Before.

"Let's go see the backyard, and I'll introduce you to the guys." They both eye me curiously. "The dogs are back there. They're also house dogs, so I hope that's okay with you."

"Uh… about that…" Petra hedges.

"I thought you loved dogs." I challenge her, probably with more vehemence than is necessary.

"I do! I just wonder how you feel about adding one more to the mix. He's really a sweetie, and he's out in the car."

"Well don't leave your dog in a cold car. Go get him and we'll see how everyone gets along." I'm shaking my head in my mind. Poor dog. At least it's not snowing anymore, but you never know about early spring in Indiana.

"I'm sure he's fine. He has a heavy coat," she retorts. "I'll go get him now." Turning and muttering something that sounds like "I hope he hasn't chewed up anything in the car," she runs down the stairs and out the front door. I watch Callum as we follow her downstairs, and I don't detect anything but interest in his gaze. I guess he really is okay with dogs. And women. Obviously, I need to get my attraction to him under control.

In less than a minute, Petra is dragged through the door behind a smiling, drooling, and completely enormous golden retriever. I swear the dog might outweigh Petra. The dog's tail is wagging so hard, his whole butt is in motion. His friendliness is contagious, and I drop to my knees to greet him as Petra announces, "This is Gus. He's kinda… well *really* new. I recently found him at the animal shelter, and I had to get him out of there before…"

Instantly I feel a yank on my heartstrings as this sweet dog looks into my eyes. "I get it, Petra."

Petra starts speaking again with a hitch in her voice. "I had to get him out of there because the shelter is so overcrowded. When I saw your ad saying 'must love dogs,' it seemed like a sign from heaven. He wasn't microchipped, and calls to local vets and the golden retriever rescue groups haven't turned up any leads as to his owner, so I wonder if he was dropped off when someone decided they couldn't handle him. Poor guy. He is as sweet a dog as I've ever known."

"Some people," Callum mutters, "can be so clueless. He's a beautiful dog." He reaches out to pet Gus, and the happy dog looks at him like he hung the moon and then sits on his feet. Callum bursts out laughing and says, "You know how everyone always says, 'He must smell my dog on me'? I don't currently have a dog, so Gus must think I smell like something delicious since I work with food."

Petra looks at me. "Should we introduce Gus to your dogs now? He's friendly and plays well with others." At that moment the pleading look in her eyes matches the way Gus is looking at Callum. With hunger.

"Sure. Let's do it. We shouldn't have any trouble with my guys." I lead them all out back where my two are sound asleep, snuggled together on the patio furniture. "As you can see, they're amazing watchdogs. The black Lab is Goliath." We watch as he jumps down off the settee and stretches, then wanders over to Gus and immediately drops into the classic "Let's play!" pose—front legs bowing to him, butt in the air, with the tail wagging a million miles an hour. Goliath is followed by my bossy little mini Aussie who constantly wants to herd everyone together. He quickly runs laps around us, yipping the whole time. "Clearly, Dave thinks he's the top dog," I say with a laugh.

"Dave and Goliath?" Callum asks with an amused look.

"Yes." I nod and smile. "I always rooted for the underdog when I was a kid. I didn't name Goliath, so I just went with it and named Dave accordingly."

A burst of pain shoots through my heart at that thought, but I try to cover it with a smile. The truth is, Goliath seemed so pitifully sad after our loss, I wanted to get him a companion, and our vet told me about a family that was being transferred out of the country for an indeterminate amount of time. They had a young mini Aussie named Smoochie. They wanted to place him in a home with at least one other dog because they were worried that moving halfway around the world would be too stressful for a young dog, and they didn't know what kind of living arrangements they would encounter. It's worked out well having him. He made sure Goliath and I got off our butts and moved around during the day when all we wanted to do was wallow in our grief. I couldn't bring myself to call the dog Smoochie, so I quickly got him adjusted to being called Dave. Note to self… if I ever have kids, do not let them name a pet when they are five years old.

But I don't lay all of this on my prospective roommates.

Petra has already dropped to her knees and is now accepting hugs and kisses from Goliath, but soon Dave nudges his way in to take over. Petra looks so comfortable around the three dogs. Apparently, the dogs all plan to get along famously too—just as long as the people pay enough attention to them.

"You'll want to get Gus an invisible fence collar. The HOA restrictions don't allow any backyard fences to destroy the view of the pond. If he's smart, he'll pay attention to how far from the house the other dogs go. Dave will herd him back to the house if he messes up anyway. He's pretty bossy that way. The fact that he's only about a third their size won't even occur to him."

"What kind of dog is that?" Callum asks, pointing at Dave.

"He's a miniature American shepherd, also known as a mini Aussie. They don't come from Australia, though, despite the nickname. The breed was developed right here in the U.S."

"What happened to his tail?"

"Most of them are born like this with a naturally docked tail."

Petra speaks up and says, "I love all the colors in his coat. He's so pretty." She runs her hands through his silky coat and coos at him, "You're a handsome boy, yes you are!" Dave is clearly eating up the attention, and I suddenly realize how much I would enjoy that same attentiveness from her.

After seeing that the dogs are all happy together, we head into the house where the three pups flop down on the living room carpet. We then go over the lease agreement and determine that Callum and Petra are both gainfully employed full-time. They fill out some standard forms for me that I'd downloaded and write me a couple of checks that clear immediately on my phone banking app. We decide to split the grocery costs three ways, except that Petra and I will take care of our own dog food. Having some money in the bank is such a relief.

Throughout the time that I walked them through the house and talked about the rent, my phone buzzed in my pocket with maybe a dozen more calls. I ignored each one, figuring they'd leave a voicemail; I thought it would be rude to accept calls from other prospective renters while we were clearly all getting along well. As expected, ten of them left messages, and I know I have to respond to them at least by text to let them know the house was rented. While Petra and Callum filled out the paperwork, I took down the ad from the site. This whole process was exceptionally easy, and I'm feeling confident I don't have to look any further. I have a very good feeling about these two people.

"I'm looking forward to having you both move in," I tell them happily. I'm so relieved.

"I'll be back tomorrow morning with my stuff. And I wouldn't mind doing the grocery shopping," Callum tells us. "I actually like it."

"That would be fantastic!" I say. "I'm fairly hopeless concerning food except for eating it." That brings a smile their faces, and then we have a discussion of our favorite foods and give Callum an idea of things we don't like as well. We're all pretty adventurous it appears, and I take that as a good sign. Callum looks jazzed about doing the cooking. Luckily, no one has any serious peanut or shellfish allergies or anything like that. And we all agree that pizza and pineapple do *not* belong together.

"We'll have to rearrange a few things in the garage so all three cars fit, so maybe you can both help me with that in the morning. It's not a lot of stuff—just a few things that need to be stored better. I was only planning on one extra car, but the HOA doesn't like cars parked all the time on the street or driveway, and I'm sure you'll both like your cars to be inside, especially when it snows."

Petra nods in agreement and Callum says, "Sounds great." He reaches for my hand to shake, saying, "See you in the morning."

Once again, I notice how good his hand feels in mine, and give it an extra little squeeze. I swear his eyes light up at that. Finally, I can't resist and say, "Nice shirt, by the way. Now I get it."

Callum laughs good-naturedly and explains, "My sister gave this to me for my birthday. I don't actually wear it very often, but everything I own was in the dryer when I left the house."

Thinking that I wouldn't mind kissing the cook at all, I give him a house key, he says thanks, and I'm left with Petra.

"When can you move in?" I ask her.

"Uh… now?"

I laugh at her eagerness. "Then let's go get your car parked in the garage and bring in your stuff." She looks so relieved, I have to ask, "Were you on super-bad terms with your former roommate or something?"

Rolling her eyes, she answers, "You have no idea. She practically tossed me out this morning and told me she was changing the locks and having professional cleaners come to get rid of the dog hair. It didn't matter to her that I vacuumed every day."

"Charming."

As we stow the final boxes into Petra's new bedroom, she tells me, "I'm so glad to be out of my former apartment.

Fortunately, I didn't have to live there very long. She hated it when I brought Gus home because he barked a couple of times, and she came unglued about it."

I shrug and say, "Dogs bark. It's a fact of life. If it gets too bad, though, we'll work together to do some corrective training. We'll manage it." I haven't heard a peep out of Gus so far, so he doesn't seem like a big barker to me. "So, what kind of work hours do you keep? You said you work from home, right?"

"Yes. I try to keep the hours between nine and five, but I'm flexible. Working as a ghostwriter, sometimes I have phone calls at odd hours, but mostly I call the shots. Once in a while, I work late at night if I want to take the day off for some reason. It's a pretty great gig."

"That's interesting. I'll leave you to unpack now, but I'd love to hear more about that sometime." She smiles and nods, looking at her pile of boxes and suitcases. I turn to leave, but then remember something. Facing her once again, I say, "We'll need to get Gus an electric collar as soon as possible and have it set to the fence's code. They're expensive, but unless you trust him to never wander off, having one is essential."

Sighing, she asks, "Can you show me where to order one online? I don't even know him well enough to know if he's a wanderer. We'd better get him one."

"If you like, I can go pick it up for you. The company isn't too far away, and that's going to be a lot quicker than waiting to have someone send it to you. I can even take Gus along so they can fit it for his neck properly."

"You'd go to that trouble for Gus and me?"

"I don't want to worry about him, and he'll need to be able to play outside with the other dogs. I'm happy to. I also need to have an extra key made because I was only planning on one extra person, so I can do that at the same time. You can just write me another check when we get back since I don't know the exact cost."

Petra agrees and locates a leash for me, and Gus and I set out to take care of his business. Dave and Goliath look at me like a traitor when I leave the house with this interloper. "I'll be back soon, guys," I tell them. "Go keep Petra company while she's unpacking."

Two

PETRA

I AM SO HAPPY TO BE MOVING AWAY FROM MY PREVIOUS situation. I never should have moved into that apartment, but I had to find something quickly—not unlike this time, unfortunately. I hope I haven't been too hasty. I have to wonder what it will be like to live with *two* men—two gorgeous men, if I'm honest—but it's a done deal now.

Seriously, though—wow are they attractive. One of them has already offered to do the grocery shopping and cooking, and the other is stepping up to run errands for me. I'll need to keep a lid on my heart—or libido—with these guys around all the time. I need to be focused on work. I'm a little behind with a major deadline looming, but I had to get my living situation under control. At least Gus seems to adapt well to new situations, and he seems happy to be here. I'm so relieved to have that dog for company.

I'm just putting my last things away when I hear Weston and Gus barreling up the stairs. Weston lets out a great booming laugh, so I take that to mean that he and Gus have been hitting it off. I'm not surprised. Gus is a great dog, despite what my previous roommate had to say about him.

My door is open, and Gus bounds in and jumps onto my bed where he nearly crashes into Dave and Goliath. They'd already taken up residence after I'd made the bed up with fresh sheets. Someone who *didn't* love dogs would be miserable in this house, for sure.

Weston laughs and says, "He sure has a lot of energy. He's a good boy, though." He hands me a receipt for the collar and the key to the house.

"Thank you so much for doing that for us, Weston. Can I treat you to dinner later?"

"Um, well, sure. Take-out or go out?"

"Let's do take-out. I'm a little too frazzled to go out." So we discuss menus and discover we both have a huge craving for Mexican food. Apparently, there are fixings for margaritas and plenty of beer in the house already.

I hope this guy isn't too good to be true. Loves dogs, has a trusting and kind heart, and enjoys tacos. My kind of guy. And did I mention handsome? Lordy. His wavy brown hair almost reaches his shoulders and looks like silk. And those eyes of his! I could dive into them. Bright and intelligent, they're the color of rich coffee, sparkling with happiness most of the time. Sometimes, though, I detect a melancholy he might be trying to disguise. It's not my business to pry, I remind myself.

He has a muscular—but not bulky—build, and is pretty tall, though not quite as tall as Callum. But everyone looks tall to me—I'm such a shrimp. It's his smile, though, that really knocks me out. He smiles like he has a secret or a joke playing in his head, and his expression is just the right mix of cocky and amused. With dimples. Gah! I'm already almost a goner, and I barely know this guy.

And then there's Callum… ye gods! A blond Adonis who looks like a cute nerd and cooks? I hope to hell he doesn't turn out to be gay. Oh, who am I kidding? That might be the best thing. I don't need to be falling for my new housemate *or* my landlord. In fact, the gay thing might really be on the table. I thought I detected some kind of spark between the two of them when they were shaking hands…

None of my business, I scold myself. Anyway… we'll see.

"I'll call for the delivery," Weston tells me, pulling me out of my lust-filled and very inappropriate reverie. "Then I'll get started on a pitcher of margaritas as soon as the dogs are fed." Did he just wink at me? Oh my. There go those dimples again. Where's that margarita?

After he makes the call, I follow him downstairs, and we take care of the dogs. When they're done, we put a spiffy new green collar on Gus and head outside with them. The dogs do a lot of sniffing around, and Gus seems delighted to be off his leash for once. He stays with the other two and never once tries to bolt, although they all three get close to the apparent fence and return inward immediately.

"He's already been trained to an electric fence, I see," Weston says with a thoughtful nod. "I hope there isn't some family with little kids who are missing the heck out of him right now. He's a great dog, just like you said."

"Yeah, well, I've done everything I can think of to find them if they exist, and I came up with a big, fat nothing. All the people at the shelter knew was that a man dropped him off saying he found the dog in his yard, and he hadn't been wearing any kind of collar."

I'm so attached to Gus at this point, it might break my heart to have to give him back to anyone. The idea makes my stomach hurt.

We lead the dogs inside again where they flop down with each other to sleep off their dinner.

Soon we hear the doorbell, so we go grab our dinner and bring it into the kitchen nook to eat. "This is the life," I sigh. "I think I'm going to love it here." We arrange ourselves so that we're side-by-side facing the view of the property and pond. It's a beautiful evening.

Weston gives me a dimpled smile and a wink, and I feel flutters.

We then proceed to stuff ourselves with an assortment of carne asada and pollo asado tacos and a generous portion of guacamole and chips. Weston politely keeps my glass filled from the pitcher of margaritas he made. I'm getting a definite buzz from the tequila, and it makes me feel mellow. "I haven't felt this relaxed in days," I sigh. "Maybe weeks, if I'm honest."

"Feel like watching a movie when we're done?" Weston asks. "I forgot to show you the setup downstairs. We can get something from Netflix if you like."

"Sure. Sounds great." I wonder what kind of movies he likes. "Just nothing scary, please."

Weston gives me a look that says he's about to call me a chicken and then thinks better of it. I don't want to get into why I avoid scary stuff, but it would not be my first—or fiftieth—choice for entertainment. We then have a discussion about our favorite movies and decide to watch *Forrest Gump* after a spirited debate about the pros and cons of the book vs. the movie. I'm privately impressed that Weston seems to be an enthusiastic reader of a variety of genres. I'd love to ask him if he's read any of the novels I've worked on, but I'm sworn to secrecy about what I've ghostwritten, and the corporate work wouldn't be anything he'd seen. Maybe I can work it into the conversation without being obvious. Or not. I'm possibly looking for trouble if I do that.

Three

I'M SO GLAD TO BE MOVING TO CARMEL. MY NEW JOB ISN'T far from Weston's house, which is a heck of a lot better than my current hour-long commute from my parents' house in Crawfordsville. Besides, it's high time to move out now that my job is squared away. What a relief. I won't be sharing with my little brother Declan in a half-messy room that smells like gym socks all the time. I keep telling him to do his damn laundry, but he ignores me. I hope he figures it out before he heads to college next fall. Anyway, it was nice of my parents to let me move back in after graduation for a while until I found a steady job. And I love my job! I cook and teach classes three days a week and sell kitchen supplies the rest of the time. I have a lot of freedom with what I teach, as long as I stick to their general plan. I won't get rich this way, but it's giving me great experience, and it'll help me eventually move up to something more lucrative. I hope to eventually have my own restaurant, but that's years away.

During the drive back to Crawfordsville, I stop and buy towels and sheets, and the whole time, I think about how fortunate it was that I noticed the alert on my phone for a new Carmel rental. The apartments I've looked at wouldn't have been nearly as much fun as sharing a house with those two. Now I'll have two people I can test out recipes on, and they have terrific dogs. I think this is going to be fun. I need to keep my attraction for *both* of them under wraps, though.

If Weston is a psychologist, I wonder if he likes to be called Dr. Alister. That's kinda hot. I wonder how he managed to buy that house at his age. It's not a huge house, but it's a really great property, and it's in a fairly expensive neighborhood. Maybe he's really, really good at his job. His vibe makes you want to open up to him, so I can imagine how his clients—or are they patients? Whatever. —How his people like talking to him about their troubles and worries.

As for Petra Feeney… Hmm. Our Petra seems to be wound a little tight. She sure is pretty, though. She looks like a china doll with that porcelain skin, kissable, pouty lips, and big brown eyes. That almost-red hair of hers is stunning, and her tight little body just begs to be… oh I have to stop thinking about her that way. We can't turn our living situation into some kind of orgy, although a guy can dream. I can't help chuckling to myself at that idea. It's time to focus on my job, not getting laid. And certainly not where I could mess up our living situation.

As soon as I get to my mom and dad's house, I start packing up all of my crap. I'm sure my brother will be thrilled to have the rest of his bedroom back—at least until he leaves for college. As much as I love Declan, I'm sure glad to be leaving his dirty laundry smell behind.

While packing, possible menus run through my head. I can't spend a fortune on groceries since I'll be sharing the cost with the others, and I'm not sure about their budgets yet, but I want to knock their socks off with my skills. And maybe not just cooking skills, if I'm honest. Geez, there I go again—fantasizing about things I ought to ignore. Maybe I should find a place to live where I won't feel so tempted. Too late now, though. I've signed a lease.

I can't deny that during college I was kind of a player, and I sampled everything that was offered. I practiced safe sex, but lots and lots of it. Good times. I thought maybe I'd figure out what I preferred if I tried both men and women, but more and more I realized I craved both equally. It was a very liberating discovery. I finally discussed it with my family, and they were cool about it. They didn't seem at all surprised, so I wonder what clues I gave. Anyway… doesn't matter. I am what I am.

As I watch the pile of junk I'm taking grow, it occurs to me that I ought to be starting a second pile I can drop off at one of the charity places. I don't need a lot of this crap. I just need my clothes, linens, the cooking equipment I have here at the house, and a few items for entertainment and communication. This whole process of having a great job, moving, and purging my junk makes me feel like a new man who's ready for a new adventure. Look out, world! Callum O'Malley is coming!

I bet my parents will be even more relieved than my brother when they see me move out on my own finally. I'm anxious to tell them as soon as they get home from work.

Four

"So how did you wind up getting Gus from a shelter, Petra?" I ask as I grab another excellent taco. I'm surprised when her face colors, and she suddenly seems at a loss for words. We've been having a comfortable conversation up until now, but it's as if the light has gone out of her pretty eyes. Strange.

With her eyes fixed firmly on her plate, Petra answers in a small voice, "I just… felt like I needed a dog. Like that would… um… help. Maybe."

I lean in. "Help what? Were you lonely? Scared? Wanting to get more exercise and thought taking a dog for a walk would fill the bill?" She looks miserable, so I ask, "What am I missing here?" She carefully sets her half-eaten taco onto her plate and puts her hands in her lap and twists her napkin. She hasn't met my eyes yet, so I prompt, "I'm like a vault, you know. If there's something you want to get off your chest, I listen to people for a living. I don't mean to pry though, so if I'm overstepping, just tell me to back off."

Taking a deep breath, she finally raises her eyes to mine, and the depth of worry and perhaps a shadow of fear I see in them rattles me. "A couple of reasons really. First, I've always wanted a dog, and I was especially lonely after breaking up with my fiancé," she finally blurts out in a sad voice. "But also, he had this friend."

She swallows hard, and I feel my protective hackles rising. "Did he hurt you?" I rasp.

"No, he didn't..." Petra starts. "But he was strange. Obnoxious. And I did worry, I'll admit, that I wasn't completely safe. I wanted a dog around for possible protection, although I think Gus might just lick anyone who got near me." She laughs a little at this idea. "And the worst damage he'd do is leave a bunch of hair on someone's clothes. I don't know if he has a protective bone in his body. When I started looking, I was focused on a pitbull, or a German shepherd. But then I found Gus, and it was love at first sight. I couldn't just leave him there and find a more ferocious-looking dog when I might not even really need protection." She lets out a huge sigh. "Oh, I don't know. I just knew that Gus needed a home and someone to take care of him." She smiles sadly and adds, "Plus, he looked at me with that face."

I can't help it. I reach out and take one of her hands. "Gus might surprise you. Even the mildest mannered dogs can sense when there's danger. And I think it's great that you found him. He's lovable and great company, and I bet you need that more than a watchdog. But… now you have three of them—not that any of them seem aggressive—and you have me. And Callum. We'll all do what we can to watch out for your safety." Although I hope there isn't any real danger involved in this scenario, I like the feel of her hand in mine, and I can't help myself from stroking her with my thumb. I'm telling myself that it's me offering comfort, but I'm taking as much pleasure from the feel of her as I'm soothing her, I'm sure.

Petra doesn't remove her hand. She just looks at it for a moment and offers a small smile. "Thank you, Weston. I could use some reassurance that I'm safe. Living here with you, Callum, and the dogs feels really good to me."

"Do you want to elaborate on that?"

She seems to have given up on her dinner for the time being, so I continue to stroke her hand softly. She sits up straight and answers, "I was engaged to be married, and I was living with my boyfriend Ben up until about four months ago. We were planning to save up and get married in two years. We weren't in a big hurry, and we wanted to be practical. But Ben had this creepy old friend from high school named Randy, who started showing up at our place at weird times and often seemed to be high or something. Ben spent more and more time with Randy, and when I was around, Randy always looked at me like I was a piece of meat. He gave off the strangest vibe, but he never did it in front of my fiancé. In fact, when we were all three together, he'd mostly ignore me." She lets out a long sigh. "Over and over, all that had to happen was that Ben might get up to go to the kitchen or the bathroom, and in those few minutes, I would be treated to sexual innuendo, and Randy would tell me to 'dump the loser and try out a real man.'" She makes air quotes with her fingers, and I'm sorry to lose contact with her hand. "At first, I laughed it off figuring he was teasing, but when he wouldn't stop, I told him to knock it off. But it went on and on, and Randy became bolder and would try to touch me.

"When that started, I tried telling Ben about it, but he wouldn't believe his buddy would act like that. It totally pissed me off that he didn't believe me, and I tried to tell Ben his so-called friend had nothing good to say about him and insulted him behind his back, but he didn't believe that either. I have no idea why I turned into the one who was supposedly lying, but I'd also noticed a change in behavior in Ben, like maybe they were both getting high and trying to hide it from me. He knew my feelings about that, and it was just another nail in the coffin for our relationship.

"Finally, Randy became so bold and nasty, he'd do things like grab me by the hair or my boob and curse in my face, accusing me of thinking I was too good for him. He tried to get my attention once when I walked away from him and grabbed me so hard, he left bruises on my arm that I showed Ben. Ben refused to believe me no matter what, and said I was just clumsy. I felt like I had no choice; I broke off our engagement and moved out. I heard from a friend a couple of months later that Ben stopped going to work and got fired from his job." She shakes her head sadly. "Randy was such a bad influence on him. He went from a nice, upstanding, hard-working guy to a loser, just like Randy characterized him. Ben has some trust fund money and won't end up starving, but he is far from wealthy, and certainly ought to be working to support himself. I just wonder how Randy managed to get to change his behavior so badly." She looks heartbroken as she says, "I was devastated to watch someone who professed to love me disintegrate before my eyes and accuse me of lying. It was horrible."

"Wow. I'm awfully sorry to hear this. Life can certainly deal us some blows, can't it? Have you heard any more from either Ben or Randy after that?"

"Not Ben, but Randy showed up at my apartment one day and tried to talk me into letting him in. He acted so sure I'd be happy to see him and said we were lucky I broke up with 'that pussy Ben' so we could be together." She gives a shudder. "I absolutely refused to talk to him beyond telling him to leave, but then after that, I started having some awful things left on the doorstep. Of course, it's not certain they came from him, but it's a possibility that he felt rejected and wanted to retaliate. He certainly has the personality to come up with something gross like that."

I am curious about the disgusting doorstep presents, but I don't want to push her too hard, so I ask instead, "You tried to have Gus in an apartment? I can imagine how well that went."

"Yeah. Not well. I had to take him out on a leash several times a day, but he needed a lot more exercise than I had the time to devote to him. That's one of the reasons a house with a yard and at least one other dog sounded so great to me. He already seems calmer, and it's the first day. Anyway, my roommate got all upset a few times when Gus would start randomly barking in the middle of the night for no apparent reason. That's when she told me I needed to leave. The last time it happened was two nights ago, and the next morning there was a dead bird on the doorstep. It might have been left by a neighbor's cat, or it could have been something else. I planned to clean it up and not tell her, but she caught me in the act and was pretty grossed out."

"If it was Ben or Randy, how did they know where you lived?"

"I stupidly gave the forwarding address to my ex, thinking something important might show up in the mail or something. I now use a PO box for all of my business dealings. I doubt he'd have bothered to forward anything anyway, so it was a dumb move on my part. If it's not him, Ben could easily have left my address lying around for Randy to see. I don't know for sure, but I think they live together now." She gives a small snort. "Maybe that's what Randy wanted all along—a place to live. I was so stupid."

"It sounds more trusting than stupid to me. I'm sure you loved Ben at some point, so you had to have trusted him."

Petra shrugs. "I guess. In retrospect, I wonder if I did love him or if I just wanted to be engaged to someone because it seemed like the time to do that. As I said, I wasn't in any big rush to tie the knot with him. That can't be good. And I'm awfully glad to be rid of him. I should have felt some regret, shouldn't I? I mean other than missing regular sex?" She gasps as her face goes beet red, and she blurts out, "I can't believe I just said that. Please erase it from your mind."

I smile and answer, "Done. But Petra, there's no right or wrong in this kind of situation. Feelings aren't correct or incorrect; they just are what they are. The important thing is to learn from them and grow. Maybe next time you'll keep your eyes open better before you get involved."

"Listen to you being all psychologicalistical," she says with a teasing look.

"Says the person who uses words for a living. That's a new one. Feeling a little buzzed?" I nod toward her margarita. We both laugh and finish our tacos.

As soon as we're done, we clean up and head downstairs to watch the movie. I know I'm feeling pretty mellow after the margaritas we drank, so it feels good to let the dogs out and flop down on the big, cushy sofa with Petra. I've always loved this movie, but I tend to forget the great music it has in it too.

We laugh together as we both recite lines with the actors for a while.

"Want another drink?" I ask. "I can run up and grab some more."

Petra rolls her eyes. "I've had enough, but thanks." Then she laughs as we see three doggie faces staring at us through the sliding glass door at the back of the room.

I get up and let them in, closing the drapes behind them, and of course, all three dogs come barreling to the sofa and take up residence on either end. Gus lands his head in Petra's lap, and my two dogs spread out next to where I was sitting. I'm barely left with any room in the middle with Petra. Not that I mind.

"Sorry," I mumble as I shift Goliath over a little. It's a tight squeeze, but Petra doesn't complain. I'll have to remember extra dog treats at bedtime, I think, as I mentally fist pump.

Petra's eyes seem to droop toward the end of the movie, so I slide an arm around her and bring her toward my chest —telling myself that I'm just being friendly. *Yeah right.* She lets out a little sigh, and her whole body relaxes into mine. Wow, does this ever feel good. Her gorgeous hair smells like flowers—or maybe it's coconut. Either way, I try not to be conspicuous about sniffing her to decide. It's been a long time since I've either held anyone or been this attracted. But Petra has been through a lot, and she deserves to feel safe in her home. I'll have to watch my step and make sure I don't put my attraction ahead of her comfort.

It's so warm and cozy surrounded by dogs and Petra, I find myself nodding off too. It's not until Petra lets out a long whimper and begins to tremble that I wake up and realize it's hours past midnight. I can't stop myself from kissing the top of her head and giving her a gentle squeeze. "Petra," I whisper, "we need to get up and go to bed. It's really late."

She jolts awake and sits straight up with a confused look. She looks at Gus and then at me with questions in her eyes and then visibly relaxes. "Oh, Weston. I'm sorry I fell asleep on you. I guess everything just hit me all at once."

"No apology necessary."

"Hmm, you say so." She snorts a little. "But I think I drooled on your shirt."

I look down and see a definite wet spot. Shrugging, I assure her, "No harm done, but we need to hit our beds so we're not all stiff tomorrow from sleeping sitting up." I can hear the sound of some distant thunder, so I pull out my phone to check the weather map. "Looks like a storm is blowing in, but there aren't any tornado warnings. We don't need to stay down here."

We all trek up two flights of stairs and head to our rooms. I feel this sudden need to give Petra a kiss but decide it would be completely inappropriate, so instead I tell her goodnight and lead Dave and Goliath into my bedroom. She mumbles something and closes her door. She looks beat.

However, about twenty minutes later, the thunder has rolled into our neighborhood, and it's deafening. My dogs are fortunately unaffected by it, but I worry about how Gus is handling it. I wonder whether I ought to check on Petra when I hear a light knock on my door. "Come in," I call out over the sound of the storm. It must be hailing because it's loud out there.

"Weston? I'm so sorry to bother you," she says sheepishly. Petra walks into my room, closely followed by Gus, who is panting a little, but mostly looks like his normal, happy self. So he's not the problem. "I feel so silly asking, but… I'm kind of scared to stay in my room," she tells me. "The wind is blowing a tree limb into the house, and it keeps banging really hard on my window. I'm afraid it's going to shatter the glass."

"Do you want to stay in here with me? I'll do something about the tree in the morning, but it's way too late to do much of anything else right now. The other options would be for you to take a blanket and sleep on the basement couch or on the uncomfortable futon in my office," It's dark, but I can clearly see that Petra is wearing a tank top and some sleeping shorts, both of which hug her body beautifully. "I promise to be a gentleman, and there is plenty of room in this bed."

Petra only answers, "Thanks," and she is crawling under the covers before I can even finish my statement about not groping her. Gus also hops up and curls himself into a big hairy ball at her feet. "Night, Weston," she murmurs as she turns onto her side facing away from me. At least my dogs have their own beds; it would feel like a mob scene if all five of us tried to sleep here. I'm certainly not lonely, though—that's for sure.

The thunder begins to peter out gradually, but now I can definitely hear the tree hitting the house, just as she'd said. That one's going to be a pain to fix, but as Petra lets out a little sigh of contentment, I can't find it in me to be annoyed.

Five

Callum

I'm so excited about my new place to live, I'm up by six and ready to go in no time since I'd already put most of my stuff into my car last night. I give my parents a hug on my way out the door. We're all early birds in this house, so seeing them up at this hour makes sense. They wish me well, and I'm outta there after promising to come home to see them a lot.

This almost feels even better than when I headed off to college. It's like a whole new chapter of my life is beginning this morning but without the fear. I'm hungry, though. On the way to Carmel, I decide to stop and pick up some essentials for breakfast at least. Maybe I can surprise everyone with a nice meal.

Traffic is light, and the market is nearly deserted as I fill up the cart with fresh fruit, eggs, and the fixings for omelets, waffles, and a few other things I have brewing in my head. I wonder briefly if Weston has a waffle iron, but then decide that if he doesn't, I'll just make pancakes or scones instead. I'll have to get one for the future; Sunday brunch isn't the same without a Belgian waffle covered with fresh berries.

By the time I get to the house, I'm so hungry, I decide to make breakfast before unloading anything out of my car. There's a sizeable branch that blew down last night and is taking up some of the driveway, so I get out and drag it out of the way. I guess we're going to have to do some serious yard cleanup today after that wild storm we had last night. It's kind of a mess. Typical Indiana springtime storm.

I haul in the groceries, happy to have my own key, and get to work putting everything away and getting organized to cook. In perusing the cupboards, I'm delighted to find a vintage waffle iron with a cord that makes me wonder if it's older than I am. But it seems to be in good shape—no fraying wires or anything—so I decide to take a chance. The house is quiet; it seems pretty obvious that everyone, including the dogs, is still asleep. It is Sunday morning, after all.

I get the waffle batter ready and prepare the eggs and fillings for the omelets. I make some bacon and brew a pot of coffee, and I make sure the table in the breakfast nook has everything on it we need. I'd considered squeezing orange juice, but the bottled stuff is good enough if you get the right kind, especially if you're making mimosas, so I skip that step. Eventually, I'm all ready to go except for the final last-minute cooking and decide it's time to go wake up the household. I hope they're not upset with me, but it's almost nine a.m. now, and I'm starved.

As I get to the top of the stairs, I hear voices and a feminine laugh. Petra then opens the door to Weston's bedroom and steps out with a huge smile on her face. She sees me and jumps about a foot in the air, clutching her chest. Gus barrels around her, all smiley and wagging his tail a hundred miles an hour. He comes right up to me and sits on my feet. I am so shocked, I don't know what to say, but the words, "Wow, it didn't take you guys long!" pop unbidden out of my mouth before my brain catches up to the idea that what they choose to do in bed is none of my business. Petra is wearing the tiniest speck of sleepwear I've ever seen—certainly nothing I'd ever refer to as pajamas. They leave nothing to the imagination, and I can't stop staring at her.

Weston quickly appears behind Petra, and his glorious broad chest is on full display, as all he is wearing is a pair of low-slung pajama bottoms. He's beautifully ripped and obviously takes care of himself. My eyes shift to him, and I take in the sight greedily. I can't stop myself. A rush of profound jealousy courses through me as I acknowledge how striking they are together, but I don't even know who I'm jealous of.

Weston interrupts my confused thoughts by saying, "You have the wrong idea, Callum. Not that we need to defend ourselves, but this looks a lot more suggestive than it was." His voice is raspy from sleep, and it only makes him sexier. Then he tacks on a comment that makes me wonder what on earth he means. "I'll need you to help me fix a tree today."

Not knowing what else to say, I tell them, "Breakfast will be ready in ten minutes." And I spin around to head back to the kitchen. What is wrong with me? Why does my chest hurt like this?

Behind me, Weston asks in a groggy voice, "Would you mind letting the dogs out? I need to take a piss, and I bet Petra would like to put some clothes on. And thanks for breakfast. We'll be right down."

He says "we" like they're already a couple or something, and I've never felt so left out. At least the dogs all seem to like me; they beat me down the stairs in a mad rush to the kitchen door. Tails are wagging—well, except for tailless Dave, who makes up for it by hopping up and down. And their happy faces greet me eagerly as they wait for me to let them out.

Ten minutes later, I'm dishing up freshly made waffles and plating omelets as Petra and Weston wander into the kitchen, still looking sleepy. I don't want to think of why they didn't get much sleep.

"Oh my God, Callum," Petra exclaims. "This looks amazing! You went to a lot of trouble for us." She comes up behind me and hugs me. The feel of her almost makes me feel a little better, but then I hope it isn't some kind of a consolation hug for the loser in the room.

"Wow, thanks, Callum!" Weston says with a brilliant smile as I hand him his plated omelet. His big brown eyes look to be full of amusement and happiness, but then he gives me a wink that makes my insides melt. He's so cocky; he came to breakfast in jeans and still shirtless. I mean… I know it's his home and all, but he seems to be advertising just a bit. At least Petra put on a T-shirt and yoga pants. She sure has pretty legs and hair, and… well… everything.

"Last night was scary," Petra exclaims as we all tuck into our food at last. "It was hailing here, and the wind was terrible. The thunder kept waking me up all night too. Did you get bad weather over in Crawfordsville?"

"Oh, um, yeah, we had a tornado watch, but nothing was spotted, so it never turned into a warning. That's pretty typical," I answer. "I was just happy I wasn't out driving in the hail."

"The tree I mentioned earlier was threatening to bust right through Petra's window in all of that wind. It wasn't safe for her to stay in that room. We need to see about trimming off a long branch that's hitting the house if you're up for that today. I should have done it sooner. I'm sorry, Petra."

Now I'm getting a better idea of why she was coming out of his room this morning, but they still looked pretty couple-y. Anyway, it's not my business. I nod. "Sure. Happy to help." I'll just have to see if she stays in her own room after we get rid of the branch. "I dragged a big tree limb out of my way when I got here this morning. It was blocking the driveway."

Petra chuckles and says, "If we're lucky, it will be the same branch that was hitting my window. Could be that the storm saved you some work. I did hear a lot of cracking and crunching sounds all night."

No such luck, of course. After cleaning up the kitchen, Weston and I tackle the offending tree branch. It takes us a while to wrestle the thing down and safely away from the house. We're both sweaty and covered in sawdust by the time we're done. I wonder privately whether Weston would have preferred to leave it so Petra would be tempted to visit his room more often. I need to forget that train of thought. It just serves to make me feel grumpy.

Six

ALL THROUGH BREAKFAST I CAN'T HELP BUT NOTICE THAT Callum has his nose out of joint about last night. Well, he can just get over it. Being a gentleman and not doing something with her was a real test of my willpower. She was restless all night, and if that and the thunder hadn't kept me awake, her light coconut scent in my bed and remembering how she felt in my arms while we watched the movie certainly did. I must have counted a million sheep to keep from fantasizing about her. My brain kept telling me, *She came to your bed. She must want you too*, but I know it was because she was frightened about the window breaking. And rightfully so.

I think Callum finally gets the picture when we have to haul down the branch outside. He seems to relax a bit and acts friendlier, especially after I compliment him again on the amazing brunch he fixed for us. I'm also glad to see that Petra pitches in and picks up the sticks and debris around the yard while we work. I think they'll both make good roommates if only I can keep my attraction to them in check. The last thing we need is for someone to get jealous, although I'm definitely getting an interesting vibe from both of them.

It takes less time than we expected to handle the yardwork, so we decide to tackle rearranging the garage and then help Callum bring in his stuff. He doesn't have much, so that's easy. When we're done, we leave him putting linens on his bed and head off to take showers. Petra says she has some stuff she needs to write down before she forgets. I guess that's what it's like sometimes when you're an author. Strike while the iron is hot and all that. She must have been thinking pretty hard while she was walking around collecting sticks. And, as a matter of fact, after her shower, it's a couple of hours before she emerges from her room.

Callum, on the other hand, has spent what's left of the afternoon making a sauce and cutting up a bunch of stuff for our dinner. He says he's making chicken Cacciatore tonight— whatever that is. Man, I could really get used to having him around permanently. One day of his cooking, and I'm already hooked. He's also so easy on the eyes. I've noticed Petra looking at him when he's not aware. She looks at him like he's just as delicious as his food. I tend to agree.

"Would you guys like to watch a movie tonight?" I ask as we do the dishes after an amazing meal that we have outside.

"I've heard about a great series on Netflix," Callum tells us. He explains what he knows, and we all agree it sounds great. "I'll bring dessert downstairs while you get it set up," he tells me.

"I'm going to go toss a ball around for Gus for a few minutes. He seems restless," Petra says. "I'll meet you both downstairs in a little bit." She looks at the dogs and says, "Come on, all of you. Let's go have some fun. It's nice outside now."

I can't stop watching her as she heads out the door surrounded by a pack of excited pups. Her cute butt jiggling in those yoga pants is something to behold, and I'd sure love to grab a handful of it. Callum catches my eye and smirks.

"She's something, isn't she?" I ask him in a low voice. His eyes widen as he acknowledges my question.

With a nod, as soon as Petra is out the door, he asks, "You think she has a boyfriend?"

Wondering if he'd like to take over that position, I say, "I know she doesn't, actually. She can tell you her story herself, though. All I'm going to say is we need to be careful and keep a watchful eye out for anyone strange hanging around the house. She's had a bad breakup, and it spooked her. I promised her we'd do what we can to keep her feeling comfortable and safe."

"Oh! Things are making more sense now about the dog and the sudden need for a new place to live. I hope no one followed her here."

"We'll find out, I guess. You'll want to get Petra to fill you in on more of the story."

Seven

In the basement, we all arrange ourselves on this great cushy couch. Weston and I sit on either side of Petra. The goofy dogs seem miffed they can't crowd in as well, but Weston orders them to lie down on the carpet. We all have fresh berry cobbler while the show starts. Finally, we're all done eating, and we kind of spread out all over the couch. I notice that Petra seems to want to scoot close to Weston, and that makes me feel left out again. I promptly get up and take the dessert dishes back into the kitchen. I need to get my head on straight, so while I rinse the dishes and stow them in the dishwasher, I give myself a talking-to. *There is no room for jealousy here.*

When I get back, however, the dogs have taken up residence right where they want to be—on the couch. Weston and Petra look pretty satisfied with themselves all snuggled up to each other. They look at me, and Petra says, "Gus, you need to scoot over and make room for Callum now."

The dog lets out a dramatic sigh as Petra pushes him over to make room for me. I had been planning to just sit on the floor, but I'm happy to squeeze in between her and the dog.

Weston slings his arm around Petra's shoulders, and we settle in like that for a while. But then I feel his hand on the back of my neck. He's not stroking it or anything. It's like a friendly hand resting on my skin, but it instantly makes me hard. I feel his eyes on me, and I chance a look at him. He raises his eyebrows as if to say, "This okay?" So, what else can I do? I love the feel of his hand on me, so I smile back and wink. Now I wonder if he's interested in Petra at all. He looks down at my lap and smirks. I wasn't aware I was so obvious, and I feel my face flame. Then I get a squirrelly notion. I scoot even closer to Petra and take hold of her hand. I hear the tiniest intake of breath from her. Her eyes get huge, and she looks at me, then looks at Weston.

Nothing else happens through the rest of the show—which turns out to be pretty good. But as soon as it's over, Petra disentangles herself from the two of us, and announces in an all-business tone, "Night, guys. I'm exhausted. Come on, Gus." She practically runs up the stairs, leaving us with Weston's hand still clasped around my neck.

"I thought you were looking kinda lonely over there for a while," Weston says softly. "You know, there really isn't anything going on between me and Petra, but, I'll admit, I wouldn't mind if there was."

Even as he says the words, he gently strokes my neck with his fingers, sending chills down my back. It feels so good, I find myself leaning into his touch.

"So," he adds, "who was the boner for?"

My face burns red, and I suddenly feel as if I'm about to swallow my tongue. I don't even know how to answer that question. "Uh…" I answer brilliantly.

"Sorry. None of my business." Weston also jumps up suddenly like the couch is on fire and calls his dogs. "Night, Callum. Thanks again for a great dinner. You rock."

I feel like I have whiplash.

This has been a long and very strange day. Tomorrow, I have to go to work, and I wonder what my two work-at-home roommates will get up to while I'm out. No telling. But leaving them alone all day makes me feel weird. I wish I knew how to handle my attraction for both of them and could put a lid on it.

I watch a few more minutes of TV, but I'm just staring at the screen rather than enjoying it, so I shut it off and head upstairs. Weston is coming out of the laundry room with a basket of folded clothes, and we smile at each other in a bland, friendly way that gives nothing away. We silently head upstairs side-by-side, followed by Dave and Goliath. As we enter the upstairs hallway, there is a faint buzzing sound coming from inside Petra's room, and someone is making soft whimpering noises. We stop dead in our tracks and hear a long moan and some whispered unintelligible words. The buzzing stops.

I'm so hard now, I can barely walk, and I would hazard a guess that Weston is as well, although the laundry basket blocks my view of his body. We lock eyes on each other and smirk. He cocks an eyebrow at me and tips his head toward his room, silently asking me to follow him in. I am so tempted, he must see it written all over me, but I shake my head and slip into my own bedroom.

The sexual tension in this house is going to be the death of me, but I find myself excited about it. There's something about living here with the two of them that makes me feel alive like I've never felt before. It's like an electric current zipping through me.

But I need to be professional. I need to be serious. I'm not a college kid anymore. It's time to… oh fuck. I have no idea what I'm telling myself. If I don't get laid pretty soon, I'm going to explode.

Eight

IT'S BEEN SEVERAL WEEKS SINCE CALLUM AND I MOVED IN, and I have to say that things have been running pretty smoothly. Callum's cooking is amazing, and he truly seems to enjoy feeding us. He watches the grocery budget thoughtfully, too. The guy works with food all day and then comes home and cooks beautiful meals, or sometimes brings home leftovers from the classes he teaches. We've been treated to some rather exotic dishes this way. I'm not complaining, but I've had to increase my workouts to combat the extra calories I've been consuming.

Callum has gone home a few times to have dinner with his family, but he makes sure we have leftovers to heat up when he's gone. When he gets back, he always seems refreshed somehow. It makes me wonder what it's like to have a real family.

It's great that Weston has a set of weights and an exercise bike I can use when he's not working in that room, plus I do some yoga. I'd like to add a run in the morning, but I got out of the habit when I started worrying about being followed by Randy. The idea just gave me the willies, thinking I'd be away from home on foot and might be accosted by that creep. I'll talk to Weston about it. Maybe he'd like to take up running with me. Or maybe Callum would.

These guys. Holy cow. Weston's such a kind-hearted, gorgeous, sexy guy. I know he likes me too, but he seems conflicted about that somehow. He's always looking out for us, making sure everyone is happy. And Callum may be a few years younger, but he seems so focused on his career—like cooking for us is his ticket to a Michelin star or something. He's always asking questions about how we like what he fixes and if it should be different in any way. And what a sweetheart. When he's not cooking or feeding us, I see him making entries all the time in a notebook he keeps. I asked him why he doesn't use a computer for that, but he laughed and said he often gets inspired to write something down while he's cooking, and he got tired of having to clean smudges of flour and whatnot off his keyboard. Makes sense, I guess. Anyway, he sure is a hottie. Seems mature for a fairly recent college grad too. I wonder how old he really is. Maybe he started college late, and he's older than I assume.

It's only in the evenings when we watch movies together that everyone seems to really relax around each other. We always snuggle together on the couch like a pile of puppies, and there has been plenty of hugging and innocent-seeming cheek kisses going around. This is always my favorite time of all. I can't deny the true affection we each have for one another, but the growing sexual tension is about to make me combust if I'm totally honest. I've noticed both guys getting hard, but no one seems to want to broach the topic or do anything about it. It's confusing to me. I kind of love it in a way, but often I end up using my vibrator after the movie is over. A girl needs some release, after all.

Weston is getting busier and busier with his counseling. At first, I would sit at the desk in my room to write, but I was uncomfortable hearing him talk to his clients online. It wasn't like I could hear everything unless someone on the other end of the conversation started yelling, but I quickly decided to take my laptop downstairs or head outside for a few hours when the weather warmed up. Once it gets too hot or too humid, I head in and sit in the hearth room to write. It always seems homey and comfortable to me. Gus seems to like this arrangement. He's getting along perfectly with Goliath and Dave, even though Dave still wants to herd the bigger dogs. The little squirt cracks me up.

I vaguely remember Callum saying something about leftovers and lunch today as he left the house, but I hadn't had enough coffee yet to really process what he said. I was up too late writing last night, I guess. But I'm definitely feeling hungry, so I save the work on my laptop and call up to Weston to ask if he's ready to help me get lunch together. We may not be great cooks, but we can nuke Callum's goodies like nobody's business.

"Be right down!" he calls. Almost immediately, he thunders down the stairs with his dogs following him. He absently shoves a lock of hair out of his eyes, and I get the unbidden urge to do that for him and run my fingers through his silky tresses.

As usual, he's not wearing a shirt. He's barefoot and wearing shorts today, but some days it's jeans. So this time, I ask in a flirty tone, "Are you allergic to clothes or something? It's not as if I mind it, but…?" I can't help but stare at his torso with a grin.

Weston looks down like he wasn't even aware he was half-naked and laughs. "When I talk to clients, all they can see is my chest and face, and I always wear a dress shirt to look professional. I don't want to wear it any longer than I have to, so as soon as I'm done with calls, I take it off and hang it up. It saves a little on laundry that way. But if it makes you uncomfortable, I can go grab a T-shirt. I'm sorry. I just got so used to doing this when I was on my own, I stopped thinking about it."

Laughing, I tell him, "Maybe you'd increase your business even more if you left it off during the calls too."

Weston spears me with a look that makes me all fluttery inside. "So, you like what you see?"

"Weston, don't be a dope." I roll my eyes. "Any female with a pulse would enjoy that view. Plenty of men would too." I wave my hand up and down indicating his deliciousness. "False modesty is ridiculous. I also see you working out every day to maintain that ripped physique." I feel my face suddenly flaming as I try to squelch the memory of fantasizing about his body when I use my vibrator. Maybe I've given too much away, so I quickly change the subject. "I've been meaning to ask, do you ever run? I'd like to start doing that in the early morning before it's too hot, or if Callum would join me, maybe after he's back from work in the evening." I look down. "I'm still too much of a chicken to go on my own because…" I trail off seeing that Weston understands immediately that I'd never want to run into Randy—or even Ben—out on my own.

"Have you filled Callum in on your story with the losers?"

"Yes. He knows about them. It's been nice not having any contact with either of them since moving here. I'm probably safe from them because they don't know how to find me."

"I wouldn't bet on it. Those kinds of people can be pretty fixated as well as resourceful. And I get the sense they both may have wanted money from you given that you think Randy might have something to do with drugs and Ben lost his job.

They sound like real opportunists who might even do you some harm."

"Now you're scaring me."

Weston moves closer and gently wraps his arms around me. "I certainly don't mean to frighten you. Sorry. We just need to stay careful." He leans down and kisses the top of my head, and I don't know what comes over me. Well… I do, but I'm not ready to admit to myself that I have a severe itch that needs some scratching. I raise my face up to look him in the eyes and open my mouth slightly. I hope he gets the message without too many cue cards.

Weston's eyes dilate and he tilts his head, then slowly leans in for a proper kiss. It's gentle and sweet. But I'm not in the mood for gentle or sweet. I nibble his lip and lick it. And that's it. His kiss goes from zero to sixty in about two seconds. It's hot and probing. He tastes divine, and his tongue… oh God. It's everywhere at once, and the pressure of his lips… Oh. My. God. I've never been kissed like this in my life. It's as if nothing exists in the whole world but his mouth on mine. Finally, he pulls back a little and I breathe, "Weston." I feel drunk on his kisses.

"Tell me to stop," he growls. He sounds so sexy I can't believe it. I have to close my eyes.

Nine

"DON'T STOP," SHE SAYS ALL BREATHY, AND I WONDER what's happening to me. All of the good reasons I had for staying away seem to have flown out the window with one little kiss. Petra is the epitome of female delight, and I have this overpowering need to protect her. She's smart, talented, and so gorgeous, she's like the perfect birthday cake. Beautiful to look at and delicious too. I suddenly want to gorge myself on her. I tighten my grip on her and practically ram my tongue down her throat. Instead of shying away from my aggressiveness, she whimpers and presses herself against my bare chest. The feel of her tits against my body is heaven.

I'm such a liar. That business about the dress shirt was a

load of malarkey. Yes, I wear one for my appointments, and I hate having to iron shirts, but I also know that walking around the house half-dressed all the time has made both of my room-mates pay attention to me. I also know that I would look perfectly professional in a polo shirt or a Henley and wouldn't have to worry about ironing. I'm no idiot—just a little full of myself. I've seen how they both look at me, and I generally sport a semi whenever I notice their expressions of lust. I'll have to knock it off when the weather gets colder, but for now, I'm enjoying the silent praise. And Petra has now openly confirmed her attraction. Before today, I could chalk it up to just friendliness or being generally cuddly.

But now… wow. Kissing Petra is taking on a life of its own. I can't get enough of her moans and whimpers, so I slide my hands down her body, grab her cute butt and lift her up. She's as light as a feather as she springs up, and her legs instantly wrap around me like she wants to be even closer. The heat of her burns through my shorts. I swear I'm immediately as hard as titanium.

Finally breaking the kiss so we can come up for air, I growl in her ear, "I want you so fucking badly right now. You have no idea."

"I have a pretty good idea, actually. Shall we skip lunch and just go for the good stuff?"

I lean back a little and look at her face. Her lips are swollen and wet, and her eyes are filled with pure lust. "Are you sure, Petra? I don't want to step out of line and make you uncomfortable or do anything that would make you want to move out. I like having you here too much."

"And I like the idea of you having me. Let's go upstairs. I can only take so much of you flashing your body at me."

I turn to leave the kitchen and almost collide with the dogs, who are all trying to beat one another to get to the back door. In what feels like slow motion, Petra and I turn our heads toward the kitchen door as it opens, and in steps Callum carrying a large, sturdy shopping bag. The room fills with an amazing aroma. "Ready to eat?" he asks and then stares at us. "Oh."

Petra is still in my arms with her legs wrapped around me like she's a dancer and I'm the pole.

"What are you doing here?" I ask Callum. *Nice to sound so accusatory, asshole.*

He frowns. "Nice to see you too. First of all, I live here. Second, I told you both I had the afternoon off today, so I was planning to bring home the leftovers from this morning's class for lunch. But I guess you both had other… things on your mind and weren't paying me any attention."

Petra slides out of my arms and rushes to him. "I'm so sorry. I was barely awake when you left this morning. That's a dumb excuse, but it's all I have. Thank you for thinking of us again, Callum." She reaches for his arm, but he avoids her, heading for the kitchen table instead. His face is full of dejection as he begins to unload food packages.

"You both look wide awake now. I'm sorry if I interrupted your plans."

"It's not what you…" Petra starts and stops. We both know it *was about to be*.

"It's okay. If you two want to mess around, I can mind my own business."

"That's not a very nice way of putting it," I tell him.

He levels me with a stare and asks with a derisive snort, "What would you call it? *True love?*"

"Well, maybe not yet, but…" I don't know how to make this less awkward, and I don't want to hurt anyone's feelings. Petra gives me a funny look, so I say, "I just remembered, I have another appointment in a few minutes. I'll leave you two to have lunch, and I'll be back down later to fix my own." I feel like a jerk, but avoidance seems the prudent course of action at the moment. It's official: I am complete chicken shit. Now they're both probably upset with me.

Ten

Petra looks me in the eye and asks, "What's going on with you, Callum?"

The frank question takes the wind out of my sails. I go from angry and jealous to resigned in one second flat. I press my hands to the kitchen countertop and sigh. "I don't know. I'm all messed up in my head. I walk in here expecting to have a nice lunch with the two of you because I brought home a new recipe I came up with, and I find you wrapped around each other like you want to crawl into Weston's skin. If the two of you are getting it on, it's not my business. I know that. We've been over that before, but I just feel… I don't know what."

"Left out, maybe?" she asks in a kind voice.

I give her a sharp look and it hits me. She's right. I'm not sure I feel like admitting that though. Right at this moment I want to pick her up the way Weston had her and kiss her so hard, she'll forget his name. But the stupid thing is, I also want to do that to Weston. I'm a mess. How can I explain this? I know I need to focus on my job and making something of my cooking—not worrying about who I'd like to fuck. Neither of them seems inclined to want to fuck me as much as they do each other, but they also both give me mixed signals. What's with all that touching the back of my neck from Weston? Or the way Petra lets me hold her hand?

I want them both—I'm honest enough to admit that, at least to myself. But I don't want to mess up our living dynamics in the house.

Instead of manning up and admitting anything, I go on the offensive and ask, "I've been meaning to ask, do you think you could shop around and find yourself a quieter vibrator?"

Petra's jaw drops with a gasp, and her face floods with red. "Y-you can hear it?" she squeaks.

"I'm sure we can both hear you. It's damn distracting when I'm trying to go to sleep, if you must know."

She screws up her face and asks, "How do you know Weston can hear me too? Did you guys talk about it?"

"No." I don't bother to tell her we didn't need to discuss it because we were both standing outside her door when we heard it together the first time. "But I doubt the wall between his room and yours is any thicker than the one between yours and mine."

She covers her face with her hands. "Could the ground just swallow me up right now, please? I can hear his client calls sometimes, and that's across the hall. That's why I don't work in my bedroom very often anymore. Oh God, I'm sure you're right. I just never considered that I was making noise. The ad for the vibrator said it was 'discreet.'" She groans into her hands again.

I feel like a complete jackass, so I backtrack. "Look, Petra. I'm sorry. I'm making things worse. That was totally out of line for me to say that or even to bring it up. If you want to use a sex toy, it's up to you. Hearing you just makes me… you know… want things. Things I shouldn't want. You're clearly into Weston, and he's into you, and whether or not *I'd* like to be a part of that… oh crap." I see the surprised look on her face. "Now I've *really* made things worse."

"Callum, are you saying that you're bisexual?"

The question sets me off again, and I turn my back to her as I say, "Well, I didn't mean to be saying that, but yes. I'm bi. If you think there's something wrong with that, it's your problem, not mine. I was born this way and can't do much about it."

Petra's hand curls around my arm and she pulls, turning me to face her again. "No, Callum! I'm not put off by that at all. Please don't think that."

I narrow my eyes at her. "You're sure?"

Laughing, Petra replies, "I'm a ghostwriter, remember?"

"So?"

"A lot of what I write these days is romance. Sometimes whole books, sometimes books from notes and outlines I get from a publisher, and sometimes I get hired by individual authors to write particular scenes they aren't comfortable writing."

"Still not following."

"Sex scenes. I've written about couples, ménage scenes, and every combination of genders you can imagine. That has required a lot of research, so there is very little that shocks me. It's all good. Now do you see?"

"Um. Okay. When you say research, what do you mean exactly? Have you tried…?"

"No! I've never done anything other than normal—I mean *regular*—I mean MF sex."

"MF?"

"One male, one female. That's what we call it in romance book descriptions. There are lots of acronyms to describe the various combinations as well as tropes and genres. MM, MMF, MFM, FF, MFF, et cetera."

I nod like I know what she means. I guess I sorta do.

"I didn't mean to imply that anything other than MF sex is abnormal or wrong in any way. It's just… um… different." She looks down and then raises her eyes back up to mine. "It's all actually pretty hot. But when I say I've researched it, I mean I've done a lot of reading and sometimes I look at videos for… inspiration." She blushes.

I'm warming up to this idea, and when I say "up" I mean I'm starting to get hard thinking about Petra watching porn and taking notes like it's for an exam. I can't help but wonder if she uses her vibrator then too.

But then Petra breaks the spell by asking, "How old are you?" and I deflate like a week-old balloon.

Not understanding how that's relevant, I answer, "Twenty-six. Why?"

She suddenly looks relieved, and I'm not sure why. "I thought you were probably about twenty-two since you recently graduated."

Oh, so that's why. She thought I was a lot younger.

"I'm the oldest of four kids who've all wanted to go to college, and our family doesn't have a lot. So I worked and lived at home for a while after high school to save money, and then I scraped together some scholarship funds and student loans. Finally, I could swing it and move into the dorm, but working full-time and going to school made me take an extra year to get all of my credits. I have one sister at Stanford now on an athletic scholarship playing volleyball, and my little brother will start in the fall playing football at Ohio State. Our other sister joined the army to get her education paid for."

"Wow. What do your parents do?"

"My dad's a firefighter, and my mom's a nurse."

"It sounds like you have a terrific family." She sounds a little sad as she says it.

I smile and nod. "I think you're right. What's your family like? Are they around here?"

Petra's expression closes off immediately. "No."

"Where are they?" I begin to wonder if she has any family at all.

"I have no idea about my sperm donor. He took off before I was born, and my mother wasn't much of a caregiver. She moved to Indonesia a few years ago to follow her 'great adventure.' She isn't the best about keeping in touch with me about her whereabouts."

Jeez, that sucks. "Siblings?"

"None that I know of, though I could have a whole bunch of half-siblings spread all over the country, thanks to my sperm donor. My mom never wanted any more kids after she had me." She raises her eyes to mine. "Don't get the idea that I was brought up by some poor, dedicated single mother who had to work four minimum wage jobs to keep a roof over our heads. My mom came from money. That's probably why my so-called father wanted to be around her to begin with. That, and she's gorgeous. But when she got pregnant and wouldn't marry him or even name him as the father, he apparently left. She probably told him, 'Thank you for your donation, now take a hike.' Or maybe she even paid him off to leave, for all I know. She's always been pretty independent. I was raised by a string of nannies with little input from my mom and went to boarding school for high school so she could travel. I've often wondered why she even wanted to have me in the first place. And before you speculate, no, she hasn't shared any of her wealth with me other than paying for private school and then college. After graduating from the University of Iowa where I studied writing, I was on my own, and that's fine with me. It makes me work really hard to support myself. I ended up in Indiana because I got a job here writing trade manuals that I quit when the ghostwriting took off."

"I see." I honestly don't see it at all. My parents are the best, and I'm so lucky to have them. I've always known they both love me unconditionally. My heart breaks a little for Petra —who obviously has no clue what she's missed out on. Or maybe she does, at least a little. "Have you ever tried to find your dad?"

"He's not my *dad*. He was only there for the sex. That was the sum total of his contribution. So, no. I don't know where he lives or even his last name. I've never seen a picture of him, so it's no different than someone whose mother was inseminated by a sperm bank. I asked my mother about him a few times, but she never had much to say other than 'good riddance,' so I didn't pursue it with her."

"That's so sad," I can't help saying.

Petra shrugs. "Not really. I don't feel rejected by him since he never knew me. Sometimes I did wish I had a daddy to spoil me like some of my friends had."

The look on her face belies her words. How could she not

feel rejected? Her father disappeared and never looked back, and her own mother would rather gallivant around the world than be a mother—*and* she prevented Petra from having a father. That's fucked up. No wonder Petra got herself involved with a loser boyfriend. She has no example of how a relationship ought to work. And if she writes romance, she might have a pretty skewed idea of how things in real life aren't always happily-ever-after scenarios.

Wondering how I could show her how caring people and real families ought to work, I ask, "Would you mind getting us some drinks and setting the table for lunch? I think I need to go apologize to Weston and get him to come down and eat. The lunch is a cold dish, so there's nothing to heat up. I'll be back down in a moment."

"Sure, but he said he had a call."

"Yeah, right. He was just getting out of the way. I'll go find him." I start to leave and then pause. Turning to Petra, I give her a quick hug and kiss her cheek. "I think we all have some talking to do." I leave her blinking at me as I walk out of the room.

I take the stairs two at a time and find Weston sitting at his computer with the door open. I can tell he isn't working, but I'll play along. I whisper, *"Sorry to bother you. Lunch is ready, and we'd like to eat with you."*

He gives me a half smile and says, "Hold on while I put this red seven on my black eight."

"I knew you weren't working."

"Yeah?"

"You forgot to get dressed."

"Petra said it would be good for business if I left my shirt off."

"Smart girl," I say and wink at him. "I like the look." Then I add, "I'm sorry I broke up your fun and acted like a jerk about it."

"No worries." He rubs his hands over his face as if to wipe his thoughts clean. "I shouldn't be messing around with her anyway. Even if she is as hot as fuck. It's just that sometimes when I look at her, all of my reservations fly out the window."

"Come back down and have some lunch. Maybe after we eat, we can clear the air a bit." As Weston rises from his chair, I let my eyes travel down his muscled body. He really is a work of art. He and Petra together are like perfection. I want them so badly. I shouldn't want them. But… I'm only human, and they are both delicious. I get an idea then and ask, "Did you turn off the AC today? It's pretty hot in here, especially for this time of year." As we head down the hall, I grab the back of my shirt, drag it off over my head, and toss it into my bedroom where it lands on the edge of my bed. Weston's steps pause momentarily, and his eyes roam over me. I try not to smirk because I know how I look. Weston doesn't have the only six-pack in this house. I quickly toe off my shoes and toss my socks. "Much better," I say, and we continue down the stairs. I can hear him chuckling.

Eleven

I'm just finishing up pouring some sweet tea into the glasses on the table when I hear the muffled sounds of bare feet pattering into the kitchen. I'd already shooed the dogs outside so we could eat without looking at their pitiful begging faces at the table, and I see them all lounging in the shade at the back of the house. So I smile and turn to the men... and just about drop the pitcher. So much manly flesh is on view, and it's all exquisite. I knew Weston was ripped, but Callum was hiding under those shirts of his he wears to work. Oh. My. Lord. "Wh...?" I start to ask.

"It's Topless Tuesday," Callum announces as Weston snorts.

"It's not Tuesday," I protest weakly.

"Then it's Fabulous Fun Times Friday," he counters. "We were hot."

"Yes, we are," laughs Weston, and he looks at Callum like he'd like to lick his chest. Then he turns to me and adds, "Feel free to join us," and he winks.

"Uh…" I don't have words. Seriously, they've short-circuited me with their masculine scrumptiousness. "Let's eat?" It comes out a little squeakier than I'd planned.

We sit down and enjoy an amazing concoction of curried chicken salad in papaya boats with delicious little orange-flavored muffins on the side. I don't know what I'm enjoying more—the food or the view. There are so many happy *mmm* sounds and lascivious looks flying around the table, I can't believe it. It's like a plug was pulled, and all of our wishful-thinking ideas are floating around our heads like thought bubbles.

"Seriously, Petra," Weston says again, "it's awfully warm in here. Why don't you get rid of your shirt and get comfort-able? You're looking rather red-faced like you're way too hot. And I do mean that *you're hot* too."

"Did you turn off the AC on purpose?" I ask.

Weston smiles enigmatically, and Callum snorts at him.

"So, Callum," I say, "have you ever discussed with Weston what you told me a little while ago?" I want to get the focus off of me for a while as I'm not sure I'd be comfortable having lunch topless right now. Or ever, actually. It just sounds weird to me.

"That I'm bisexual?" He turns to Weston whose eyes light up. "It hadn't come up in so many words, no."

Weston blinks a couple of times and then grins.

I look pointedly at Weston and see clearly how interested he is in this. Suddenly, I feel all squiggly inside like eels have invaded my tummy or something. And I feel an even deeper blush creeping over my face. "Do you have any response to that, Weston?"

"Hot damn," Weston laughs. Then he adds, "I bet Callum is as yummy as his muffins. I'd love a taste, wouldn't you, Petra?"

Ignoring that question, I ask, "Is anyone surprised?" I look between their faces and see that their eyes are locked on each other. Now I'm getting the sense of how Callum felt when he entered the house. I suddenly feel like the spare tire that's stuffed in the trunk. But as soon as that sensation registers, both men look at me without changing their expressions. "Oh!" I breathe. This is heady stuff being under their combined scrutiny. It seems they weren't joking about my shirt and topless dining. I take a cooling swallow of sweet tea.

"I bet she's as sweet as the tea. What do you think, Callum?"

"Would we be too much for you, Petra?" Callum asks. "You said you'd researched certain… ah… configurations."

"She has?" Weston asks with a grin.

"Indeed, our Petra here is a self-proclaimed expert on sex with multiples. Didn't you know?"

Squeezing my legs together under the table and squirming in my seat, I say, "I wouldn't go *that* far."

"You refuse to experience a ménage?" Callum asks with wide eyes. "Why not?"

"No, um, what I meant was I wouldn't go so far as to call myself an expert."

"So you *would* be open to ménage sex," Weston crows with a huge grin. "Outstanding."

"You're both putting words into my mouth." I am so flustered and, quite honestly, turned on right now, I can't stand it. "I explained to Callum that I research various multiples for sex scenes that I write so I can get things straight and make them sound realistic. I haven't actually ever *done* anything like that."

"But you'd be willing to?" Callum asks.

I take a deep breath. "Maybe if the right opportunity arose, I'd be game for some… experimentation. I can't deny thinking about it."

"Why don't you start by expressing your appreciation to Callum for this splendid lunch he brought us. I'm sure Callum would like that," he directs his eyes to Callum, who seems to be eyeballing me, "wouldn't you, Callum?"

Callum scoots back from the table. "Sounds perfect," he answers as he opens his arms to me. "Come sit on my lap, Petra." Then he adds, "Now that you know I'm not several years younger than you, and you wouldn't feel like a cougar."

"I'll just get rid of these dishes while the two of you get comfortably acquainted," Weston says, laughing. He quickly stacks everything into the sink in less time than it takes me to stand up and move to Callum.

I feel as if I'm moving through space in slow motion as I shift over to Callum wondering, *what the heck am I doing?* I carefully perch myself on his knee, but Callum is having none of that. His muscled arms wrap around me—wow do they feel good—and he draws me against his bare chest.

"Did you like my cooking?" he asks as his lips graze my neck.

"I…uh…yes, I did."

"Can I get a kiss for my efforts?" He nibbles that tickly place just below my ear, and a feeling of intense lust spears through me. *Oh my.*

"I'll thank you properly," Weston announces as he sidles up to us. He bends down at the same time as Callum raises his face. "Petra, Callum goes to a lot of trouble cooking for us, and we never thank him enough. We need to show our appreciation." Weston's lips are just millimeters away from Callum's as he says this. Then he closes the gap, and *oh my.* There is nothing hotter than this. Weston and Callum start kissing each other like it's the best idea they've ever had, and my eyes can barely take it all in. If I had eels in my tummy before, now I have elephants performing ballet to the "Dance of the Hours." I'm just inches from their faces as they go at it. Weston takes my hand and places it on Callum's pec. It's hard and warm, and Weston's hand is firm as he presses me to Callum's body.

Finally, Weston pulls back and suggests, "Let's go somewhere a bit more comfortable and without a table in the way. My back's getting a crick from leaning over."

So I pop off of Callum's lap, expecting him to let go of me, but he doesn't. His arm remains wrapped around me. He stands as well and wraps his other arm around Weston and looks at me, asking, "What acronym would this be in one of your books?"

"It looks to me like MMF. I'd have said MFM before the two of you locked lips, but, damn, guys, that was hot. Please don't stop."

Weston looks confused. "What are you talking about with all of the Ms and Fs?"

"In romance books, MMF stands for male/male/female. MFM stands for male/female/male. Big difference. In the former, the guys interact, but in the second one, they only pay attention to the woman. I don't think that's very genuine, but some readers prefer it."

"Oh, well," Weston says with a chuckle, "equal opportunity sounds like more fun to me as long as no one is left out. Are you both on board with that?"

"Just what are you proposing here, Weston?" I ask.

"It's too early for a proposal," he laughs, "But I'm ready

for some group groping. I'm just suggesting we have some fun. Let's at least go downstairs and sit on that comfy couch."

I'm relieved he didn't suggest a bed. It was one thing to end up in one with Weston but with both guys? That's a bit much for me. At least for now.

Just then the dogs show up whining and scratching at the door, so Weston breaks away and lets them in. As he refills water bowls, he looks at us and says, "Downstairs, now."

"Ooh, he's bossy," I tell Callum with a tiny laugh. Callum's eyes seem to be shining with anticipation. He grabs my hand and pulls me toward the stairs.

Twelve

CALLUM

IF I'M DREAMING, I MAY NEVER WANT TO WAKE UP. I'VE BEEN telling myself to stay away since the moment I moved in with these two, but my resolve has been shattered now that I see they both want me as much as I want them. I just don't know if this will be a one-off experience or something that has legs. But I know for certain I'm going to enjoy today to the hilt. Petra's face is flushed, and her mouth positively demands to be kissed, and Weston looks like he's stalking us down the stairs like a hungry wolf.

"Happy birthday to me," I say with a laugh as Weston gives me a gentle shove onto the middle of the couch. He settles on one side of me, and Petra snuggles up to me on the other. "I'm going to try to bring home lunch more often if this is what happens around here in the middle of the day."

Petra's sweet laugh rings out like a bell. "It doesn't— believe me. I always have my nose in my laptop writing, and Weston has his clients to deal with. We usually grab something to eat when we need to take breaks, and it's rarely even at the same time. You're the catalyst here, Callum."

"But what about what I saw as I entered the house? You were clearly ready for… something together."

"That was a new development," Weston assures me. "I think you've been putting an aphrodisiac in our food. All of a sudden, I couldn't keep my hands off of her, and now I feel the same way about you."

"So you're bi too?"

Weston's face squinches up a little. "I guess. Maybe? I was at least bi-curious in college and messed around a little, but nothing since then, and I never felt the need to 'come out' or anything like that. I just haven't been tempted. But… my life has been pretty difficult for the past couple of years, and I didn't have any girlfriends either."

"Want to talk about it?" I ask.

"Later maybe. It's all irrelevant now, and I want to get back to having Petra and me show you our appreciation for the wonderful job you've been doing feeding us these amazing meals. I feel so… cared for." Weston looks away for a second. "It's nice. No one has done much for me in a long time."

I feel Petra's soft hand stroking across my belly, and

Weston leans over me. He kisses my neck, and then his lips trail a path up to my mouth. I can't help but reach for his head, threading my fingers into the silky strands of his hair as I encourage him to kiss me harder. Petra scoots even closer to my body, and I let out a satisfied moan.

Weston keeps kissing me as Petra's hand makes leisurely patterns on my bare skin. Then she seems to resolve to do something more as I feel her hand going toward the front of my jeans. And then, hallelujah, I feel the button pop open. I smile into Weston's mouth, and he pulls back a moment to take in what's happening below. As Petra draws down my zipper, Weston makes a happy sound in his throat. "Mmm, Petra has the right idea, I see."

I am fully erect as I feel two hands reach for my waistband and tug. I lift my hips up, and suddenly I'm sitting there in nothing but my boxers. I'm so hard, the tip of my dick is protruding out of the top of my underwear, and I am not even remotely embarrassed. My heartbeat speeds up, and I watch the two of them look at each other and then slide to their knees in a beautifully choreographed motion.

We are momentarily distracted as we see all three of the dogs lumber down the stairs. They look at us with no interest whatsoever and find comfy places to conk out on the carpet.

Resuming their focus on me, Weston and Petra begin to stroke me through my boxers. I am hyperaware of the heat of their hands and the feel of them, but then they sort of lose track of me for a second as they find each other's lips and kiss deeply. God, they're beautiful. With one hand on me and one hand on each other, we make a triangle of bliss. I have to touch them, so I reach out and stroke whatever I can reach. Petra needs to take off that darn shirt of hers. I want to see more of her in the worst way.

Not really wanting to lose the hands on me, but needing more of her, I reach out and take the bottom of her shirt in my hands. "Get rid of this, Petra," I command as I tug her shirt upward.

Her look is compliant, so Weston jumps right in to assist. He whooshes the shirt up and over her head, giving us both a view of her glorious tits spilling over the top of a lacy bra. Her nipples look so tasty through the sheer fabric, I swear my mouth waters. Weston grabs her and kisses the daylights out of her, deftly unhooking her bra while she continues to stroke my erection. Then he puts his hand back on me as well. I haven't had this much fun in… well… ever. Weston's hand is much larger than Petra's, and together they feel like heaven.

We both take a moment to ogle her lovely breasts. They're perfect. Simultaneously, Weston and I take her nipples into our mouths, and Petra shivers and moans delightfully.

I lean back finally, and they kiss each other once more. Apparently, they like that a lot.

Feeling pretty forward by now, I raise my hips once again and slide my boxers right off onto the floor. They both stop kissing long enough to stare at my dick, and I am not too modest to say they both look at it with appreciation. I'm well-groomed and on the generous side down there, so I can't help but gloat to myself a little. But then, oh *then* they lean over, perfectly synchronized once again, and start to lick me from base to tip. I can't help letting out a protracted moan. Seriously, is this really my life? I would close my eyes in sheer bliss, but I don't want to miss even a fraction of a second of this kind of action.

When they get to the tip of my cock, they pull off and once again lock lips. This becomes a pattern of licking me like a stick of hard candy and kissing each other until I can barely take any more of it without whimpering.

I desperately need more, so I request politely, "Fucking suck my goddamn dick, one of you. Right now! I can't take it anymore."

They both crack up, but Weston grips me around the base of my cock and engulfs me immediately. He goes straight to deepthroating me, and I swear I see stars. Apparently, he's no stranger to this—giving head like a champ must have been included in his college extracurricular activities.

Petra starts playing with my balls. That never did much for me because they're ultra-sensitive and too prone to feel pain for my taste, but suddenly gentle ball play feels interesting with her nimble fingers. I can tell she's enjoying the exploration, so I relax and let her continue.

They keep this up for a while until Weston pauses and looks questioningly at Petra. She nods, and Weston pops off of me.

Not even a full second later, I'm once again engulfed—this time by Petra's mouth. This woman has some skills with that tongue of hers, I can tell you that. She doesn't deep throat me the way Weston did but concentrates more on the sensitive head of my cock. I am now a moaning mass of goo.

But just to make things even more delicious, Weston sticks his fingers into his mouth and then slides them underneath my balls to my asshole. Oh. My. God. It feels incredible as he massages around it while Petra's quick tongue salsa dances on me. I feel that glorious sensation building in the base of my spine as my orgasm approaches. Because I'm polite that way, I decide to clue Petra in just in case she doesn't want a load of cum in her mouth, so I strangle out the words, "I'm about to blow!"

Much to my surprise, she grips her hand around me tighter and takes my dick deep into her mouth. At the same time, Weston presses his fingertip against my hole and shoves it inside a little way, just as I bellow something profound like, "Ohhahhhnngggh!" and feel myself coming like a raging river. His finger pushes inside of me deeper and hits my prostate as a second jolt of ecstasy plows through me. "Fuuuuckk!" I cry out. I can't help it.

My chest heaves and they both pull back looking at me with smug expressions. Petra has a dribble of cum on her chin, and it hits me that it's the sexiest thing I've ever seen. Weston sees it too and, oh my God, he bends over and licks. It. Off.

Even sexier.

So this is what it's like to have two lovers at once.

It's official. I'm dying here of ambrosia overload, so I choke out the words, "I promise you both, I am your sex slave from now on."

Petra slithers up my naked body and kisses me like she's starving for me. I taste my own saltiness on her tongue, and I swear I'm *this* close to getting hard again. My dick twitches, and I wrap my arms around her. I love the skin-to-skin contact with my chest. Weston chuckles and then makes a disparaging sound. We pull back and stare at him.

"Sorry. I just looked at the clock. I have a client call in about five minutes, so I'm going to have to leave you two and go upstairs. I have just enough time for a one-minute cold shower so I can get my head in the game a little before trying to make sense of this guy's problems. He's a pretty big mess." Weston leans over and kisses first Petra and then me, and says, "Be good, kids. That was fun." He wiggles his eyebrows at us. "See you later." He stands and heads toward the stairs. Dave and Goliath follow right behind him.

Before he can leave, I call out to him, "Hey, Weston. Welcome to the Queer Club. It's official. You're a member."

He turns and eyes me. "In that case, I can't wait for the initiation ceremony." He winks and jogs up the steps.

Petra looks serious all of a sudden and scoots off of my lap. "Well, he seems happy, but that wasn't too much for you, was it?"

"Are you kidding? That was the most incredible thing

that's ever happened to me. I'd like to do it over and over, but I'm afraid it would be too selfish of me to expect it. I know you both worship me, but…"

She snorts and pokes me playfully in the ribs. Then she asks, "Do you think he really did have a call this time?"

"I do. He looked genuinely sorry to be leaving. Doesn't he usually have afternoon patients?"

"Yeah, he does. I guess I'm just taking everyone's pulse to see if this is going to mess us all up somehow. I sure don't want it to."

"Are you sorry about it?"

"Not at all. Just nervous. I loved it, but I'm a little surprised at myself for doing it."

"Petra, you and Weston can do that to me anytime the mood strikes you, and I'll probably just fall in love with both of you for it."

I can't believe I just said that.

Petra blinks at me and settles back in for a snuggle. It's amazingly comfortable like this. We sit quietly like that for a while, and I wonder if she's drifting off. Sadly, however, she finally sits up and says. "I'm sorry to say that I have to get back to work. I have a deadline to meet, and this book isn't going to write itself."

I'm so sad to watch her put her bra and shirt back on. That was such a nice view. But I have the sneaking suspicion that we'll be seeing lots more of our beautiful Petra's tits in the future. She may be a bit shocked at herself, but she certainly embraced what we did with a flare.

She gives me a friendly smooch and says, "I'll be in the hearth room if you want me."

Chuckling as I pull up my pants, I answer, "I always want you." Leaning back, I close my eyes and decide to take a much-needed nap for a while.

My final thought before drifting off is, *What an amazing day. I love my life.*

Thirteen

I CAN'T BELIEVE I HAD TO LEAVE THEM AND GO TALK TO A whiny client who tries my patience like this clown manages to do. He doesn't have any real problems other than he's selfish and spoiled—and probably lonely. And he expects the world to do his bidding. I'm not getting through to him very well that it's time to grow a pair and grow up because he'd rather cry about his latest litany of perceived injustices. I can see why his parents are paying for his counseling. They're probably sick of trying to make him take some responsibility for himself. He's a thirty-five-year-old man who has the maturity of a kinder-gartner. And just my luck, he seems to like me. I steel myself to get into the mood to be polite and talk to the guy. I know I need to have empathy for him, and I normally have no trouble with that, but this guy…

At least my client load has picked up tremendously. I've been networking and making contacts that have given me a bunch of referrals. It's like having Petra and Callum move in was a good luck charm and the kick in the butt I needed to get my act together. What a relief.

I dash to the shower where I'm in and out in a minute, run a brush through my wet hair, and streak down the hall to my office with a shirt and sweatpants in my hand. Looking at the clock again, I panic because I'm a stickler for appointments starting right on time. I fling myself into my chair, and I'm still buttoning up my shirt when the call connects. I didn't even have time to put on the pants yet. If anyone could see me, they'd think I was some kind of pervert or something.

I never knew this seat cushion was kind of abrasive, but immediately I have the urge to scratch my butt cheeks. That's not going to fly, so I try to put my discomfort out of my mind while I welcome the patient politely. "How's it going today, Gavin?" I ask, and just as I expected, the guy barely comes up for air. He complains about a driver who was crowding his lane at a stoplight and who gave him a dirty look when he flipped him off. The drugstore has stopped carrying his favorite candy brand, and he has to drive two extra miles to buy it. (He doesn't need to be eating candy. He needs to lose weight and brush his damn teeth.) His mean parents are threatening to start charging him rent unless he stops cranking up the AC so high. They claim they can't afford the utility bill, but he gets so *hot*. His coworker wears stinky cologne that makes him gag. He says he can't get a promotion because his work is being negatively affected by this smelly person who reminds him of his fifth-grade social studies teacher who gave him a D when he failed to memorize the Pledge of Allegiance for a test. When I break in and ask him finally if he can request a different location to work in, he says, "I like my space. It's close to the vending machines. I don't want to move."

On and on it goes, and a couple of times, I can't stand it. I *have* to scratch. The third time, Gavin asks me, "What's the matter? Why aren't you taking notes like you usually do? Where do you keep putting your hands? Why is your hair all wet and you keep making faces? Are you even listening to me?"

I gaze dumbly back at him and give a nervous cough. The movement makes my cheeks rub on the rough cushion even worse, so I bite the bullet and say, "Gavin, could you please excuse me for just a second?" Without waiting for an answer, I slam the laptop lid down—immediately regretting that I just disconnected the call—and grab my sweats. I jam my feet into the legs and stand up to haul them up, just as I see Petra walk by the open door. *Why didn't I shut the door? Oh yeah, I'm a dumbass who was in a hurry.* The reminder of why I was in such a rush comes flooding back as she pauses and gapes at me with a surprised and then lustful look on her face. I stare back like a deer in headlights, and my dick immediately swells up to a nice boner. I groan as I have to stuff it into my pants.

"Weston? I thought you had a client call," she says with some confusion. "Were you just trying to get away from us after all?"

"Yes, I... I mean no! I can't explain right this moment, Petra, I'm in the middle of a session now."

She frowns at me and blinks at my disappearing boner, then gives a pointed look at my closed laptop. "Right. It must be some call. Don't let me keep you." Clearly thinking I'm full of shit, she bolts away into her room and a few seconds later, she leaves again with the charger for her laptop. She doesn't look at me on the way back down the hall.

I went from being on top of the world to the pits of confusion in just fifteen minutes. I'm going to have to do some serious explaining, but right now I can't. I open the laptop and redial Gavin, ready to apologize profusely. I see that he is now eating an ice cream sandwich, and it's dripping all over his hand, down his T-shirt, and onto whatever surface his computer is sitting on. He looks like he's ready to cry as he says, "I wasn't sure you were coming back, Dr. Alister. You've never left me before." He has ice cream on his face and chocolate cookie bits in his teeth. I suppress a shudder.

I apologize as professionally (and effusively) as possible for the interruption and try to salvage our session. At least my butt stopped itching, and I resolve to keep a towel over the cushion for any future pants—or non-pants—emergencies.

The only further catastrophe happens when Gavin drops a blob of ice cream onto his keyboard and gets panicky about that. The idea of sticky keys with food in them frankly turns my stomach, but just like everything else, he brought it on himself.

After talking him down from that, we try to get back on track. I suggest a relaxation technique he might try when things start feeling like they are too much for him to handle, and he seems satisfied with that. Finally, I tell him I'm looking forward to speaking to him in a couple of days, and we disconnect.

Shaking my head, I think to myself, *Some days are a challenge.*

♡♡♡

OVER DINNER THAT NIGHT, I EXPLAIN THE ENTIRE SCENARIO TO my roommates—without breaking any confidentiality rules for Gavin. Petra and Callum can't stop laughing their heads off. At least I'm forgiven, and they believe me. Callum even wiggles his eyebrows and offers to massage my butt cheeks for me, and just the thought gives me a shivery feeling.

We're just finishing up the dishes when Petra's phone

rings. She looks at it and says, "Huh. It's Darleen—my old roommate." She shrugs and takes the call.

"Hello?" She listens and frowns. "Why do you think I have anything to do with that?" Silence. "I assure you I have no idea, but if you're worried about it, why don't you install a doorbell camera? I think you can get one that's pretty inexpensive." She listens and frowns even more. "No, I'm not paying for it! I have nothing to do with it. Take it out of my cleaning deposit that you refused to give back because you didn't think I vacuumed enough!" She listens some more and then answers, "Look, I'm sorry you're grossed out, but I don't live there anymore, and it has nothing to do with me… *What? Why would you take me to small claims court for that?!"* By now she's shaking with anger. "Okay! You're being an unreasonable bitch as usual, but if it will make you shut up and leave me alone, I'll see if I can have one installed." She ends the call with an abrupt jab at her phone and reaches into the refrigerator.

Cursing under her breath, she pulls out a bottle of wine, pours herself a tall glass, and plops down at the kitchen table. Callum and I sit down with her, and I ask, "What's going on? Can we help?"

She sighs. "Either someone who's pissed at me is still hanging around, or some animal is pulling some pretty gross shit. She keeps finding dead birds and rodents on her doorstep. I tend to go with the idea that it's a cat, but on the off chance it has to do with me, I guess installing a doorbell camera might help me to figure out who's doing it. Since my car hasn't been anywhere near the apartment in quite a while and no one has seen me come and go, I sincerely doubt anyone I know is doing this. It's just not plausible. But she says she's going to sue me if this doesn't get resolved because it never happened before I moved in. I'd rather take care of it than waste my time in stupid small claims court over dead critters. She is *such* a vile person, but hopefully, this will get her off of my case."

"My dad and I installed one of those for my parents' house," Callum says. "They aren't difficult. We can swing by Best Buy tomorrow where you can get one, and Weston and I can install it for you. It can be synced up to both of your phones, so you'll know firsthand what's going on. You won't have to take her word for anything."

"You'll do that for me?"

"Of course," I reply immediately.

"You guys really are the best," she says. "Thank you."

"We're happy to help," Callum assures her.

I'm just about to suggest some nighttime fun when she stands up and announces, "I desperately need to get back to my manuscript, guys. I'm getting further and further behind. Thanks for another great dinner, Callum." And with that, she scurries up the stairs.

"You think she's okay?" I ask.

"Maybe a little freaked out about everything. Or… she could actually *be* busy and behind schedule. I know I wouldn't have been any good to get much work done this afternoon if

I'd needed to." Chuckling, he adds, "I basically passed out. You guys were amazing, and maybe she needs to regroup to settle her head. Or… maybe what we did gave her some inspiration for her writing." He winks at me.

Nodding, I say, "I'm going with the last option. I like the sound of that." Not really wanting to initiate something just with Callum, I tell him, "I guess I ought to go write up some notes before I forget everything I talked about today in my last consultation." I think for a moment and add, "I like what we all did. A lot. But I think I'd feel best about it if we maintained a three-person rule for any future… ah… shenanigans. I don't want to foster any jealousies, and besides, it was fucking *hot* that way. What do you think?"

"I think that sounds amazing. And I can't wait to return the favor to you and Petra. Oh, and speaking of her, I messed up. I was in a shitty mood and mentioned that we can hear her when she uses her vibrator, and that embarrassed her to death. I apologized profusely as soon as I said it, but it was a dumb move on my end. I'm so sorry I didn't keep my big mouth shut."

"Hm. Well, I guess we'll have to make her feel special and make it up to her together, if you know what I mean." I wiggle my eyebrows and get a smile out of him. "We can suggest she uses it *with* us. And you can use your big mouth for something better than embarrassing her."

Nodding, Callum stands up and says, "That sounds good. If everyone is busy tonight, I guess I'll go downstairs and read for a while. Gunnar Dahl's newest Lance Wannamaker mystery is tempting me from my Kindle."

"Oh, you're a fan? I like his books a lot. Have fun. Good night, Callum." And then, just because I can't stop myself, I kiss him on the lips and sprint up the stairs to my office.

So much for keeping my distance when Petra's not around. Both of them are under my skin in the best way possible. I guess Callum's right, and I am queer after all. It's surprising how good I feel about that.

I think about what it would have been like to "come out" to my family and how they would have reacted to a bisexual son and grandson. They probably would have been fine with it. I never had any reason to think that what I did would have caused them to turn against me. I was lucky that way.

Too bad my luck ran out with them. Suddenly, I feel that stabbing sensation where my crushed heart lies in my chest. Some things just plain suck, and there is nothing you can do about it. Put one foot in front of the other and keep going. That's what Granddad would've told me. As I sit down to type up my notes, I have to wipe some moisture from my eyes. Must be because I just yawned. Oh, wait… I didn't yawn.

All three dogs file into my office, and I give each of them a good snuggle and scritch. One by one, they position them-selves around me and lie down to take a nap. It's funny how they clue in so well when I'm feeling melancholy and need them. At first, Goliath needed me as much as I needed his comfort, but the other two are great about it too. I'm glad he's not feeling alone. Thinking back… No. I'm not going to think back. It hurts too much. Time to focus on work for a while, then I'll take the dogs out and go to bed early.

Maybe I can even avoid bad dreams. I'll concentrate on the fun we had today instead.

Fourteen

Petra

When I show up at my old apartment the next day with the guys, my former roommate Darleen is suddenly graciousness personified. I'll concede that she's stunning to look at, but this new cordial side of hers is as phony as her boobs. She clearly has the hots for both of them and wants to impress, so she zips into her bedroom and puts on more makeup and a tighter, more revealing top while they work. When she returns all spruced and fluffed—showing a lot more cleavage—she stands too close when she offers them cold drinks.

Shrinking away from her like she has cooties, they both politely refuse without checking out her assets. Inwardly, I'm fist-pumping.

When Callum asks her for her phone number as they finish the job, she preens and flirts with him, sticking out her boobs. But her expression looks crestfallen when she realizes it's for the system they've installed, and he did not enter her digits into his phone. Finally, after he explains how the system works to her in a very businesslike manner, she blurts in what she clearly thinks is a sexy voice, "Wouldn't you like my number for yourself?" Wiggle, wiggle, wink, wink. She seems to be going for a Marilyn Monroe act, but to me, she sounds more like Minnie Mouse.

Callum smiles blandly at her and answers, "Not really. Thanks anyway." He turns to Weston and me and asks, "Ready to leave?"

Darleen looks flirtatiously at Weston then, and before she can open her mouth, he says, "Don't even ask. But I am glad you kicked Petra out. Your loss is our gain. These two are the greatest roommates anyone has ever had. And that dog of hers? Gus is the best."

Trying not to laugh in her blinking, incredulous face, I tell her "I'll be in touch if anything shows up that's important. In the meantime, please don't bother me again. And you're welcome."

As we load into the car, Callum seems deep in thought and then asks, "Would either of you mind if we stopped at the market and did a little shopping? I want to make something special for dinner tonight, and I need a few things. Since the grocery store is on the way, this would save some time. I could actually get stuff for a few days."

"Sure thing," Weston answers. "Market District?"

"Yes. Thanks. You don't need to get right home for anything, do you Petra?"

"No, I'm good for a while. And it might be interesting for Weston and me to see you in action."

The market is huge and high-end. Weston and I get a kick out of watching Callum discuss cuts of meat and types of fish with the butchers, who seem to recognize him, and we watch as he pores over the produce, examining each item carefully. He discounts plenty of pieces of fruit that I'd have just tossed into my cart, so I'm beginning to get the idea that the reason our meals are so divine is because he is not only a creative and very talented chef, but he also cares about every last tiny detail. Knowing his level of concern warms my heart.

Weston and I trail around behind Callum as he shops, and Weston can't help but touch me over and over. It's sweet that he'll wrap his arm around my waist or hold my hand, but then he'll get distracted and pick something up from the shelf. Several times he asks Callum, "What the heck is this, and what is it used for?" Some of these questions are directed at strangely shaped fruits, and some of them are jars of things in the international food aisle. Each time Callum has a quick answer, and a couple of times he offers to use the item in a recipe soon. It's quite the education, and I've never had so much fun grocery shopping before. It's more like we're on a field trip than merely buying food.

When he's not completely engrossed in looking at the groceries, Callum also bestows little touches and flirty looks on Weston and me. It's sweet really. He says a lot with those gorgeous eyes of his. They seem to be full of promise.

About half an hour into our excursion, I get the strangest sense of being watched. A shivery feeling starts at the base of my scalp and runs right down my back. I grab the back of my neck to see if it's wet—that's how strong the sensation is. But there is nothing there. With one arm draped around Weston's shoulders, Callum is explaining chutneys to him, so neither of them pays any attention to me. I pivot around quickly and look up and down the crowded aisle. It's a busy store, but no one is staring at us. I chalk it up to my imagination until we get to the frozen food section. In this aisle, Callum is explaining to Weston the differences between custard, ice cream, sherbet, and sorbet when I get that sensation again. This time I think I see a man dart around the corner, so I take off after him. He seemed to be heading back toward the middle of the building, so I walk quickly in that direction. I see absolutely nothing out of the ordinary. Shoppers of all ages are milling around. Couples, singles, hired shoppers, moms with babies—just normal people buying groceries. I contemplate slipping through the door to the liquor department at the back of the store to see if anyone is hiding in there, but I don't want to worry the guys, so I head back to the frozen food section.

Weston is piling several pints of ice cream into the cart, and he looks up at me.

"Where'd you go?"

"Oh, I thought I saw someone I knew. False alarm."

He narrows his eyes at me. "Then why do you look so freaked out all of a sudden?"

"Okay," I huff. "I thought someone was following us and it felt creepy, so I decided on a whim to go investigate. I came up with nothing."

He grabs me and pulls me to his chest. "Petra, if you ever have that feeling, tell us. And don't go running off like that. I couldn't live with myself if anything happened to you!"

"It's not as if anyone could do something to me in the middle of the market," I protest in a crabby voice.

"You don't know that for sure!" Weston says way too loudly.

"What's this?" Callum asks as he drops a couple of boxes of frozen fresh fruit juice bars into the cart. I eye his goodies skeptically and he shrugs with a smile, "We all deserve an easy guilty pleasure now and then, and I love both the lime and the mango bars. Now why are you two arguing?"

"Petra thought someone was following her. I think we ought to leave."

"Now don't jump to conclusions. I just said I got a creepy feeling that someone was watching us, and I thought I'd check it out. I ended up seeing nothing. And besides, if someone *was* following us, they sure took off in a rush, and that's not terribly threatening, is it? Just odd. Anyway, you know I have a vivid imagination since I'm a writer, so let's forget it and finish shopping before all of this frozen stuff turns to mush, okay?"

"I don't like it," Callum states in a flat voice. "I trust gut feelings. We have what we need, so let's get out of here."

And that's what we do. While we're piling the groceries into the car, I know all three of us are sneaking looks around the parking lot for anything suspicious—even though not one of us knows what to look for. On the way home, I keep craning my neck around to check for a familiar car, but there is a lot of traffic, and all cars tend to look alike to me anyway. I breathe a sigh of relief when we pull into the driveway and see that no one seems to be tailing the car—at least not up close. Still, it's nice that we can unload the groceries from inside the garage with the door closed. By the time we're done, I decide that I was being melodramatic and promise to put the whole thing out of my mind.

As we unpack all of the bags and start to fill up the refrigerator and pantry shelves, Callum asks, "Weston, do you really need fifteen boxes of Kraft macaroni in your pantry? I know the company says it keeps indefinitely despite having a use-by date on the box, but I can feed you better than this."

Weston stops what he's doing and opens his mouth to say something, but there is a long pause. Finally, he says, "I ah… used to… ah…" When no more words come out, he turns and walks out of the kitchen. He swipes a tear from his eye as he goes.

"Okay, sorry!" Callum calls to him. "I won't throw this stuff out. I was just trying to free up some storage space." He looks at me with a questioning expression, and I merely shrug.

I have no idea what just happened.

Fifteen

THEY BOTH MUST THINK I'VE LOST MY FREAKIN' MIND. WHO *cries* about macaroni? I'm not a two-year-old. As I lie on my bed staring at the ceiling, the memories flood back whether I want them to or not, and my heart breaks all over again. I'm getting tears in my ears. Isn't there a song about that? Whatever. If there is, it's probably a country song. My life might make a good one of those, come to think of it.

I don't know how much time passes, but I guess I finally must have fallen asleep when I hear a soft tapping on my door. I quickly wipe my face off with my T-shirt and sit up. "Come in."

The door opens and I expect it to be Petra, but it's both of them. "You okay?" she asks.

Callum looks apologetic and careful as they walk into the room.

I sigh and tell them, "I'll live. I'm sorry about that."

"You have no reason to feel sorry," Callum protests. "I was the one making disparaging comments about your food choices and trying to throw away something that belongs to you. I'm really sorry, Weston."

"No, it's okay. Honestly. I probably ought to explain a few things though, so you don't think I've flipped my lid. I'm not a diehard fan of macaroni or a huge shareholder of Kraft Foods stock." I try to interject a laugh, but it comes out like a grunt. "Those boxes are really just… uh... leftovers that I hadn't gotten rid of yet."

"Hm," Petra says while Callum waits for me to say more.

"Have a seat," I tell them, patting the bed. We all pull pillows out and prop ourselves against the bedstead getting comfortable. Callum is on one side and Petra is on the other.

Then the dogs barrel into the room and leap onto the bed with smiling faces and wagging tails. Gus tries to lick Callum's face, Goliath starts to circle around like he's settling in for a long nap, and Dave hops over our legs several times before trying to dig a hole in the blanket. It's terribly crowded and definitely not relaxing, so Petra tells them, "Come on. Get off, you guys," and points to the floor where Dave and Goliath reluctantly retreat to their beds. Gus flops down between them on the carpet with a grunt. If this keeps up, maybe he needs a bed in here too.

When our laughter subsides, I take a deep breath and say, "I don't want to depress you, but you may as well know what makes me… ah, makes me the way I am."

"Only if you want to share," Callum assures me. "I won't lie though… your reaction to old macaroni boxes caught us both off guard, to say the least."

Nodding, I begin, "My mom taught me how to make that when I was about six years old. It was my favorite food back then, though I eventually lost the taste for it. I remember standing on a stool so I could reach the counter. She would boil the noodles for me and then let me stir the rest of the ingredients together. I was always amazed at how powdery orange stuff and slimy noodles turned into food. I felt like a big kid when I made it because she'd tell me what a great job I was doing and all that shit little kids eat up."

"I'm sure she was sincere and proud of you, Weston," Petra says. "Where is your mom now?"

I clear my throat. This is hard. "I'll get there."

"Oh, sorry."

"No worries. Anyway, I bugged her all the time to let me make it, and it was something I loved to eat. Real comfort food. Sometimes she'd toss in extra ingredients like extra cheese or bacon, or whatever, and that was even more fun to stir up. Sometimes when we'd visit my grandparents, she'd have me whip up a batch—that's how she'd say it—to take over there to add to their dinner. My granddad always got a kick out of it when I showed up looking all proud of myself and carrying a casserole dish full of that stuff." I look at Callum and try for a smile. "See, you're not the only famous chef in the fam… ah… house." He gives me a kind smile, and I get lost for a moment in those expressive hazel eyes of his.

"When I was nine, my grandmother started having small strokes. She could still function pretty well—only her speech became compromised, but gradually she began having mobility issues. My granddad was still working then. He had to be up in Chicago on a day she had a doctor's appointment and needed a ride to get to it. So my parents agreed to take her. I was supposed to go straight from school to my next-door neighbor's house to play until they could get home. My mother was a stay-at-home mom, and my dad worked nearby. He wasn't sure my mom could handle her mother on her own, so he took the afternoon off to help.

"I don't have all of the facts, but what I remember being told was they were… ah… heading home when an ice storm hit. It had been a regular winter day one minute and then black ice the next. My dad's car was crossing a bridge when a semi went out of control… and hit them, knocking them clean off the bridge and onto the interstate below. It was a pretty horrific accident that involved several vehicles from what I understand."

"Oh, Weston!" Petra gasps and grabs my arm.

Callum takes my hand on the other side. It seems strange,

but I feel their caring energy pouring into me with their touch. It helps me get through the rest of the story.

"I had to stay with the neighbors until Granddad could get home. The ice storm lasted all through that night, and the major roads were impassable. The poor guy had to be positively ruined. He'd lost his wife, daughter, and son-in-law all in one fell swoop. I was so distraught, they had to call my pediatrician who prescribed a mild sedative, but no one could drive out to get it, so I just sobbed all night long. I can't even begin to tell you how awful it was. I was terrified and flattened by grief.

"When Granddad finally made it home, he quit work on the spot. He had this house and he'd saved up for what he called a rainy day, so he knew we'd be okay. He became my mother, father, and best friend until the day he died."

"When was that?" Callum asks.

"A few months before you moved in. It was awful. He was a such good man, and I never once doubted his love for me, even when he was chewing me out for being a dumb fuck." I smile sadly at the memory of his gravelly voice. "He encouraged me to get great grades and always do my best so I could get an excellent college education. Fortunately, I had scholarships and insurance money that took care of tuition, even though the accident settlement should have been better than that. I'd have preferred to go to some cheap Podunk school if it meant I could have had my family intact, but that's the way life goes sometimes.

"He always told me he was happy enough, and he was proud of me. He never complained about being lonely, but when I was a senior in college, he got Goliath to keep him company." I smile at the memory, "He had some pretty funny stories about raising a puppy at his age." I look fondly over at the dog who's snoring and twitching his legs, probably dreaming about playing fetch.

"Granddad's heart started giving him trouble when I was in grad school. I offered to quit and come home to take care of him, but he wouldn't hear of it. He said he'd move into an assisted living facility, so I came back during Christmas break, and we looked at places. All of the nice ones were full, and the ones with vacancies were gross. He refused to give up Goliath to go live in any of them. So I arranged for caregivers to come in regularly to help take care of him. Those people are really expensive, so his life savings were dwindling pretty quickly. I worked as many hours as I could while I was in school to take some of the monetary pressure off, and I encouraged him to sell this house or at least take out a mortgage on it. He wouldn't think of it because he said this was all he had to leave to me and didn't want to saddle me with debt. I'm pretty sure he didn't think he was going to last very long with that ticker of his. He actually did better than he expected, I believe.

"Each time I came home for a school break, I could see that he'd faded away a little more. When I was a kid, I thought he was a huge bear of a man. He'd always had a broad chest and big strong arms, but now he seemed to be shrinking. What he needed was a heart transplant, but at his age, he wasn't given a lot of hope for that. He'd probably been having trouble long before he admitted it to me.

"As soon as I was done with my Ph.D., I moved back in here to take care of him so we could cut back on the caregivers a bit, and it frankly shocked me to see how feeble he was by then. I set up counseling calls with the few clients I had and tried to do what I could." I make a disparaging sound as I continue, "I *had* a long-distance relationship with my girl-friend because that was the best I could do right then. But she was less than enthusiastic about the lack of attention I had to give her and promptly started to cheat on me. So we ended our two-year romance in the blink of an eye. Good riddance, I guess. My life had become a real country song at that point."

I feel Petra and Callum stroking my arms, and it gives me the strength to go on. I notice too that Gus has silently crept back onto the bed and is now lying with his head in Callum's lap looking up at him with pure doggie adoration.

"Granddad used to ask me all the time to fix that 'orange crap' that tasted so good. It was about all that tempted his appetite in his last weeks. So I always made sure there was plenty of it on hand, and we ate so much of it I thought I would turn orange." I try to wring out a small laugh, but it's not at all funny. "One night he… ah… took a couple of small bites then apologized and said he couldn't finish and wanted to go to sleep." I have to pause and clear my throat before going on because it's closing up on me. "In retrospect, I wonder if he ate it all the time to try to make me feel useful or good about something. He was completely bedridden at that point, and he could barely speak. His voice sounded like sandpaper."

I have to steel my emotions to get through telling the rest of this, and my voice comes out pretty shaky. "I told him goodnight and took his dish away. The caregiver helped him get ready to go to sleep and then took off for home. Later that night I heard Goliath… ah… howling. He was making a noise I'd never heard come out of him, and I knew instantly that it was over. Granddad was now gone too, and I had no one left to love except his dog. It occurred to me then that getting Goliath was probably Granddad's plan to have someone to keep me company and make me get out of bed in the morning. He knew how sick he was even back when he got the puppy." I try my hardest not to choke up, but it's impossible. Callum and Petra silently support me by surrounding me in a tight hug.

It takes me a while to compose myself so I can continue.

"All that was left to do then was bury the man who was everything to me, but I honestly can't even remember the funeral—only that it was another dreadful one I had to endure. After that, I spent a lot of time donating and tossing out his stuff and then fixing up this place. At first, I expected to sell the house and move into something cheaper, but each time I came into this room it made me feel closer to him, and it somehow relaxed me, so eventually I decided to move in here permanently and make it my own. It's mostly all new furniture, so it's not as if the room is some weird shrine to him or anything, but I did keep photos and a few souvenirs. The king-size bed frame was his, but I replaced the old mattress and springs. He hadn't even slept in it in a long time because we'd rented a hospital bed for him, but I wanted to start fresh.

"I took stock around the house and realized it had fallen into some pretty bad disrepair. Most of all, it needed a new roof, but also the air conditioner and the furnace were old and unreliable. I had to face the fact that in order to replace these, I needed to take out a mortgage. That was a sad day for me to get a loan against the house that Grandad had tried so hard to keep debt-free." Shaking my head, I continue, "It was the only way at that point.

"I decided to adopt Dave so poor Goliath wouldn't be so lonely. It was a hard adjustment for him, but Dave is so pushy, it gave Goliath a new lease on life just to try to stay ahead of the little squirt." We all smile at the dogs. "I can't deny that I spent a lot of time moping around and feeling sorry for myself, and I'd ignored my business too much. Finally, one day I realized if I didn't do something in a hurry, I was going to be flat broke, and I'd default on the mortgage. I also faced up to the fact that I was extremely lonely, even with the dogs. So I listed the house on the roommate-finding app. And that brings us up to meeting the two of you. I'm so glad the app brought us all together. I feel more whole now than I have in years. Thank you." I look down for a moment and ask, "Do either of you believe in fate?"

"I'm not sure," Callum answers. "Certainly there are times when circumstances seem controlled by it. But… life just happens, and sometimes you get lucky. What about you, Petra?"

"No. I don't like to think that what happens to me is outside of my control by some predetermined fate. I agree, though, that sometimes we all just get lucky. And I feel extremely fortunate to be living here with the two of you, with Gus and his new buddies."

"Well," I tell them, "I think I'm the luckiest. My business was in the toilet, my personal life was a trainwreck, and I was going broke. Then these two amazing people showed up, and everything turned around. It's like the two of you waved a magic wand over me."

I turn and kiss the cheeks of one and then the other of my friends. Lovers? We'll see. If all we have is an amazing friendship, it will be great, but I'm beginning to see the potential for so much more.

And just as if they want to reassure me that there is plenty more to us, both of their free hands begin to roam. Callum nuzzles my neck and Petra nibbles my earlobe. She slides her hand under my T-shirt—yes, I am still wearing one today since we left the house—and caresses my abdomen and chest, and Callum strokes my thigh.

Then they change directions, and both hands converge on the waistband of my shorts. Callum pops open the button, and Petra lowers the zipper. It sounds like music to me. Together they tug down my pants as I raise up my body to give them access. And suddenly I am experiencing the same ecstasy that Petra and I bestowed on Callum. Two hands stroke me as one. Oh God, it feels so delicious; I can't stop the moan that rolls out of me.

Apparently, Gus doesn't like all of the movement and jumps off the bed to join his buddies. Fine with me. More room to maneuver.

Petra asks, "This isn't insensitive considering the conversation we just had, is it?" She gives a little squeeze to highlight her question.

"It's definitely not insensitive. It's just what I need, so don't you dare stop," I groan.

Callum chuckles and Petra scoots even closer so she can put her lips to mine. She kisses me playfully at first, but I crave more and thrust my tongue deeply into her mouth. Immediately she sucks on it the way she might suck my dick, and I am gone. I'm so freaking hard right now I could hit a homer with this bat of mine. I scoot down so I'm prone on the bed and nearly beg, "Petra, take off your clothes and sit on my face while Callum takes care of my dick. Please."

She leans back with a pretty blush, but quickly whips off her clothes. Smart girl—and she is breathtaking.

Meanwhile, Callum has removed his shirt and pants and is leaning over my cock with stars in his eyes. "Have you ever fucked a guy?"

"No. I wouldn't mind trying it though. Any ideas about that?"

"I'll be right back." He dashes out of the room, and we both ogle his tight buns as he jogs away. In less than a minute he's back with a condom and a bottle of lube. I see what he's thinking, and my insides feel like they're liquifying.

But it's almost too much to think about now because Petra is following my instructions like a champ and is positioning her sweet little body over me. I kiss up her thigh and grab her hips to position her over my mouth. I look up to see her pinching and pulling at her own nipples with the hand that's not holding the headboard for balance. She's already squirming as I tongue her delicious pussy where her bare skin is as soft as flower petals. I think to myself, *Ya gotta love a woman who waxes.*

Meanwhile, I feel Callum's tongue slide up and down my shaft, and then he engulfs me in his mouth. I can't help but moan into Petra's pussy, causing her to squirm even more. I latch onto Petra's clit and begin a barrage of tonguing and sucking that makes her shiver and quake. She makes the sexiest sounds. I think I must have died and gone to heaven as this onslaught of sensation overtakes me. I am almost ready to come in Callum's mouth when he pops off. "Fuck, man! Where'd you go?" I ask in a desperate voice. Petra groans in displeasure as well because she was clearly winding up for a spectacular orgasm when I stopped the ministrations on her clit.

"Hang on, Weston. I gotta get myself ready for you. It won't take long." We turn and look at Callum who lubes up his fingers and then crams one into his own ass. I am just about to swallow my own tongue because I have never seen anyone perform such a personal—and arousing—act. He closes his eyes, and Petra's jaw drops as we see him remove his finger and then jam two large, lubed fingers into his hole. He winces a little and then pops his eyes open. Seeing our expressions, he chuckles, "Normally, I would leave this to my partner, but I wanted to move things along." He pumps in and out a few times and declares, "Okay, I'm ready. You can go back to getting our beautiful Petra off now and leave the rest to me."

Callum then quickly rolls a condom onto my stiffy and positions his body over me. Just as I resume sucking Petra's tasty little clit and eating up her moans, I feel Callum grab my boner and hold it steady while he slowly slides his body down onto my shaft. His head is thrown back as if in rapture, and he's making a humming noise. I guess he really loves getting fucked.

"Holy shit!" I cry out as I become encased in his hot, tight ass. He slowly adjusts to my size and settles onto my body. I have to pant a little before I can resume playing with Petra. This is the most arousing and exciting sex I've ever imagined in my life, and I think my heart is going to pound right out of my chest.

Petra cranes her neck around to see what it looks like to

have Callum on top of me too, and she grins. Callum sweeps his hands around her body to play with her tits as he begins to rise and fall on me. She grinds her pussy into my face over and over, keeping time to the rhythm Callum sets.

I'm so turned on; I know this won't last much longer. As soon as I feel Petra's muscles contracting and she bends over convulsively with a huge groan, I let go. Over and over I feel myself shooting into the condom to the point that I finally wonder if my brains are leaking out as well.

Just when I think I am drained for life, Petra gets up and reverses her position, still straddling me. She bends over and sucks Callum into her mouth, eliciting a smile and another humming noise from him. I have an interesting view of her pretty butt as she sucks him off, and I can't help but touch her. I push one finger into her pussy, making her moan again, and then I use my other hand to play with her backside hole. I mean… it's right there in my face, so why not, right? I reach over and grab Callum's lube, necessitating me to remove my finger from her, but once my other hand is properly lubed up, I replace the finger that's fucking her and carefully push my other finger into her butt. I tell her in a rasping voice, "This is what it would feel like if you let us both fuck you at once."

Making a noise that sounds sort of like an enthusiastic "*uh huh,*" (though it could just be my hopeful imagination) Petra has hold of the base of Callum's cock as she sucks him off. She clamps her other hand onto her clit where she starts rubbing in quick circles. I suddenly get the image of a three-ring circus and then blurt out that thought to them and start to laugh. This is so much fun! I truly have not felt this happy since I was a little kid. And even then, it's debatable.

Soon Petra is writhing with another orgasm, and I watch Callum's face as he watches her. It's almost as if there is love pouring out of the man's eyes. He shifts his focus to my face with that same warm expression. But then his eyes close and with a shout, he discharges his release into Petra's mouth. He looks completely blissed out. Nothing… I mean it, *nothing* is better than watching the two of them when they're turned on like this.

Carefully I extract my fingers from Petra, and she sits up and then climbs off of me. She flops down on one side of me, looking as satisfied as a cat in a sunbeam. Callum flops down on the other side of me and kisses my shoulder. "Amazing again," he whispers as if in awe of us all.

I'm so relaxed, I can barely move, so I don't. I'm feeling pretty drowsy when I say, "That was a hell of an initiation ceremony. Wow."

Sixteen

I HAVE NEVER EXPERIENCED ANYTHING LIKE THESE TWO MEN. Sure, I've read and written about this kind of sex, but to read about it as opposed to actually doing it is *way* different. I never knew how strongly I would feel about seeing Callum and Weston being affectionate with one another, for one thing. Obviously, I've read MM books, and often the love stories are sweet and heartwarming, but to physically see them and be able to reach out and touch them together… *holy cow*. They seem so uninhibited about what they want. It's refreshing. My former fiancé was, now I realize, unimaginative as well as downright dull in the sack. Sex with him was just… adequate (maybe), whereas sex with these guys is explosive, mind-blowing, and so much fun, I can barely stand it.

I get the feeling we've only scratched the surface of what we might do together. Weston actually broke out laughing and explained that it was because he was so happy. He called us a three-ring circus. What a riot. I wonder who's supposed to be the ringmaster.

I've read about compersion—the good feeling one gets by watching their partner give or receive physical pleasure from someone else. Now I finally understand it. There is no way I could feel jealous when I watch them pleasing one another. It's thrilling, arousing, and heart-warming, actually. I'm happy for them—just as happy as when they turn their attention on me. I'd have a hard time explaining this to someone else, I'm afraid, but it's definitely part of the equation now. I hope they're on the same page with me.

I feel so free! These men are both kind and giving, and I am equally attracted to both of them. To put my hands—and mouth—on two men at once? *Holee bejeebers!* It's amazing. I get all mushy inside thinking about what Weston alluded to. DP! I'm quivering inside just thinking about it. It's not something I ever thought about much before for myself, but now… well, I am certainly thinking about it, and surely the guys are too. I hope we can try it sometime soon.

I'm incredibly glad Gus and I got here in time to move in with them. I can't imagine living anywhere else at this point. However, I can't help but wonder if the newness of our sexual awakening together will wear off a bit, or if it will escalate into something deeper. What does one do with two boyfriends simultaneously? This is real life for us, and we'll need to figure out how to navigate a relationship if that's where we're headed. And frankly, I do hope we're headed that way. Do the guys? It's probably something we need to get out into the open pretty soon before anyone gets hurt feelings, or we have a misunderstanding.

This is all running through my head when, sounding like he just woke up, Weston says, "Let's go take a shower. The one in here ought to be large enough to accommodate all of us."

So we all amble into the master bath. It's nice and roomy, just as he'd said. I've never been in here other than the quick peek he gave us the day we showed up. I watch as Weston gets rid of his condom, chuckling at the rather huge amount of cum trapped in it. We all pile into the shower, looking both worn out and tremendously satisfied. Being surrounded by so much male skin and muscle makes me… well… tingle. I want to rub up against them like a cat.

So… I do just that.

Seventeen

CALLUM

SEEMINGLY OUT OF THE BLUE, PETRA LEANS INTO ME AND says, "Callum, I'm sure Weston and I would be fine about it if you wanted to take the night off from cooking tonight. You've been so generous with your time and talents since we moved in, wouldn't you like break? We could take you to a restaurant or order takeout."

Stroking her soft skin, I look at both of them and answer, "Are you tired of my cooking already?"

"No!" she gasps.

At the same time, Weston protests, "Not ever!"

"We just want to make sure we're not taking advantage of you," she assures me.

"Well, I might take you up on it soon, but not tonight."

"Why not tonight?" she asks.

It's a fair question, and suddenly I feel rather sheepish about this. "We have company coming. In fact, they ought to be here in about an hour. I'm sorry I neglected to tell you. I got sidetracked with everything we had going on today. But that's one of the reasons I wanted to go shopping for stuff for dinner."

"Who's coming?" Weston asks.

"Oh, um… just my mom, dad, brother, one of my sisters, and my grandmother."

"And you didn't tell us?" Petra squeaks, taking a step back.

"Uh… sorry?"

She nudges us out of her way so she can rinse her hair and dashes out of the shower hollering, "I need to get ready, and the house needs to be vacuumed, and the table needs to be set, and…" her semi-hysterical voice becomes inaudible over the sound of the shower as she zips out of the bathroom heading toward her room. The dogs all chase her down the hall, ready for action.

"What's the big deal?" I ask Weston, who has an amused look on his face.

"I guess she's nervous about meeting the fam. And you did spring it on us pretty last minute. Admit it, did you want to keep us from worrying about it all day?"

I sigh and reluctantly confess, "It may have crossed my mind. I didn't want to stress either of you out anymore than you're already feeling, but my mom insisted that this was the only time they all had when everyone could come because of their crazy work schedules. They all want to see this place and meet you, and my brother and sister have to leave for school soon. Anyway, they're a relaxed bunch. They never expect much, and they don't pass judgment, so it ought to be pretty painless. I planned a simple main course that won't take a lot of time to put together, and they're pitching in with side dishes and dessert."

"It's fine with me. I'd love to meet them all, but I get the sense from Petra that she isn't always great in family situations."

"Makes sense since she's never had much of one to deal with. We'll have to do our best to make her feel comfortable." As I speak, I become distracted by Weston absently soaping up his dick and balls, so I step closer to him and take the soap from his hand. His eyes light up as I lather my junk up too and press against him. I take hold of his dick along with my own and use both hands to soap them up together, rubbing them as one. It's convenient that we're close to the same height because we're a perfect fit. Weston makes a happy sound, and boom, I'm hard. He's hard. We're the hard(y) boys. I lean in to kiss him and keep stroking up and down on our shafts.

The friction feels *so* good.

Things are starting to feel really, *really* good when we hear a snort coming from the bathroom door, "Come on out of there you two sex maniacs! We have company coming, and the house needs to be cleaned up. The dogs need to be fed, and most of all, you two need to get dressed!" Petra is on a tear now, and I guess the shower fun time is over. Too bad. We turn to look at her, and she's already dried her hair and gotten herself dressed in a pretty outfit I've never seen. She looks incredible. Boy, that was fast. Or maybe we've been messing around and lost track of time. I give Weston a regret-filled kiss, and we rinse off.

"The house is clean enough, Petra," he says as he wraps a towel around himself. "We just vacuumed and dusted two days ago."

She seems momentarily distracted by the water droplets making their way down his sculpted torso, and asks, "Huh?"

Then she shifts her glance to me when I step up behind him, saying, "Plus, we can eat outside since it's great weather this evening, and I planned to use the grill."

God, she's gorgeous and responsive to us. The look on her face says she's ready to lie down and do the deed right this moment. But she gives her head a minute shake and asks, "Is the downstairs bathroom clean?"

I smile at her. My family would crack up if they knew how seriously Petra is taking their arrival. We're just a simple Hoosier family who loves to get together to eat until we burst and drink lots of beer. I know they'll love Petra and Weston. And the dogs.

Besides, my parents already know that I love Petra and Weston. It seems I can never keep my mouth shut.

Eighteen

To say the next few hours are going to be hectic is putting it mildly. Callum's family are all tall, good-looking, loud, and affectionate with one another. They pile into the house in a big, smiling, jabbering herd of O'Malleys, laughing and talking a mile a minute. Callum's brother Declan, who looks like a younger, broader version of Callum, swaggers in exuding a "football player" aura from his very soul. He and their equally athletic, volleyball-playing sister Gracie immediately start a rambunctious game in the backyard with the dogs. No one seems to know the rules or the goal, and it doesn't matter in the least. It just requires a lot of running around, much to the dogs' delight—Dave is especially pleased, bounding up and down on the lawn. Everything seems like a good-natured competition with them, and they laugh at each other nonstop.

When their crazy game winds down, Declan starts to wander around the house and loudly exclaims, "Jeez Louise, Callum, you really lucked into a great deal here! This is a fantastic house, and the scenery is pretty amazing too." He eyeballs Petra with an exaggerated leer, giving her a red face and a fit of stifled giggles. He reminds me of an overly friendly, exuberant puppy.

Gracie is a *bit* more reserved, but she's been giving me the eye too. She sure is pretty with those long, tan legs of hers and… oh, who am I kidding? She's lovely, but she doesn't hold a candle to our gorgeous Petra. I'm such a goner for that woman. Gracie's still a college student, so I'm polite to her and don't return the heated gazes.

Callum's grandmother, who insists we *all* call her Grammy, is just what you'd expect. She's tall and energetic and peppers everyone with personal questions from the minute she bestows her "pleased to meet you" bear hug. Petra and I become de facto grandkids immediately. I'm grilled into giving up the information (the quick version) about how I can afford such a nice, big house (I inherited it from my grandfather), what kind of money I make as a psychologist (I try to be vague), and whether or not I'm single. That is the one I have the hardest time answering, so I just say, "Things are…ah… really new so far in that arena," and that gets a wicked grin from her. She seems to somehow intuit that I am coming off of a sex coma from earlier in the day. That may have been prompted by Petra's crimson face. Right away I adore the woman, and judging from Petra's reaction to her, she feels the same way.

Grammy's questions to Petra are equally probing, but Petra is awfully good about keeping her ghostwriting private. Even after being badgered, she doesn't reveal anything. "I'd be sued if I broke my confidentiality contracts," she explains politely and shifts the questions back to Grammy, asking about her hobbies and what she likes to read. *Well done, Petra.*

We discover that Grammy has a taste for sizzling romance, and that launches them into a discussion of favorite authors. One they laughingly agree upon is Dolly Gunn, and Petra swears on a Bible that she's never ghostwritten any of those books, but she loves them. She blushes again, so I wonder what's in those books that has them both fanning their faces and giggling.

Callum's parents Dylan and Liv are warm and loving, and it makes me so happy to imagine what kind of a childhood he had growing up in their household. I don't exactly feel jealous, but I do feel the hurt in my heart thinking how short a time I had with my mom and dad. When his mom asks me where my parents live, I answer quickly that they both passed away several years ago, and I get up to go refill my glass. It doesn't need refilling, but I needed to clear my head for a moment.

The hushed voices in my wake let me know that Callum is filling them in.

When I return to the living room, the sympathetic looks I'm getting make me feel worse, so I immediately ask Callum's dad to tell me what it's like being a firefighter. He's apparently a captain, and he's been at it for a long time. He launches into one story after the next, and I'm relieved to have the pressure off me for now.

While his dad is speaking, Callum politely excuses himself to go turn on the grill and start the kebabs he's had soaking in some fancy marinade. Callum's mom and Petra leave to go arrange all the other dishes and place settings on the outdoor table.

When we all sit down, I see that there is enough food here for at least twenty people, and it all looks amazing. Dinner is a chaotic, joyful meal with a table full of very nice people. I understand Callum better now. I get his confidence.

At one point, Gracie stands up and announces with a poorly suppressed burp that she's had too much beer and needs to find the bathroom. I direct her to the one right off the kitchen, but she waves me off. "I've seen it, thanks, Weston." She heads inside the house, and no one gives it another thought.

However, in the amount of time it takes for Goliath to wag his tail once, the whole complexion of the evening changes.

Nineteen

I'm laughing so hard I have tears in my eyes. Declan is telling a ridiculous story about one of Callum's early kitchen disasters. I guess there was a lot of smoke and a very loud fire alarm, besides the charred mess and lots of frantic running around. Their dad was not present, and for that, they are grateful since it turned the kitchen into a fire hazard. Callum looks like he's trying to be somber about it, but he's actually amused at his brother and himself.

We're all making a lot of noise laughing and don't even pay any attention to Gracie as she returns to the table. As we all realize she is being followed by someone, one by one we stop laughing and look at who just arrived. Gracie—who is blocking my view of the guy—has a big smile on her face and announces, "Petra, look who was knocking on the front door! It's your fiancé! I explained to him that he was late for dinner." She steps out of the way, and there's Ben—looking smug.

"Oh, no he's not!" I cry and jump up from my seat. Callum and Weston stand with me. Callum grabs one hand and Weston wraps his arm around my waist. "He is *not* my fiancé. Ben, what are you doing here? How did you find me? You need to leave. This is a private party. Leave. Now."

"It's so good to see you, babe," he croons as if he didn't just see me come unglued. "You look nice. I brought you these." It's a large bouquet of calla lilies that look all wrong for something he could afford—or any sensible man would pick out for his girlfriend. They look somber, like a funeral bouquet—not romantic at all.

"I don't want your flowers or *anything* from you ever again. Did you steal that arrangement?" Wow, even I amaze myself for going there so quickly.

His face reddens and he says, "Of course not! I got them for you because I know how much you love… uh… orchids."

Glaring at him and muttering, "Idiot," I stomp toward Ben and root around in the flowers until I see a card buried in the middle of them. I snatch it up and pull it out of the envelope. His eyes get shifty as I read aloud, "'Our sincere condolences.' It's signed 'Marv and Daphne Greenbaum.' How did you swipe this, you jerk? Should we call the florist? Did you even know that people who send flowers *put cards in them*? I'll say this one last time. Get. Out."

Apparently deciding to deflect by going on the offensive, Ben says, "What are you doing with these two fags anyway, babe? I saw you all in the grocery store when I went to buy some donuts. They couldn't keep their hands off you, and then they were all over *each other*. Weirdos!"

I'm so mad at that, I'm shaking. "What I do is none of your concern. And you owe these very fine men an apology for that slur. Then you need to leave and forget about where I live and anything else you imagine you know about me. Shall I call the police and have you physically removed?"

By now, Callum's dad and brother are also flanking me and looking like they want blood. I see when it finally registers, and all of the color drains out of Ben's face. I'm definitely supported by a lot of muscle. The dogs also join in, advancing on Ben with low growls. Dave even goes so far as to bare his teeth and nip at his legs. I could kiss each one of them.

"Ben, have you been leaving dead animals at my previous apartment? That's just sick!"

"Of course not! Why would I do that? And besides, I wouldn't touch a dead animal." His shudder and horrified look actually lend a ring of truth to that statement, but the rest of what he says just digs him deeper in trouble. "Look, Petty. Come back home with me and get out of this house with these creeps. I need you, babe."

I see red—and not just in his bloodshot eyes. "For what? To pay your bills? Have you found a new job yet? Have you spent everything you have getting high?" I see him flinch slightly at that. "Why don't you get your best buddy Randy to pitch in since he never leaves your side these days? I want nothing to do with either of you. I made that clear when I moved out months ago! And don't call me by that stupid nickname. How did you find me here anyway?"

Looking sheepish, Ben answers, "Well you've blocked my calls, and your old roommate wouldn't give me your address..."

"She doesn't know it," I snap at him.

"She refused in any case, so when I saw you all at Market District, I figured it was fate. I followed you back to this house. I didn't try to talk to you then because I wasn't sure what I wanted to say yet." He hangs his head.

"Yeah, that isn't creepy at all, Ben."

Everyone is glaring at him until Grammy finally stands and removes the flowers from Ben's hands saying, "We'll just give this florist a call and let them know one of their arrangements ended up in the wrong hands. It's time for you to run along, young man. Try your best to stop telling lies and stealing things and maybe one day you'll find a lovely girl who can trust you with her heart. If you keep this up, however, you're likely headed for jail time. No decent woman wants to marry a con." She turns to Callum's dad and brother and orders them, "Escort this poor, confused man to the door, and lock it."

Before they can leave, I have to add, "Ben, don't you ever *dare* tell Randy where I live. That guy is a total sleazeball."

"He's okay," Ben protests. "What did he ever do that was so bad?"

"He was creepy and abusive to me, and you know it. You're just too stoned most of the time to see it. Now *get out* of here!"

As they take him firmly by his elbows and propel him toward the door, I sink to my seat. "Thank you, everyone. He's bad news. Did anyone else think he looked high?"

"Yeah, now that I think of it, he might have been," Gracie says. "Sorry I let him in."

"I wouldn't know," Grammy demurs.

Callum's mom just looks at me skeptically and asks, "Were you ever actually engaged to that… person?"

I'm so freaking embarrassed right now, I want to cry, but I force myself to sit up straight and explain, "He wasn't always such a loser. It was only when an old friend of his, Randy, started coming around that he started getting high. I even wondered if Randy purposefully got Ben hooked on some-thing so he could control him. It was really weird. Before that, he had a good job and acted responsibly. I left when Randy horned in and wrecked what we had, and then everything fell apart. Leaving was the best decision I've ever made, obviously. I am so sorry you all had to see that. I've never been so ashamed."

Grammy speaks up in a gentle tone, "You have nothing to be ashamed of. He's a handsome young man, and you were probably attracted to him at one point. It's when they stop being on their best behavior and their true personalities finally show up that things get bad. I've been divorced for over forty years from a man I never should have married in the first place. The only worthwhile thing he ever did was get me pregnant with Liv, and then he made my life miserable until he took off for good. Our lives were vastly improved by his absence. Be happy you dodged a bullet, sweetheart."

"Your story sounds a bit like my mom's—or at least what I think she may have gone through."

"Sorry to hear that."

The faces around the table are all as somber as can be when Callum breaks the mood finally. "Who's ready for dessert?"

A LITTLE WHILE LATER, WE ALL HEAR THE DOORBELL RING, SO this time Weston rushes off to answer it. He grabs the floral arrangement on his way. When he returns, he explains to us, "The poor delivery guy was beside himself. He was dropping off a bunch of flowers at a house around the corner, and he left the truck open in the driveway so he could make a several trips to the door easily. When he got back to the truck to grab more of the flowers, he saw that the calla lilies were gone. To say he was grateful is putting it mildly. He just kept asking me, 'What kind of a jerk steals flowers meant for a wake?'"

"Good question," Callum answers. He looks at me and his eyes show nothing but understanding, so he gives me a quick hug and a little snicker. "That wasn't a very great gift, but I guess you could have had worse. We actually have a really awful—and hilarious—running contest in our family to see who can win the worst gift award."

"Oh yeah?" I ask. "What are some of them?" I need to be cheered up by something funny after Ben showed up and put a huge damper on the party.

Dylan and Liv start laughing, and Dylan explains, "I have a brother who's a little eccentric, and one Christmas he went to Costco and bought a bunch of packages of bar soap. Then he divided up the bars and gave them all to everyone in the family according to how important we were to him. I only got two bars, but he gave our mom six. So then we all got into a competition to see how many everyone got. It was so dumb and at the same time comical. Who gives stupid discount bars of soap as a Christmas gift?"

I can't help but get the giggles over that story.

It's obvious that everyone is eyeing Liv as if waiting for her response, but she looks at me and asks, "Have you ever been given anything odd, Petra? I mean other than purloined funeral flowers to try to win you over?"

I wrack my brain, and all I can come up with is, "My mom travels a lot, and sometimes she sends me weird stuff from other countries. One time she sent me a candle that was supposed to ward off vampires. I'm not sure what she was thinking." That gets me some laughs and strange looks. "What about you, Weston?"

"My grandmother used to knit me a sweater every Christmas. I would never wear them to school though. They could have won any ugly sweater contest ever." He looks down. "I wish I still had them actually—even though I was just a little kid at the time."

I reach over and give his hand a squeeze.

Callum breaks the tension by saying, "Okay Mom, tell your story." He has a look of suppressed mirth on his face.

Liv seems to agree that it's time to let us know the all-time winner. She clears her throat and says, "My grandmother was a piece of work. A true original. We never knew if she was as thick as a post or as dumb as a fox because she never seemed to react the way everyone else did about anything. She was famous for cheating at cards and giving us all strange things that we never knew if she was serious about or meant as a joke. She often passed around things like chopped-up Jerusalem artichokes from her garden. She'd put pieces in a jar —not canned or preserved in any way, just stuck in something like an old mayonnaise jar, so that by the time she'd hand them to you, the contents would be all moldy." Liv laughs. "It was gross and hilarious at the same time, but she seemed oblivious. I never knew who ate those awful-looking things anyway, but someone must—just not the ones she gave out from her garden.

"Anyway, one Christmas she gave my cousin a box of old plastic dishes. That wouldn't have been that bad, but there was dried-up food stuck to the plates." Everyone makes faces and disparaging noises, but Liv is finally ready to deliver the worst part. She suddenly can't stop laughing.

"My cousin thought that was the worst until I told her my story years later. When I was thirteen," she stops to wipe her eyes, "we were all opening gifts around the tree on Christmas morning. I took the paper off the gift from Nana to me and thought to myself that she'd used a rather *odd* box to put a present in." She pauses for effect and looks around at everyone. "I opened the box only to discover that she'd given me half a box of sanitary napkins."

My jaw drops.

"I closed that box so fast and ran to the bathroom to hide it in the cupboard. I was mortified. I didn't even tell my own mother about it for months."

"I was also not amused when she told me. I'd been a victim of her so-called 'generosity' my whole life," Grammy says drily.

"It was just so wrong for a young girl of that age," she says with a laugh. "It took years for me to see the humor in it, but I eventually did."

"You win." I declare as I stare at Liv. "Worst gift ever."

Then I look around at the faces of Callum's beautiful family, and I am stuck by the absolute rightness of them being here and the affection they show one another. They can tease and poke at each other, and the love shines through it all. I know I've never had this in my life, and suddenly I crave it more than anything. This reality stabs me in the gut so hard I almost double over, so I quickly stand up and say, "Thank you, everyone, for tonight. This has been amazing. I'll just get started on cleaning up now." Grabbing a stack of plates, I head toward the kitchen before anyone can respond. Then I stop and add, "Weston, why don't you take everyone downstairs and play ping pong for a while? Maybe you can have a round-robin tournament or something."

When I look at Weston's expression, I suspect he's feeling an emotion similar to mine.

Twenty

WESTON

I'M SO BLOWN AWAY RIGHT NOW. CALLUM IS AMAZING. HIS family is absolutely the best. I know I've been missing my own family for years and years, but the longing I have for them has never been so acute as right at this very moment. Petra just asked me something, and I didn't even hear her; I was I caught up in my head.

"Huh?" I grunt stupidly at her.

"I said, why don't you take people down and have a ping pong game? I'm going to start cleaning up since I didn't do any of this terrific cooking. It's only fair."

"I'll help Petra," Liv says. "We planned to leave the left-overs here for you, so I'll just put most of this into the refrigerator, and Callum can get the containers back to us later."

So Callum, Declan, Gracie, and I all take off for the ping pong table, and Gracie shouts at her brothers, "I get to be on Weston's team! He probably knows more about ping pong than you two doofusses." The rest of the trash-talking proceeds me down the stairs, but I can hear Grammy announce, "I'll help too."

"Why don't you and Dylan just relax and have a glass of wine or another beer?" Petra asks. "We have it covered." She probably doesn't want to wear out Grammy, although the woman does seem as though she's still full of plenty of energy. Grammy must be close to ninety. Amazing.

"Nonsense. I don't need another drink, and Dylan is driving us all home." With that, she and Dylan stand and start hauling dishes and cutlery back into the kitchen too.

And we begin a hilarious ping pong tournament with lots of hollering and laughter. It's almost as much fun as what the three of us did earlier today… but not quite. When was the last time this house was filled with so much activity and joy? Maybe never.

We play and play, getting wilder and crazier with our shots. At one point I see Dylan come down the stairs with the dogs on his tail and a bottle of water in his hand. He smiles at me and positions himself in front of the TV. After some channel surfing, he settles on something, looking relaxed and satisfied.

Each of us is sweaty and red-faced from laughter and exertion. Finally, Callum and Declan are declared the tournament champions after winning two out of three hard-fought battles, but it was certainly close. Callum and his brother high-five each other and Callum crows, "Winner, winner, chicken dinner!" at the top of his voice.

"Oh, don't gloat. You kept serving before I was ready," Gracie complains.

"No one likes a sore loser," Declan says, shaking his finger at his sister. "Come on, let's go grab a beer. This made me thirsty."

"You're too young to drink, Dec." She pokes him in the ribs as he rolls his eyes at her. And on and on it goes.

I love watching them.

Twenty-One

As soon as the guys are out of earshot, the inquisition begins. Oh sure, it's polite and friendly, but I'm feeling pretty grilled in any case.

"Weston and Callum both seem pretty taken with you, Petra," Liv mentions breezily. I can feel Grammy's eyes staring a hole in the back of my head with her laser focus.

"I'm pretty taken with them too," I admit, deciding not to hold back.

"Hmm," Grammy says. Liv looks at her and has no discernible expression on her face whatsoever.

"They also seem pretty taken with each other," Liv continues after zeroing back in on me.

I nod as I start loading dishes into the dishwasher. "Yes, I believe they are."

"I think I'll go find a TV and watch the game," Dylan announces to no one.

"You'll find it downstairs," I tell him. "The remote is on the coffee table." I have absolutely no idea what game could possibly be on right now, but in true man-fashion, he'll find something, I'm sure.

He nods and leaves the kitchen quickly, and the dogs trot out with him. Apparently, we haven't been accidentally dropping enough food on the floor for them to want to stick around.

"Was there any truth to what that young man said—the one who barged in and unsuccessfully tried to sweep you off your feet?"

I lurch upright and feel my hackles rising. "Ben is a complete idiot, so I hope you aren't referring to his calling the guys… um… you know… a derogatory slur."

"Petra, I am fully aware that Callum is bisexual. I'm his mother, and I wasn't born yesterday. We all love him and accept who he is. I just don't want to see him, or you for that matter, get hurt."

I blink at her for a moment and answer softly, "Neither do I."

"So there is something serious going on with the three of you?"

"I think you ought to be asking Callum that question. I'm feeling rather ambushed right now."

"I've actually spoken to Callum, and I know he has strong feelings for you *and* Weston." She looks at me kindly then. "You seem like a lovely person, though I know nothing of your background or much of anything beyond your writing career. I just think all three of you ought to be careful with each other's feelings. It's true we live in a more progressive world now, and alternative lifestyles are more acceptable than when Dylan and I were your age, but I can't help but worry. I suppose it's exciting to be fulfilling some kind of fantasy you all might have about a ménage or throuple or whatever it's called today, but be careful. That's all I want to say."

I decide then to lay some truths out for Liv, so I take a deep breath and begin. "I pretty much grew up without anyone to nurture me. I never had a father, and my mother preferred far-off, exotic destinations over caring for a daughter. I had a series of nannies and later boarding school—never any siblings or cousins, and that was it. I've made some colossally poor choices with men, as you so clearly saw when my ex showed up this evening. I met him through a dating app and lived with him for six months after he proposed, but I could never make myself settle on a wedding date. The fact was, he bored me to death, but I didn't know any better. I thought maybe all men were like that. I was spoiled by reading and creating book boyfriends who are too good to be true, so I disparaged ever finding a man like that for myself. I was of what I considered marriageable age, so I accepted Ben's ring and agreed to marry sometime in the not-too-near future… until I caught him in a series of lies, and his horrible friend virtually moved in with us and kept trying to convince me to hook up with him behind his best friend's back. Ben accused me of making up stories when I told him about it, and that was the last straw. I also suspected that his friend dealt drugs, and I wanted to get as far away from that as possible.

"Eventually, I found my way to this house at practically the same exact moment Callum did, and we all clicked within minutes. Not one of us *tried* to begin a relationship. We were all happy and obviously fond of each other, but we were also all super attracted to one another. I mean… look at them!" I laugh and Liv's eyes crinkle with humor. She's losing some of her Mama Bear attitude little by little, I think. "There was some harmless flirting and some couch snuggling for several weeks, and nothing more than that. And then we all just sort of caved in at the same time. I'm not sure what happened, but we each just chose not to fight it anymore."

I make sure I'm looking right into Liv's eyes when I admit, "This is the happiest I've ever been in my life. Those two men are both so considerate and generous with themselves. I've never felt so protected and cared for, and it's a beautiful thing to see the affection they have for each other. I feel incredibly lucky."

I reach into the refrigerator for a bottle of water and take a swig. "Is this serious between us? I would have to say it probably is in that I would never intentionally do something to disrupt our harmony or hurt either of their feelings. Do I want it to continue? You bet I do."

"Well, I must say that I appreciate your candor, Petra. And I hope for everyone's sake that you can maintain what you have started. I wish you all good luck."

Grammy then adds, "If I hear that you've done anything to hurt Callum, I'll personally come and steal that anti-vampire candle of yours and let them at you!" Then, laughing, she wraps her arms around me and gives me the kind of hug I always wanted—but never got—from my mom. How could I not fall in love with Callum? I'm already completely in love with his entire family.

♡♡♡

Not too much later, the O'Malleys leave in a flurry of hugs, kisses, promises to talk soon, and thanks for everything.

"They're really terrific," Weston says as we wave at their departing car. "Thanks for inviting them over, Callum." He puts his arm around both of our waists and asks, "Is anyone else as ready for bed as I am?" He wiggles his eyebrows and flashes those killer dimples at us.

"You bet," Callum answers.

"Absolutely. I have to say too that they're wonderful, Callum, and despite the grilling I got from your mother, I am crazy about all of them. Thank you for having them all come over tonight. It was honestly a real treat."

"Sorry, she felt the need to grill you. I hope she didn't overstep."

"She's a caring Mama Bear who's looking out for her cubs. I love that about her. No harm in anything she said. You're so lucky to have a mom like that."

Twenty-Two

Callum

Petra sure is a good sport. I can imagine what my mom asked. After raising four kids, she has no boundaries. But I'm not getting any negative vibes from Petra, so I guess I ought to be thankful for that.

"I'm going to let the dogs out," Weston says, "and I'll meet you both upstairs as soon as they come back inside." He gives us a wink.

I weigh our options and tell him, "If it's okay with you, I think your bed is our best bet. It's the largest. Petra and I will be ready for you when you get back." I can't help running my hand down her arm and love seeing the reaction she has to my touch. She presses into it like I'm giving her pleasure with the smallest caress. When I add, "I'll bring some lube," her cheeks flame with a rosy blush. "If I recall correctly, Petra had a request."

She gives me a heated look and then winks at Weston.

"Okay, boys!" Weston calls to the dogs. There's a little crack in his voice as he adds, "Let's… ah… get this nighttime business done quickly! Last one back is a rotten dog bone." He heads to the back door, careful not to step on Dave, who's twirling, and the retrievers whose tails are wagging at warp speed while they bounce up and down. Gus is panting and smiling, and Goliath is making *woo-woo* noises with curled lips. It's a happy, somewhat chaotic sight. Dave spins around the other dogs and herds them through the door, yipping at them. The bigger dogs seem unfazed by his bossiness.

Petra and I head up the stairs, and she says, "I think I'd like to take a really quick shower."

"Want some company?"

"Um… sure. Okay."

So I begin peeling off my own clothes as we head up. By the time we make it to our shared bathroom, I'm down to my boxers, and she's laughing. Petra shucks her own outfit a little more carefully and puts her hair up in a bun while I adjust the shower. I suspect she wants to shave, but I'm surprised when she gets under the spray with me and doesn't go for a razor immediately. "Not shaving?" I ask. Then, come to think of it, I realize I've never seen one sitting in the shower.

"Don't need to. I splurged a couple of years ago on laser

treatments. It's great because I never have any razor cuts or itchy stubble this way. Also, I don't have to keep waxing."

"Doesn't the laser treatment hurt?"

"It depends on the part of you that's getting lasered. Some parts are pretty awful, and others are no big deal. I'm sure you can figure out the differences without me spelling them out. But the beauty of it is, it's permanent. I just keep the landing strip trimmed, and that's it."

For the next few minutes, we help each other lather up all those hard-to-reach—wink, wink—areas with some delightful body wash she always has in the shower. It has a coconutty, fruity smell to it that makes me feel like we should be sipping rum drinks on a Caribbean island. I can almost hear the steel drums, and it makes me smile. I start to fantasize about an island honeymoon, and mentally slap myself. *Cut it out!* I'll admit to opening this bottle more than once while showering so I can imagine fucking Petra while I take care of my morning wood. It never fails to start my day out right.

When we're sufficiently buffed, I take the showerhead off its holder and spray her down, leering at her reaction when I direct the spray between her legs. She hisses and then doubles over slightly, grabbing my arm for balance. "Did I hit a nerve, Petra?" I ask innocently.

Just then, Weston opens the bathroom door and asks, with a laugh "You really have a thing for showers, don't you Callum? Come on out, both of you. We have some *stuff* to do."

"You could come on in too," Petra says invitingly.

"Not enough room. You should have been in the big shower."

I laugh and say, "This one was closer."

As Petra and I step out of the shower, Weston strips down to no clothes, and as he steps past me, he says, "You smell just like Petra now," and grins. "So, if everyone else is all freshly scrubbed and smells delicious, I don't want to reek like I've been sweating through a ping pong tournament for the last hour."

"I'll go grab you a clean towel," Petra tells him.

"Oh. Yeah. I… ah… forgot. Thanks."

Within moments, we've brushed our teeth, and we're all refreshed and dry. We pile onto Weston's big bed.

I've grabbed a stack of condoms and a large bottle of lube.

Petra has gone back to blushing and reminds me of a delicious ripe strawberry. I'm anxious to sample her sweet juices.

"So, Petra," I begin. "I seem to remember Weston making a suggestion to you about both of us fucking you at the same time, and you sounded agreeable to that idea. Any second thoughts? Are you still willing?" I watch as Weston eyes her greedily. He must be thinking what I'm thinking. What a beautiful thing this could be for all of us to express ourselves with one another simultaneously. Plus… this whole scenario is sexier than fuck.

"Yes," she answers with no hesitation. "I want both of you inside me at the same time, and I want you to feel each other inside me, so we can experience our shared desire together."

"Weston?"

He takes Petra's hand and says with reverence, "I would love to be in that gorgeous, tight little ass of yours. I've been fantasizing about it for weeks, actually."

Blinking at him, she asks, "You've been fantasizing about me?"

"You and Callum. I can't get either of you out of my mind."

"Oh my." It's a tiny gesture, but she shivers at his words. "How… stimulating."

I grin at them. "Then let's get her prepped, shall we? Petra, lie down on your stomach and spread your legs. We need to open you up for Weston's big cock."

Petra's eyes are huge as she stares at us for a second, then she flips over. I undo the top of the lube and squirt some on my fingers. "Hold her cheeks apart," I tell Weston. "That's right." I groan at the sight of her pretty little hole and think what a lucky bastard Weston is by being the first one in there. It's hard not to feel jealous, but I will be the one inside her sweet pussy, so there is no room for complaint. I begin to massage her rosebud and lean down to kiss the exquisite dimples just above her butt. "So beautiful," I whisper and then say, "Weston, lube up a couple of your fingers too. She's going to need plenty of stretching so she's comfortable."

I can already see that Weston is rock-hard and leaking precum. It's such a beautiful thing, I can't resist leaning over and licking the head of his dick. "Mmm."

Now Weston is shuddering like our Petra. He leans down and kisses Petra deeply and then tells her, "I'm going to love this. I hope we can make it perfect for you." He sits back up and joins my hand in massaging her.

Petra makes some sexy little hums as we play with her. I'm as hard as Weston, and I can feel my own pulse thrumming through my dick.

Starting with the tip of my finger, I invade her hole little by little. I apply more and more lube and smile as I watch Petra squirm. She's not retreating in any way. She's pushing her bottom into my touch as if she's begging for more. Finally, I have one finger all the way in and begin the process of introducing a second one. She gasps a little and then calms down with a purring sound. Once two fingers are in her, and she seems to be tolerating that well, I nod to Weston, and he squirts even more lube out and gently probes her with one of his fingers. She gasps even louder with the entry of this one, and this time it sounds a bit more like a tiny cry of pain. But she instantly tells us, "Keep going. Mmm, I love it!"

"You have no idea how beautiful this is right now," I tell her. "We both have two fingers deep into you together. I know it's a lot, but we're going to stroke them in and out now, so get ready." She gives a long gasp as Weston and I slide our combined fingers almost all the way out of her and then push them back in. "Does this feel alright?" I ask.

"Yessss. I never realized… Don't stop. Please."

"Then let us know when you're ready for Weston's dick, sweetheart."

"Almost," she whispers.

Weston takes his free hand and slides a finger into her pussy, eliciting another groan from her. That looks like fun to me, so I join him with a free finger of my own. I'm so turned on by this sight, I wonder if I'll make it inside of her before I explode. "My God, she's sexy, isn't she, Weston? Look at how she's taking our fingers inside her body." I can feel her muscles clamp down on us, and it makes me want her so badly, I can barely think straight and let out a groan of my own.

Weston's response is to smile seductively and then kiss me deeply. He tastes delicious, like Petra. How did I ever get to be so lucky? We become lost in each other's kiss as we stroke in and out of Petra. After a little while, she says, "I think I'm ready now."

We pull away from each other, and I look down. Weston is still leaking profusely he's so turned on. We pump in and out a couple more times just to enjoy the view and then slide our fingers out of Petra. I can't resist grabbing Weston's dick and sucking him once again while he reaches for a condom. I slide off with a pop, and he quickly sheaths himself.

With an eager look on his face, Weston lies down beside Petra and holds the base of his erection.

"I think you'll be more comfortable if you prop some

pillows behind you so Petra can lean back onto your chest," I suggest.

Petra eyes me and asks, "Have you done this before, Callum? You seem to have all of the answers."

Chuckling, I answer, "Well…"

"Okay, I don't want to know," she says quickly. "Never mind."

Once Weston looks satisfied with his pillows and has lubed up his dick, I help Petra climb on top of him, facing me. She begins by straddling his body, so I help her balance above him while he positions himself beneath her nicely prepared butt. Then we begin the process of lowering her down onto him incrementally. I wish I could bottle the combined looks of rapture on their faces so I could keep them forever. They are beyond sexy. Weston's eyes are focused on mine with a laser stare, and he seems to be holding his breath. Petra's eyes close involuntarily as she sinks down onto his rigid shaft.

The whole time, Petra keeps up the mantra, "Ohmygod, ohmygod, ohmygod…" over and over.

"Are you alright?" I ask her.

"Oh, yeah. Never better," she finally croaks.

"You are both so perfect," I tell them. "I want you to understand that this is way beyond just sex for me. This is… well… everything." I lean forward and kiss Petra's glorious mouth, and then I slide my lips down her body, lavishing my affection on her breasts one after the other, her navel, and finally, I kiss her thighs and lean closer to tongue her swollen clit. The woman is drenched, she is so aroused. She grabs my hair as I flick her bud over and over with my tongue. She is writhing on top of Weston, who is groaning in pleasure now. Finally, I suck her stiff clit into my mouth over and over and watch as she is overcome—gasping with a colossal orgasm.

Immediately, I grab a condom and sheath myself in record time. I position myself at her entrance and shove my dick into her with a cry of bliss. "Fuck yes!" I couldn't go slowly if my life depended on it. She is so hot and wet, and her muscles are still rippling around me in aftershocks. I can feel the ridges of Weston's dick as I slide in and out feverishly. I've never been so turned on in my life. This feels like home and heaven and some high level of nirvana all at the same time. None of us can stay silent. We're all moaning and groaning, writhing, and pumping. This is life! This is… love. I feel it bursting out of me. Pouring out of my very pores. I feel on fire and like I'm floating in the sea all at the same time.

Over and over Weston groans and Petra spasms while I pound in and out—rubbing against his stiffness and relishing her glorious wet heat. At last, Weston gives a loud cry announcing, "Coming! Ahhh!" and I can see his eyes roll back as he shudders in ecstasy.

Petra rasps out the words, "Me too," as she nearly strangles my dick by clamping down with her inner muscles. I swear, the woman must practice her Kegels all day long! Her chest is heaving, and she's panting. She is magnificent.

The feeling of omnipotence overcomes me. I am on the top

of the world. I feel pleasure overtaking my body like nothing I've ever experienced before, and I explode into Petra's tight grip on me. There is heat and softness, and oh, so much love. I can't contain it all. It spills forth from me in streams and jolts of sheer delight. Over and over I ejaculate, and I feel powerful and complete.

"I haven't," I croak to them finally.

"Haven't what?" Petra asks in a drowsy voice. "You certainly came."

I'm not sure Weston has the ability to form words quite yet.

"I haven't ever done this before," I admit with my chest heaving. "I think I was waiting to do it with people I love. This was… perfection."

"Oh, Callum," Petra says softly. "I agree."

"I… ah… uh huh," Weston breathes. He is still mostly non-verbal, but we get the idea.

I climb off them and kiss Petra, then carefully help her off Weston. He has the most blissed-out expression ever seen on anyone's face in the history of everything, so I kiss him too and then tell him, "Your ass is next, Loverboy."

Weston's eyes pop open, and his dimples wink as he grins at us.

♡♡♡

I'm just coming out of the bathroom as I see Petra walking through the bedroom door with an odd expression on her face. She's carrying her phone, but she is still stark naked, and it's difficult not to be knocked over by her beauty. She looks up and says, "I heard my phone chime, so I went to grab it off the charger. So far, the alerts have always just shown my old roommate coming and going through her front door, but this time it showed exactly what I expected would eventually happen. It was our neighbor's big, fat cat depositing what looks like a gopher on the doormat. So there's one more mystery solved. Now we know who was following us in the market and who's been leaving gross presents at the door." She sets down her phone and climbs into bed between Weston and me, sighing contentedly.

"Is this okay that we're invading your bed, Weston?" I ask.

"Best thing ever. I hope you never plan to leave it."

I'm sure we all fall asleep with smiles on our faces.

Twenty-Three

WAKING UP TO TWO HOT MEN IN ONE BED IS BEYOND A DREAM come true. Let me be clear that reading about this kind of scenario pales in comparison to actually experiencing it for yourself. I feel like a different person! How is this my life?

Last night, Callum expressed some pretty deep feelings for us, and I'm sorry to say that I—the wordsmith—let my words fail me somewhat. My response was so inadequate, I need to make it up to these guys. But then, Weston was practically catatonic, and his response wasn't any better than mine. At least Callum didn't seem fazed by our silence. If anything, he looked pretty smug. He is amazingly comfortable in his own skin, and it was a relief to hear from his mother that they accept his bisexuality. It kills me when families turn against their children for not being exactly what the parents expect of them. Then again, my own mother probably doesn't give a crap how I've turned out—not out of love but more disinterest. I'm lucky if I get a sporadic email or text message from her. I often wonder what it would have been like to have had parents who cared about me.

Well, no sense dwelling on that now. What's done is done.

I'm lost in these thoughts, staring at the ceiling, when I feel stirring in the bed. My partners are waking up. Somehow, I ended up between them, and it's pretty toasty in here with these two large, hot men flanking me, but it's also more fun than I could ever imagine.

Callum starts nuzzling my neck and whispers to me, "Are you sore, sweetheart?" His arm lays across me, and his warm hand cups my boob. Something firm is pressed against my thigh.

Thinking about his question for a moment, I answer honestly, "Hmm. A little. Nothing bad."

"We need to go easy on you in any case," he tells me, then kisses me soundly, slides out of bed, and heads for the bathroom. I love watching him walk away. What a body. Considering he's such a foodie, he stays in remarkably great shape. I still need to ask him if he'll go with me for a run.

No sooner has Callum closed the bathroom door than I feel Weston pull me closer to him. He lavishes me with more kisses to my neck, mumbling in a sleepy voice, "I'm dying to kiss you for real, but I'm afraid I have morning mouth."

I laugh softly and assure him, "I don't mind." And so it begins. Weston can kiss like he invented it. Morning breath is the last thing on my mind as he invades me with his tongue and caresses me with his soft lips.

Moments later, Callum returns and chuckles at the sight of us wrapped around each other. He sits on the bed and says, "There was a time when seeing this would have made me feel jealous and left out, but now all I can think is that the two of you together are the most beautiful thing I can think of. And I think how lucky I am."

Weston pulls back and gives Callum a cocky look. Then his expression changes to alarm as he asks suddenly, "What time is it?"

"It's eight-thirty."

"Aw crap!" Weston leaps out of bed and dashes for the bathroom saying, "I forgot I scheduled a make-up session with someone for nine this morning. I need to get ready. She had to cancel…" The rest is muffled by the closed door, but we get the picture.

"Isn't Sunday morning a little odd for a session with a patient? Or client? What does he call them anyway?" I ask.

"He calls them clients. So, maybe that's all she could do, or it felt like an emergency. Who knows?" Callum answers with a shrug. "Anyway, let's get up and I'll fix everyone some breakfast. Then after that, I actually have to make up menus for the next series of classes I'll be teaching. Do you have anything you need to get done?"

"I'm a little behind on my writing, so, yes. Today would be a great day to catch up. If it's nice out, I think I'll write outside."

Weston dashes by us and grabs some clothes. He jams his legs into a pair of shorts and then reaches for a nice, ironed dress shirt. He eyes Callum and asks, "Did you make coffee last night?"

Callum stands and puts a friendly hand on Weston's shoulder. "Relax. I'll bring you a mug and something quick to fill you up while you're checking your notes. Give me five minutes. Go get yourself ready for your call." He puts his finger to the side of his mouth and says softly, "You have a bit of toothpaste—right here."

"Oh, ah… thanks."

A few minutes later, I'm coming out of my bedroom, and I catch the sight of Callum across the hall placing a tray in front of Weston. The breakfast is simple, but somehow it manages to look divine: a toasted bagel with cream cheese, orange juice, and a steaming cup of coffee. Weston is sitting at his desk trying to look relaxed as he studies the notes from his last call with this client. Callum leans down and gives him a gentle kiss. "You've got this. Plenty of time to finish eating before connecting the call. When you're done with your appointment, if you're still hungry, come find me and I'll serve you the rest of your breakfast."

After a big slug of his juice, Weston says, "What would Petra and I do without you?"

"Eat lots of cold cereal and canned soup, I'd imagine," Callum laughs at his own joke and heads back out of the room. "Are you ready for a splendid breakfast, sweetheart?" he asks me and wraps his long arm around my waist. We head for the kitchen where he shows off for me by making delicious savory crepes filled with cheesy eggs and sausage and covered with a light, delicious sauce I can't even begin to identify. Like I said, how is this my life?

I don't ever remember being this happy. Honestly, what used to seem good to me was a slight blip on the joy-o-meter compared to now. I had so-so friends at school and passable relationships that fizzled quickly. Ben was the exception, and God knows that should have been nipped in the bud. I regret having been so naïve. What a loser. Hopefully, I've seen the last of him. I just wish he didn't know where I live now. That makes me a little nervous, but definitely not enough to move somewhere else. Who could leave this house with these two men? And Gus is the happiest dog in town living here. Callum says he's done some research on dog nutrition and has even started making them special treats. That guy is amazing.

Once I've fed the dogs, Callum sits down to enjoy breakfast with me. We talk about this and that until I ask him, "How's your job going?"

"It's great, but it's not exactly what I want to be doing for the rest of my life."

"Don't you enjoy teaching?"

"I do enjoy it, actually. A lot. In fact, I'd love to have my own restaurant where I could combine cooking classes with wonderful meals. That's a long way off, though, I'm afraid."

"Hmm. What do you need for it to happen?"

He laughs. "Lots more money than I have now. Or a very flush investor. For now, I still have a lot to learn, and I'm definitely enjoying what I'm doing. I get to come home at night instead of keeping late hours in a regular restaurant setting. That's the downside to being a chef."

"What if you were to open a luncheon place that caters mostly to women? Not to be sexist, but you could also appeal to more women who'd like to learn to cook like you. Besides, one look at you, and they'd flock to your place. I mean, some men would also..."

A slow grin appears on Callum's handsome face. "Are you saying you like the way I look, Petra?" Apparently, we're done discussing his employment possibilities.

I can feel myself blushing. "You know I do. You and Weston are..." I shiver. "Hot." I take in his piercing look and blush harder. "But besides how you both look, I also know you are both incredible men."

"Well, we're *your* incredible men, you should know that."

"That's for sure," I hear from behind me. Weston is walking into the kitchen and apparently heard some of our conversation. "You could say you have us by the balls, Petra."

That makes me laugh. Then I sober and ask, "So that means we're all in this and we're exclusive, right?"

"I… ah… sure hope we are," Weston assures us as he sits down at the table. "I never in a million years expected any of this to happen, but I love every bit of how this is going with all of us. I see myself falling for both of you more and more every day. I know we're unconventional, but I don't care. I feel alive and fulfilled when I'm with you both, and I've never felt like this before. Ever."

Once again, I, the wordsmith, seem to have been topped by my men. I wish I could just spit it out and say what's in my heart. Why is that so hard for me?

Callum stretches out a hand to the middle of the table and asks, "Petra and Weston, will you be my girlfriend and boyfriend? Exclusively?"

"I sure will," Weston answers as he grasps Callum's hand. They look at me.

I reach both hands out, slide one under Callum's hand on one atop Weston's, and answer, "You guys are absolutely it for me. Exclusive all the way." I kiss Weston, who kisses Callum, who kisses me. "Well! I guess it's official then," I say with a huge smile.

"Crepes, Weston?" Callum asks hopefully.

"You better say yes," I say with a chuckle. "They're amazing."

"In that case, fill me up," Weston says.

Callum winks at him and answers, "Oh, I plan to. Over and over."

I shiver again at the implication. "I'm anxious to see that."

"Tonight," Callum promises and gives me a saucy wink too.

Now it's Weston who's blushing. I love it.

Twenty-Four

WESTON

CALLUM AND PETRA HAVE BEEN PRETTY BUSY TODAY, SO I spent a lot of time working out in the gym, and then after a shower, I took the dogs for a walk. I wasn't sure what to expect, given their differences in size and their energy levels, but it worked out when I put Gus and Goliath's leashes in one hand and Dave's leash in the other. He bounced around a lot at first, but he calmed down pretty fast.

I got a lot of smiles from passing drivers and had to stop and chat with lots of neighbors who were curious about the dogs, so we didn't exactly get too far on our walk. It was nice to be outside with them, though. After about twenty minutes, I heard some quick footsteps approaching from behind, and the dogs all whipped around and looked happy with their tails going a mile a minute (except for Dave, of course, who wiggled his butt and hopped up and down). It turned out that Petra and Callum had gotten a little bit of cabin fever and were tired of working, so they decided to go for a run around the neighborhood.

I take in the sight of their lean bodies in running clothes coming toward me. I am the luckiest guy in the world. They are smiling at me as happily as the dogs, and I smile back at them.

"How are you guys all doing?" Petra asks as they get close enough to talk.

"Great," I answer. "We've made a lot of new friends, and I've had to explain about five times that no, Gus is not a golden doodle, he's a golden retriever, and Dave is a mini Aussie. No one seems too confused by Goliath so far at least."

"Want us to both take a dog and walk you home?" Callum asks.

"Don't you want to run some more?"

"Nah, we headed the other direction for a while, and when we didn't find you, we turned around until we finally saw you. We have plans for plenty more exercise at home." He wiggles his eyebrows. Unfortunately, I can't see his eyes because he's wearing sunglasses. I miss the view, actually. Callum reaches for Goliath's leash and Petra takes Gus's leash.

"Okay. I think we're about done anyway."

As soon as we get home, Petra and Callum head for the shower, and I grab a book to read for a while. It feels nice to relax now that I've spent some time outside. The dogs are calmer too. I think they needed the change of scenery as much as I did.

Soon Callum heads for the kitchen to work on dinner, so I follow him in asking, "Can I do anything to help?" I notice that he has continued to leave his shirt off a lot of the time. Petra and I enjoy the view.

"Hmm… I guess you can set the table. Dinner is a Moroccan chicken stew that I've had cooking for a while. I've also made us a cooked eggplant salad to go with it, and we can eat as soon as Petra comes downstairs. Last I heard, she was using her hairdryer."

"She's great, isn't she?" I ask him.

"Absolutely. I wonder sometimes about her lack of family, though, and how that may have affected her ability to form relationships. You probably know more about that than I could ever hope to. Do you think we need to treat her any special way?"

"Be yourself, Callum. She no doubt needs honesty and consistency in a relationship more than anything. We both know her last one was a trainwreck. We also want to show her a lot of affection because I get the sense that was lacking in her childhood. Imagine being ignored by your parents." I give a shudder. "It was hard for me to lose my parents, but I always knew they loved me, and my grandfather proved he loved me by taking me in and raising me. Granddad was crotchety sometimes, but I never doubted his affection." I look down at my feet a moment and then continue, "For a while, I was angry at my parents for leaving me, and that left some scars, but intellectually I knew that they certainly didn't do it on purpose. I just needed to grow out of that phase."

Callum reaches past me to get something, and his bare chest brushes my shoulder. I love that skin-to-skin feel, so I lean into him a little and surprise him with a kiss. Well, maybe he's not so surprised at all. He appears to be sporting a bulge in his jeans that I can't resist stroking.

Soft chuckling comes from the kitchen door as Petra waltzes in. She's also wearing the minimum amount of clothing—just a pair of tiny shorts that hug her ass and a tank top with no bra. Her legs look longer than ever in those bitty little pants of hers, and the outline of her puckered nipples is enticing. I immediately want a taste.

"Dinner's ready," Callum announces. "Let's eat while it's hot, and then we can play." He gives us a wink.

"Wonderful idea," Petra agrees.

"Uh huh," I say because once again I've been struck semi-mute. These two people have a power over me that is incredible. I love it.

Dinner is absolutely delicious, and I tell Callum, "This might be my favorite dish so far. What's in it? It's incredible."

He starts listing ingredients I've never heard of, and Petra gets the giggles at the look on my face when the doorbell rings. "I'll get it," I tell them. "Would you mind serving me a second helping?"

When I get to the door, I open it to see an attractive woman who looks to be somewhere north of forty. She has a duffle bag sitting on the porch beside her and a backpack slung over one shoulder. She has bright red hair that I'm guessing is not natural and is currently eyeballing me from top to bottom. She licks her lips and says, "Hi, handsome. You must be Ben. I'm Maggie."

Frowning at her assumption, I answer, "I'm not Ben; I'm Weston."

"No worries. Where's my daughter? Did I get the wrong house?" She looks over her shoulder and then back to studying my body.

"Who's your daughter?" I ask, even though I'm pretty sure I can guess.

"Petra, of course. People usually think I'm her sister." She winks at me, and my stomach squeezes. Not in a good way.

"Petra's having dinner," I start to say, but she grabs her duffle and shoves me to the side as she swoops into the house. Is this woman for real?

"Good," she says, dumping her belongings in the middle of the foyer. "I'm starved. I need a meal, a shower, and a bed. I've been traveling for days." She sticks her nose in the air and, like a dog on a scent, she sniffs her way toward the kitchen. "Smells great in here." Then she stops abruptly and looks around. "This is a nice place. I wouldn't have expected it here in Corn Country, USA." Then she scoffs, "First Iowa then *Indiana?* What is she thinking?"

Twenty-Five

Petra

I'M LAUGHING WITH CALLUM OVER HIS DESCRIPTION OF ONE of his college professors' habits of forgetting people's names and making up ones he thought suited them better when I get a sudden prickling sense of... foreboding? I don't know if I subconsciously overheard a snatch of a familiar voice or smelled a familiar perfume or what, but I jerk my head around just as *my mother* flounces into the kitchen with Weston close on her heels. Weston looks confused and a little miffed, and as soon as she locks eyes on Callum, she looks like she might want to take a bite out of him.

"Mom! What are you doing here?" I ask as I stand to greet her. Still ogling Callum, she offers me her cheek to kiss but doesn't try to so much as hug me back. Her normal luster seems a bit dimmed, and her clothes could use some laundering. I guess that's what prolonged international travel can do for a person.

"I don't need an excuse to visit my only daughter, Petra. Introduce me to your friends. Is *this* one Ben?" She points rudely at Callum but gives him a come-hither look anyway.

Being a gentleman, Callum stands and offers his hand, saying, "Callum O'Malley, ma'am."

She flinches microscopically at the "ma'am" and only gives him her limp fingers to shake. A look of confusion flits across his face. I get the sudden mental picture of two people who offer half-handed shakes to each other and have to stifle the giggles thinking how silly it would look to have two hands flopping at each other because both greeters refuse to clasp the other's hand in a real shake. It's one of those situations I've pondered for years. Thankfully, Callum takes her hand as firmly as possible under the circumstances.

All three of the dogs then surround my mother looking at her curiously, and she goes pale. All of them are polite, but my mother has never allowed a pet in the house. I begged her for years to let me have a puppy. I read everything I could about raising, training, and feeding a dog. It definitely helped me when I met sweet Gus to have that knowledge, but I sure could have used the companionship when I was little. I even considered getting a dog and hiding it from her since she was gone all the time, but I was afraid she'd make me give it up if she discovered it. Anyway, as a ten-year-old, my logic wasn't always spot-on.

"Call off your animals, please," she whispers. "I don't wish to be bitten or covered in fleas."

Weston scoffs. "I assure you we do *not* have fleas either on the dogs or in the house, and not one of these dogs would ever bite you unless you were to maybe take a swing at Petra, then all bets are off." That wasn't very friendly—he seems to have sized her up pretty quickly. Nevertheless, he says, "C'mon, guys. Why don't you all go outside and play for a while?" He looks at Callum. "Do we have enough dinner left, or should I whip up my special Kraft mac and cheese for the occasion?"

I have to stifle a giggle while my mother glares at Weston, and Callum says, "There's a little left. There was more, but I just served some of it to you."

"Oops," Weston and I say at the same time.

I grab a plate and hand it to Callum and then I show my mother to the half bath off the kitchen. "You'll probably want to freshen up," I tell her and start to walk away, assuming she'll wash her hands. No telling where she's been.

She grabs my arm instead and asks, "Whose house is this? You sent me the address, but I didn't know you'd moved on from Ben."

"Yeah, long, boring story about Ben, Mom. It's one for another day. The house belongs to Weston, but we share all the expenses."

She interrupts me by asking, "Weston is the one with the dimples and long hair?"

"Um, yeah. See you back in the kitchen." This time I'm able to break loose. I really don't get her at all, but her attention to detail is unsettling—and not in a particularly good way.

"Apparently she's planning to stay here," Weston announces quietly as I return to the kitchen. "She dumped her stuff by the door like some valet would haul it upstairs for her and unpack or something." He shakes his head a little.

She has not made too favorable an impression so far, I guess. "Don't worry. She won't stay long. I don't think she's genetically programmed to stick around."

"Where should we put her? Do you want her in your room? That's awfully close for comfort to me."

Callum rolls his eyes. "Why don't we make a bed up for her downstairs on the couch? She'll have privacy and her own bathroom that way, plus she'll be two floors away. We'll just have to have movie night upstairs while she's here or something."

"That sounds good to me," I tell them.

Mom slithers back into the room—apparently trying to look come-hither-ish with her hips swaying like a hula dancer. I try to keep from rolling my eyes as I tell her, "Mom, if you need a place to stay, there are some really nice hotels nearby. Carmel is growing by leaps and bounds…" I trail off as she scowls at me.

"Really, Petra. You and these handsome men can't put your own mother up?"

"Oh, we can. I just thought maybe you'd like more privacy."

Weston pipes up, "If you don't want the expense of a hotel, we can give you the entire downstairs if you'd like. There's a full bath with a shower, and you'll have plenty of room. The couch is quite comfortable."

"Couch? I'm supposed to sleep on a *couch*? Can't one of you give up a bedroom and let me sleep in peace? There's no telling how my back will feel if I sleep on…" She wrinkles up her nose. "Furniture."

"We're actually full upstairs, but I'm sure you'll be happier down there anyway, Mom. Really." I can feel myself blushing crimson to the roots of my hair, and she eyes me suspiciously.

"The only other option," Weston tells her, "is the futon in my office, but it's small and nowhere near as comfortable as the downstairs couch, and I need the office at all kinds of odd hours, so I'd have to boot you out a lot."

I hope he sounded convincing and pray she'll choose the hotel idea. I notice that no one seems willing to admit that Callum and I have abandoned our bedrooms anyway.

Callum places a steaming plate in front of her, and without thanking him, she dives in like she hasn't eaten in a week. In fact… she looks awfully thin. I wonder what's going on with her and why she's really here. She's never dropped in on me.

Ever. She's always summoned me to her place when she's in the country and gets a notion it's time to see me for some reason. This whole thing is odd.

"So how did you like Indonesia?" I ask as she continues to stuff her face. What's the deal with her? I don't remember her ever eating like a starving animal before.

"It was magical. You ought to go there sometime. I met the most beautiful people there and had a truly enlightening experience. But… it was time to come home. And I missed you so much, Petra."

"Well, that's a first," somehow just pops out of my mouth. I start to retract my statement, but dammit, she's never given me much thought at all. It's the truth.

My mother drops her fork down on her plate and looks at me in shock. "Petra! How could you say such a thing? I've always loved you dearly."

"Mm-hmm. Funny how you rarely made it home when I was on a school break… like Christmas." I turn to Callum and ask, "Did you make us dessert? Dinner was fabulous as usual, but I'm still a little hungry." Privately I think my mom could use some more calories. I'm actually stuffed.

He has a quizzical look on his face as he answers, "I did actually. I made a Moroccan lemon cake to go with the rest of the menu. Maybe I could also cut up some fresh strawberries to go with it." I'm relieved to see that he's aware of my mom's obvious hunger too. However, given how close Callum's family is, I can imagine he finds my relationship—or lack of one—with my mother pretty strange.

Apparently, she's wisely chosen not to argue with me about her motherly attentiveness while I was growing up. "Don't you kids have any wine?" My mom looks at the glass of ice water Callum served her with a sneer.

Good grief. We're off to a great start.

I get up, pour her a glass of Chardonnay, and place it in front of her, trying hard not to smack the table with the glass. I'm attempting to keep my cool. "So, Mom, how long do you plan to stay?"

Her head snaps up from eating and she squints at me. "Darling, I just got here, and you're already trying to boot me out? I'm afraid I'm a bit hurt." She pulls a sad face with big, brown puppy-dog eyes, but I'm not particularly swayed by her performance. Then she surprises me by saying, "You know I sold the condo in Chicago a year ago. It was too expensive to keep it when I was living abroad. And you didn't seem to want to live there."

"Because I got a job in Indiana and then stayed here after I quit. You know I was engaged to Ben, and this is where he was working. But…you don't have the condo anymore? Why didn't you tell me? What did you do with all your furniture and stuff?"

"Well, I sold it mostly furnished and had someone come and clean out all the rest of the things. They sold what they could and donated the rest."

I can't believe what I'm hearing. "Mom, some of that was stuff that belonged to me. Didn't you think it would be nice to let me know so I could decide what I wanted to keep before disposing of all of it?"

"Petra! You've had plenty of time to take what you wanted out of the condo, and you left things there for *me* to take care of. I assumed that if you hadn't taken the items you wanted by now, they weren't important to you."

"I didn't have space for some of the stuff, but I guess it's too late to worry about that now. I'm flabbergasted you wouldn't at least warn me before this, though."

"There wasn't that much, really."

"I had an entire bedroom full of furniture! You gave that to me for my birthday."

"I may have bought it for the room somewhere around your birthday, but the furniture was all mine to sell. Not yours."

I throw up my hands in disgust and scoot back from the table. "Funny how you told me 'Happy Birthday' when you had it all installed then. But there were old photos, books, letters, and diaries that I would have loved to have had, Mom. I'm... well... I'm in shock right now." I look at Weston and Callum and say, "Thanks for a great dinner. I think I need to get some air." I head outside to toss the ball around for the dogs. I have to get away from this. There wasn't much from my childhood that I want souvenirs from, but I'm still shocked that the woman has no sense of boundaries. Once again, I feel as if my own mother is a stranger. This is one of those times when I wish I'd had a father or a sibling.

I feel so much more grounded and even loved in this house with the guys—human *and* canine—than I ever did before. Thank God for them.

After horsing around with the dogs for a while, I realize they'd all like to go in for a drink of water, and I can see that the kitchen is empty. So I go in and start loading the dishwasher. I assume Weston and Callum are attempting to get my mother settled downstairs. I doubt either of them would be willing to let her anywhere near the upstairs part of the house.

Once the dishes are all done, I head for the stairs, and sure enough, I can hear her flirty voice jabbering away at the guys. It sounds like a pretty one-sided conversation from here. I decide to be polite and head downstairs. When the dogs see me doing that, they all race ahead of me, spraying water droplets from their wet faces.

Gus, in his friendliest fashion, makes a beeline to my mom and smiles at her. She jumps back as his teeth are bared in a grin. More water and probably some drool is still plopping off his muzzle as he wags his tail at her and noses her in the crotch.

"What is this creature doing?" she nearly shouts. "Get him off of me!"

"Sorry. He's just trying to get acquainted," I tell her. "Gus, come." He ambles back to me and then detours to Callum and sits on his feet. He's always adored Callum. The dog has terrific taste.

After much more persuasive talk and plenty of cajoling, we get my mom to agree to try sleeping on the couch. I bring her a bunch of linens and make sure she has everything she needs. She's looking pretty beat, so we make up the bed for her.

"Thank you all. I'm going to take a shower now and then get some sleep. I'm suffering terribly from jetlag, you know."

"Ms. Feeney…" Weston begins and is interrupted immediately.

"It's Maggie, honey."

"Ah… yeah, if you want to wash some clothes, the laundry room is right off the kitchen. You can't miss it. Otherwise, you ought to have everything you need. Callum makes us breakfast in the morning, but if you're hungry before then, feel free to raid the refrigerator. We generally eat pretty early on a weekday so he can get to work."

"Well, Callum," she eyes him longingly again. "You sound like a talented guy. I bet you can make everyone very happy."

He sends me a heated look. "You have no idea."

My mom regards him hungrily. "I'd like to find out."

I am mortified.

When Callum doesn't respond, my mother looks carefully at Weston and in a calculating voice asks him, "How did you come by such a nice, big house like this on your own? Did you get the house in your divorce settlement or something?"

"Mom! That's unbelievably rude!"

Weston eyes her with a flat expression and answers simply. "No. I am not and have never been married. Good night, Ms. Feeney."

"I told you to call me Maggie, cutie pie." Her voice is saccharine.

"That's okay, Ms. Feeney. You can call me Dr. Alister, and we'll be even."

"Oh! A *doctor*. Now I understand."

"That's doubtful. Good night," he retorts and heads up the stairs. His footsteps are a little clompy-er than usual. She seems to really get under Weston's skin in the worst way. I can hardly blame him.

I start to follow Weston as I call, "Good night, Mom," over my shoulder, but as I look back, she is reaching for Callum's arm.

"Feel free to come back down, handsome, and we'll get better acquainted," she whispers to him none-too-quietly. I get the feeling she wants me to hear but wants to make the appearance of being sly about it.

Shaking loose from her, he answers clearly, "Thanks anyway. My dance card is already booked for the whole night. Sleep tight, *ma'am*."

She makes an audible gasp, and I try my best to suppress the fit of giggles about to choke me.

Callum and the dogs scurry up the steps behind me.

Twenty-Six

WESTON

AFTER DEALING WITH PETRA'S ANNOYING MOTHER, WE'RE ALL in grumpy moods, and it's still relatively early anyway. So Callum and I snuggle into the big bed with Petra in the middle to stream a movie on my laptop. "I'll take the dogs out one last time when this is over," I tell them.

Unfortunately, the movie turns out to be boring, and Petra falls asleep before we make it halfway through. Then Callum zones out well before it ends. They look so peaceful I can't bring myself to disturb them. It's been a long-ass day with Maggie showing up and demanding attention from everyone. I wonder what her real story is. She seems as fake as Petra is real. If they didn't look a lot alike, I'd swear they were from completely different gene pools.

I turn off the movie and ditch the laptop, slide out of bed, and grab a pair of shorts. Then I pat my thigh quietly to get the dogs' attention. On the way to the back door, I check and see that it's all dark and quiet in the lower level, so I assume Maggie is fast asleep. With the dogs taken care of, we make our way back upstairs where I slip back into bed.

But I can't sleep. I can't stop thinking about how Petra grew up with this infuriating woman for a mother. She comes across as self-serving, fake, and clueless. She doesn't seem to have an affectionate bone in her body, so why would a woman like that even want to be a mother? Hours go by as I ponder their strange family dynamics and decide I'm actually quite impressed with Petra's resiliency and ability to show affection given her upbringing.

Suddenly, I hear soft growls coming from across the room. In the darkness, I see the form of Goliath rise up from his dog bed and prowl toward the bedroom door. The growling becomes louder, and then Gus is also on his feet and flanking Goliath, who is now scratching at the door. Dave is still sound asleep with his head thrown back, his belly bared, and all four feet in the air. Once again, I slip out of bed and into a pair of shorts.

Ever so quietly, I open the bedroom door and see a crack of dim light appearing under Petra's bedroom door—a door that is usually left open when Petra's not in the room. Turning around, I confirm that Petra is still in my bed with Callum, so I know I didn't nod off and miss her leaving somehow. I signal the dogs to go ahead of me and close my bedroom door as silently as possible behind us. As we get closer to Petra's room, I can hear faint sounds of exasperated swearing.

I open the door and discover—much to my total lack of surprise—that Maggie is sitting at Petra's computer and the screen is open to a banking site. She does not seem to have been able to break in, however, as there is a large error message on the screen saying she has exceeded the number of attempts she can make without having the proper login information. Her body language goes instantly from frustrated to startled when she whips her head around and sees me staring at her, surrounded by two large growling dogs.

"Trying to steal from your daughter? Nice move."

"Nothing of the sort. The door was open. I'm still messed up with jet lag, so I just wanted to check my emails and make sure my daughter has enough to get by. Of course, I'm not trying to *steal* from her." She tries to convey her supposed innocence by making scoffing noises.

"You could have asked her."

"Is she in your bed?"

"Poor deflection, and none of your fucking business."

"Oh, then she must be with the other boy, and you're jealous."

"Callum isn't a boy, and I'm not jealous. Now shall we try again? What the hell are you doing in Petra's room at this hour trying to hack into her bank account? I'm about ten seconds away from calling the police."

"Do that and I'll say you were trying to rape me. Petra won't like that much, will she?"

I roll my eyes. "She's *way* smarter than that." I advance on Maggie and grab the laptop. I close it, snatch it up, and unplug it. "She has some vitally important work files on her laptop, so I'll just take this now. I suggest you head back to bed, and if you leave tomorrow, I'll refrain from telling Petra what a cockroach her mother is. If you spend one more night in this house, all bets are off."

All of her starch seems to wilt, suddenly leaving a sad, broken woman in the place of one filled with bravado just moments before. "Look, Wesley…"

"That's not my name."

"Okay, *Dr. Alister*. I'm in a bit of a bad way. I'm tapped out. Penniless. Flat-ass broke. I need help." She turns away like she can't stand to look me in the eye.

"You need help from me? I'll give you some free advice then. Get a job."

She scoffs again.

"No, seriously. Businesses around here are looking for people to work for them all over the place. You could find a job by lunchtime tomorrow if you tried. But what happened to your funds? Petra said you came from money."

"I… um… well… Are you gonna help me or what?"

"I don't particularly see any reason I should. I work hard

for my income the same way Callum and Petra do. We don't look for handouts. Petra is grateful for the education you provided her with, but it's not her responsibility to keep you in first-class tickets to Timbuktu just because you want to live beyond your means. Grow up."

"I don't live beyond my means..." she tries to convince me by taking a new approach. She stands, bats her eyelashes, and wiggles her booty.

"Oh right. You sold a condo in Chicago a year ago, and now you're *penniless*? Where did that money go? You must have had a pretty good sale."

"I don't have to explain myself to you."

"You're right. You don't. But I don't trust you, and I *don't* have to allow you to stay in my house and steal from someone I care deeply about."

"Aw. Isn't that sweet? You're jealous and in love."

"And you're on very thin ice, lady. But because I care about Petra's feelings, I'll make you a deal. If you start looking for a job tomorrow—looking for real, not faking it— I'll let you stay here for a week. But if you're just here to fleece your daughter and cause trouble, you're gone. Got it? I'm serious about calling the police."

"I haven't done anything you can report to them, Wesley."

"I told you that isn't my name."

"Whatever." She sashays by me then with a snotty look on her face and accidentally on purpose steps on my bare toes as she stomps out of the room, saying, "Whoops."

My skin crawls as I hear her giggling her way down the stairs. I probably should follow her to make sure she isn't up to more questionable antics, but suddenly I'm hit with a wave of extreme sleepiness. I can't wait to crawl back into bed and curl up next to Petra. I'd love to keep her safe all night.

In the morning we head to breakfast, and Petra calls down the basement stairway to her mom. But when she gets no answer, she goes downstairs to see if Maggie is still sleeping.

Petra reappears in the kitchen looking confused. "She's gone. And her stuff is all gone too."

Steaming with rage inside, I tell Petra, "It pains me to say that I found her in your room and had a conversation with her at around two or three this morning. She was unsuccessfully trying to hack into your banking app, so I suggest you check to see if you have any missing valuables."

Petra looks stricken but rushes to her room wordlessly. She returns to the kitchen with tears in her eyes. "My checkbook is missing and so it my laptop. What should I do?"

"I put the laptop in my bedroom, so it's safe, but call your bank immediately. It's still pretty early. Hopefully, she hasn't done too much damage yet. I'm so sorry I didn't wake you up last night to tell you, but I hoped she wouldn't take it this far."

Twenty-Seven

PETRA

THIS IS A NIGHTMARE. I REALIZE NOW THAT MY MOM ALSO took my bank card and my credit card and has already gone on a spending spree that started at about seven this morning. At least Weston secured my laptop. If he hadn't, I might be out of a job on top of everything else.

I've reported her to the credit card company and the bank —who swears that as soon as the local branch opened, *I* cashed a check for fifty thousand dollars—the royalty money I just recently deposited into the account. I don't get paid often, but when I do the payments tend to be large. Anyway, the signature matched what they had on file, and she had the proper ID, so they let it happen. According to my credit card company, she also took an Uber to the airport and bought a ticket to Chicago on American. I don't understand what's happened to her and where all of her money went. Has she ever loved me, or have I become her cash cow? I feel *horrible*.

"How could she have an ID in my name?" I ask the guys.

"Sadly, if you know the right people, a fake ID isn't that hard to come by," Weston tells me as he drags me in for a comforting hug.

Callum—who called his work and said he'd be a little late due to a "family emergency"—comes up behind me and wraps his arms around me too. I feel their comfort pouring into me, and it honestly goes a long way to making me feel better. Then Callum kind of ruins it by asking, "Do you think she may have been scamming you for a long time, sweetheart? Have you ever seen money disappear from your account before?"

"No."

"Do you want to call the police? They can probably pick her up before the Chicago flight leaves. That's an awfully large amount of money to steal."

"Callum, I…" Tears well in my eyes, and I choke out the words, "Maybe she's really in a bad way and needs the money. She's my mother, and I ought to be able to help her when she needs assistance."

Weston pulls back and has an angry expression on his face. "Petra, I understand that you might want to be sensitive to her problems, but the fact is, she stole cards and a lot of money from you, then disappeared in the night like a common criminal. She's committed ID theft, forgery, and who-knows-what-all else. She isn't worth your pity if she acts like that. And besides, the credit card company won't make you pay for what she fraudulently charged on your card, but they will want to press charges even if you don't."

I have to think about that for a moment, but Weston keeps talking. "Remember, she said she recently sold an expensive property in Chicago, so she shouldn't be flat broke. It just doesn't make sense. I'd call the police, but it's not up to me." He shifts his gaze down and then up straight into my eyes, "She wanted me to give her money last night too, but she refuses to help herself by looking for a job. Nothing about her words or her actions adds up, and she certainly doesn't appear to be a devoted mother who cares about the welfare of her daughter."

I realize I can't let this go. So I slip out of Callum's embrace and pull my phone from my pocket. I shore up my conviction and, before I can talk myself out of it, dial 911.

"What is your emergency?" I hear immediately.

"Um, well, my scumbag mother just stole fifty thousand dollars from me as well as my bank card and my credit card, and now she's apparently at the Indianapolis airport waiting to get on a flight."

We have a conversation about this, and the entire time I feel the clock ticking. She could get on that plane any minute and lose herself anywhere. She could be going back to Chicago where she may or may not actually have a place to live, or she could be going to connect to a flight out of the country. I try to convey the urgency to the 911 operator, but she has the questions she needs to ask, and I need to give a full description of my mom's appearance, only I have no idea what she's wearing. Finally, the 911 lady says the magic words, "We have officers dispatched to pick her up at the airport now, ma'am."

"Thank you," I breathe out and crumple into a chair. Callum brings me a steaming cup of coffee, a toasted bagel, and a bowl of fresh fruit.

Now we wait.

A couple of tension-filled hours later, two police officers show up at the door. Callum finally had to get to work, so it's just Weston and me left to deal with the cops.

Their expressions are grim.

"Ms. Feeney?" one asks me.

"Yes. Please come in." When they are inside and the door is closed, I ask, "Did you arrest her?"

"I'm sorry ma'am. The Uber driver definitely dropped her off at the airport. But we searched the facility with the help of airport security, and no one matching her description was waiting for her reserved flight to Chicago. The ticket she bought in your name was used, however, and we finally determined that she found an earlier flight than the one she was booked on and apparently flew standby at the last minute before we even showed up. No one we spoke to remembered her, but it's busy today, and the airline employees at the ticket counters change all the time."

"So, now what?" I ask with a sigh.

"We have no jurisdiction to arrest her outside of Indiana, and about all we can do is issue an arrest warrant. But we don't know what state she may have fled to or if she even left in the first place. She hasn't committed a violent crime, so another state is unlikely to extradite her if they even spend any time at all looking for her. So, I'm sorry to say, she's probably going to get away with it."

I nod my head and feel myself starting to shake. Once again, I feel the strength of Weston as he closes in on me to offer support. I realize then just how much I miss Callum. I'm so thankful for them and feel whole when we're all three together. I'm not sure what that says about me.

Looking at the officers, I say, "Thank you for trying. I guess I better get to work and earn back all of the money I just lost. I wish I'd already bought the CD I expected to invest in, but I'm receiving another lump royalty paycheck soon and planned on buying it then so the money would be safe. Hah. Live and learn."

"If it's any consolation, Ms. Feeney, she faces arrest if she shows up in Indiana again. The charges are serious, even if they aren't violent."

"You'll have to find her first," Weston grumbles.

Suddenly, another horrible thought crosses my mind. I did

manage to take one thing of value with me when I left home. My prized possession in fact. "Excuse me a second," I say and dash up the stairs. Opening my closet, I see the specially made box that normally sat on the shelf is also missing. My heart breaks with this new development. With hot tears pouring down my face, I find Weston and the officers and tell them, "She also stole my first edition collection of Winnie the Pooh books that I've had since I was a baby. They're very valuable, and they're… gone." I look at Weston and ask, "How could she?"

ONE THING AUTHORS ARE QUITE GOOD AT IS RESEARCH. AND I decide to do some sleuthing since the police aren't likely to find her and arrest her. The first thing I do is look into our old condo and see if she still has it and lied about it or if she really did sell it after all. What I discover makes me confused… and ill. Not only did she sell it, but she did it under very questionable circumstances. It turns out that the property was *in my name,* and my mother was just on the title as custodian. When I reached the age of twenty-one, the property was supposed to be all mine, but she somehow got around that and claimed full ownership for herself. Apparently, she's been acting fraudulently for years. No wonder she didn't want to be around me. She was ripping me off!

But now I need to figure out how the property came to be in my name in the first place. I seriously doubt it was out of her deep sense of generosity. If the property belonged to her, why would she have put it in my name to begin with?

As quickly as possible, I report the stolen books to every pawn broker, estate buyer, and rare book dealer I can locate. It takes forever, but I'll be damned if I'm going to let the one thing I've cherished my whole life be ripped away from me by my greedy, shithead mother. This is the last straw.

I've never been clear about how the Pooh books came to be in my possession because my mother's story changed a few times. Once, she absentmindedly said they were from my godmother. As a tiny girl, I thought that meant I had a fairy godmother, and that tickled me. When I asked her later why I'd never been able to see my fairy godmother, she laughed at me and asked where I'd gotten such a silly notion. She said they were a gift to *her* from her parents, and she gave them to me. When I was older, I asked where her parents were and why I'd never met them. I wanted to know more about how they got the beautiful books and if they knew how to find more. This time she skirted the issue of her absent parents and said, "The books didn't come from them. I found them at an estate sale, so quit bugging me."

One thing I knew for sure was that the cover of the special box that housed the collection was an intricate design that bore my name on it—not hers. Another thing I knew for sure was that I didn't believe my mother. And I loved those books.

Twenty-Eight

Callum

When I arrive back from a hectic day at work, I'm so sorry to find Petra in a very uncharacteristically glum mood—not that she doesn't have good reason for it. I resolve then and there to salvage the evening in some way. She has obviously been crying throughout the day and probably fuming when she wasn't weeping.

Unfortunately, I have some news of my own that, while interesting, potentially won't make for a very happy home, so I decide to store my personal baggage away for a while and let her deal with one thing at a time. I hope this decision doesn't end up biting me in the ass. I have a serious choice to make, and it's tearing me up inside. For Petra's sake, however, I'll put my issues on the back burner tonight and see if I can make her forget her troubles for a while.

Once again, I've brought home a delicious feast for dinner. I'm trying out various international cuisines for my upcoming series of classes on ways to fix chicken. It's such a staple in many kitchens, but I know most cooks have maybe two or three ways to cook it that they fall back on. So I'm hoping to offer some easy-to-make recipes that can become new old favorites.

Weston is all smiles and full of compliments about the dinner. To me, he seems to be trying just a bit too hard to lighten the mood, but I understand. He's been at home all day with Petra, and he's seen up close how upset she's been.

I decide we need some music, so while we're cleaning up the dishes, it turns into a bit of a dancing sing-along. Petra's voice is off-key, but Weston sounds great. His dance moves are spot on as well, and I wonder… "Have you ever done any theater stuff—at school possibly?"

"Me? No. Why?"

"Because you sound great, and your moves are terrific." Weston laughs as he holds Petra in his arms, and they are presently grinding on each other in what has to be called dirty dancing. If he wants to take her mind off her troubles, he has the right idea. I dry my hands, hang up the dish towel, and step behind Weston, grasping him by the hips. Petra gives me a wink and a sultry smile. I move in and begin to grind against Weston. Petra's expression changes, and I see her eyes dart downward, so I'm guessing that Weston is hard against her. Her smile turns into a wicked grin.

"So, guys, why don't we take this 'dance' upstairs and get rid of these hot clothes?"

I guess it's safe to say that Petra is cheering up.

"You don't have to ask me twice," Weston answers and starts to pull off his shirt as we head for the stairs. Frankly, I think it's a wonder he had one on to begin with.

When we make it to the bedroom that I now think of as "ours," clothes fly off each of us at record speed. Petra regards Weston with a mischievous smile and asks, "Are you up for Callum's suggestion, *Loverboy*?" I can't help noticing she uses the name I called him when I suggested fucking him. I'm so hard thinking about being the first to go there with him, so I resume my position behind him and stroke his cheeks. Petra continues, "I think it would be so hot if Callum got inside of you while you were fucking me." Her eyes close for an instant and she shivers as if to underscore her feelings. The expression on her face is captivating in its eagerness.

"Ah…" Weston begins, but nothing else comes out of his mouth.

"I'll be careful, and I'll make sure you enjoy it," I tell him as I nuzzle his neck.

"It feels *so* good," Petra tells him. "You'll like it. Just trust us."

"I do trust you, and I can't believe I'm… ah… nervous about it." Weston declares. "I've just never been on the receiving end of a dick in my butt, even if it does sound interesting to try. I already know I love fucking both of you, so… ah… let's do this."

"The minute you're uncomfortable, we'll stop," I assure him and grab the bottle of lube.

"I want to see as much as I can," Petra declares as she lies back onto the bed and opens her arms for Weston.

He embraces her and then slides down to worship her beautiful pussy. "Isn't she amazing?" I ask as I watch him bestow kisses on her sensitive flesh. Weston seems a tad eager and quickly goes for her clit with his tongue and lips. Petra positively levitates off the bed as he plunges a finger into her at the same time as he sucks her clit into his mouth. She makes the sexiest noise I've ever heard—almost a moan, but hungrier.

"More of that!" she cries. "Don't stop, please! Ohmygod." She shakes and spasms with what appears to be an extra-satisfying orgasm. It's a glorious sight. "Woo! That was fast!"

Weston puts his other hand out to the side and demands, "Lube." So I squirt a dollop onto his fingers. I know where this is going, and I love watching, but I know also that I have to prepare Weston for what is to come. I squirt a generous amount of lube onto my fingers as well and begin to massage him in just the right spot.

Weston makes it easy for me by sticking his butt in the air and spreading his legs. "I've never seen anything so beautiful in my life," I tell them. "Petra's pussy is all glistening and wet, and Weston's ass is just waiting for me. This is surely heaven on earth, Loverboy and Lovergirl." Petra giggles at her silly new nickname, but her giggles quickly dissolve into more moans and continued spasms.

I take my ministrations on Weston extremely slowly and carefully. Watching his pucker loosen and contract around my finger as I lube him up is a trip. He seems to be eager to take me because I feel him pushing back against the pressure of my hand, so I tell him, "There's no rush. We can take all night."

"I… ah… think I really *need* you all of a sudden, though. I feel empty inside and want you there. Is that weird?"

I chuckle at him and wink at Petra, who is smirking a little. "Not weird at all. I am irresistible." As I say that, I shove a finger deep inside him and revel in the groan of approval he makes.

As if he can't wait a moment longer, he plunges his dick into Petra's pussy. His hand that isn't holding himself up is still prodding and twisting in her butt. "This is so cool," he says, "I can feel my own dick inside of you with my finger in your ass, Petra."

Petra gasps and seems to be coming back to herself a bit as she watches what I'm doing over Weston's shoulder. She's drunk on bliss as she looks at me and then at Weston's reaction. "Are you enjoying this as much as I am?" she softly asks him.

Weston exhales with a shaky breath and nods. Then he says, "God, yes."

By the time I've lubed him up sufficiently, I can barely stand it any longer. I'm aching with the need to be inside him. My patience is wearing thin, but I hold back until I hear him whimper, "Callum, please. I need it. *Now*. Do it!" He's pumping rhythmically in and out of Petra at a steady pace, so I wait until he's pulled back, almost all the way out of her before I push my dick into his hungry hole. Grabbing him by the hips, I slide in past the ring of resisting muscles and gradually sink in deeper and deeper. It's a beautiful sight, but the strangled sound of bliss that Weston makes is enough to nearly make me come on the spot. I have to steel myself to hold back. I've never felt anything like this before. It's like magic.

Petra's eyes are fixed on Weston's face as he cries out, "Yes!" She again grins at me like I've just given her the best gift ever.

"This is like my favorite fantasy finally come to life," she croons into Weston's ear. And then she drops the L-bomb as she gasps, "I love you both so much. I'm not sure what I'd do without you."

While that's great to hear, my heart takes a little dive in my chest. I have things I need to discuss with them, and the deeper and deeper I get into this with them, the worse it's going to be. But now isn't the time. I can't start a heart-to-heart conversation in the middle of the most beautiful sex I've ever had in my life. These two are my best friends, my wonderful lovers, and they are precious to me. What am I going to do? Somehow my mouth takes over before my brain becomes completely involved, and I blurt out, "I love you both too!" As true as the words are, I want to snatch them out of the ether and swallow them back into myself to hide them away until they are more appropriate.

They may decide they don't love me at all. They may even hate me for what I'm contemplating.

Weston, who has become a mass of quivering lust, is barely capable of anything other than moans and groans, but he also manages to (roughly) articulate, "Ah… I… ah… love you both… ah… too! So much."

I lean past Weston and kiss Petra's lips. She pants into my mouth and then battles tongue to tongue with me as Weston pounds into her, propelled by me. Her groans take over as I pull my head back a little so I can kiss Weston's neck. I bury my face into his thick, long hair until I can taste the sweat on his skin, and I'm sure in the depths of my soul that he's as turned on as I am right now.

I can't help it. I bite him. Again he cries out, "Yes!" He takes a deep breath and commands, "Fuck me hard, Callum! Make Petra feel us both."

Releasing his neck, I double my efforts to pound into Weston the way he wants it. I hope like hell he's not too sore later, but he sure seems happy right now, judging by the noises he's making.

Petra too is making noises like I've never heard in my life, and suddenly declares, "I'm gonna come *again*! Oh, man! This is *amazing*. Nnnngaaahh! Ohmygod, ohmygod."

Then Weston cries out in his release, and that triggers mine. But just as I feel the hot spurt of cum pouring out of me and into Weston, I realize what I've done. "Oh, Jesus. Weston, I'm sorry!" I cry as he shakes and shivers with his release and accepts mine as I pull out quickly, only to watch as I paint his backside with a strong stream of cum. The sight of it is so erotic, I feel myself getting hard again instantly. Well, that's a first. Coming and going all at once.

"Where'd you go, Callum?"

"Oh fuck. I forgot to put on a condom, Weston. I got so excited, and you were so eager, I lost my damn mind. I promise I'm clean, but I'm so sorry."

"Oh shit. I forgot too. But it's okay with me, Callum, and I promise both of you that I've been tested and I'm fine," he says. "I have to admit the feeling of you releasing inside of me was a total rush. I just wish you hadn't pulled out so fast." He sort of flops down onto Petra's neck then and snuggles into her. "Did you like this, sweetheart?"

"So much. It's fine with me if you guys both lose the condoms with me too. I've been tested, and I'm willing to forgo them. I have an IUD."

"Too bad we didn't have this conversation thirty minutes ago," I tell them with a chuckle. "But the idea of everyone going bare is amazing." I back off Weston and go get a washcloth to clean up the mess I made of him. As I wipe him off, I can't help kissing his bare skin a few times. I'm so happy that we've agreed to ditch the condoms.

Now I just have to hope they still love me when I tell them what's been going on with me and the decisions I need to make.

After we're all sufficiently cleaned up, and the dogs have been let out and brought back in for the night, we snuggle into bed like a pile of puppies and sleep like we've never slept before. Declaring our love to one another probably had a lot to do with that, I think, but also... It's been a long, emotional day, and we're all beat.

Twenty-Nine

Petra

"Last night was incredible, and I want to do that again and again." I sigh as I look at the two handsome men in bed with me. How did I get to be so lucky? "Can we do it again?"

Callum chuckles at me, and says to Weston, "I think we've created a sex fiend."

Weston opens his beautiful brown eyes and regards us thoughtfully. Then he asks, "Now?"

"I think tonight would be a better idea, Loverboy. I need to get to work, you know. But I'd be happy to trade places with you this time," Callum says to Weston.

"That can be arranged. And no condoms?" Weston looks at Callum and then at me.

"That's the agreement," I tell him.

"Something to look forward to," Callum says with a wink. "Without the guilt this time of forgetting." Then he hops out to hit the shower while Weston and I doze off again for a few minutes.

ONCE WE'RE ALL SHOWERED AND FED, CALLUM KISSES US both and leaves for work as we clean up the breakfast dishes. I pensively regard Weston and ask, "Did Callum seem a little distracted to you this morning?"

"Definitely. He was deeply in his own head. I asked him to pass me the salt, and he handed me the syrup. I wonder what's going on."

"Hmm. Maybe he's dreaming up a new recipe he wants to try out. Or he was lost in his head about how great last night was."

"Could be." Weston's dimples appear as he smiles broadly at me, and then his face goes serious. "Anyway, have you decided what you're going to do about your mom?"

"Not really. I need to do some more research into our old condo to see why she'd have put it in my name only to end up ripping me off, but I'm also getting behind on my current manuscript. I'll need to put in some good hours of writing before I can tackle my own problems, especially now that she almost wiped me out financially."

"Petra, you know you don't have to worry about it if you're late with rent or anything."

"Thanks, Weston, but I've got it covered. That wasn't my only bank account—just the biggest one. I get paid so sporadically, and in such large chunks, I've spread things around. Now I'm glad I did that. But also, we made an agreement, and it's not your problem that my loopy mother stole from me. You still need to be paid rent."

"Well, I appreciate that, but I'm never going to evict you if you can't pay, that's all I'm saying."

I give Weston a tight hug and a big kiss and say, "Thank you. You mean the world to me, you know that, right? You and Callum are the best. Now, I really need to get some writing done. Callum said there was one of those big, fancy salads of his to share for lunch later. I'll see you then. For now, I'm going to head outside to work while it's still nice weather." I turn to the dogs who are all sprawled on the kitchen floor and say, "Come on, guys!" They jump to attention and thunder to the door while I grab my laptop.

W HEN WE RECONVENE LATER FOR LUNCH, W ESTON HAS A serious look on his face. He seems a bit confused, too.

"What's up?" I ask. "Why so glum?"

"I... ah... had some time between client sessions and

started to look into that property and the previous sales. I hope you don't mind, but I found something pretty curious."

"Do tell."

"Well, I couldn't find the name of any previous owner because I guess when your mom and you moved in, it was a brand-new building. But what I did find was that the deed was in your name."

"Yeah, we already knew that, Weston. So?"

"So, it was apparently paid for by a guy named Jameson Harvey. Ever heard of him?"

"Not that I recall. Why would he buy the property for us, though?"

"Petra, it kind of makes sense that he could possibly be your father."

"What? Why would you even think that, Weston?" I can feel myself beginning to shake, and he takes me gently in his arms and leads me to the couch where we sit down together.

"It's just a hunch, but who else would spend that kind of money and put the property in a little kid's name? I think it might be a good idea to try to find this guy."

"I'm… speechless." What could this mean?

"What do you remember your mom ever saying about your dad?"

"Um, well… not much. I asked her a few times, but she always shut down the questions right away."

"How did she act? Was she angry? Sad? Shifty? Matter-of-fact?"

I furrow my brows and try to concentrate on the memory of my mom's face when I asked her about this. She certainly was not forthcoming with any valuable information. "I'm trying to picture it. I… can't remember her being particularly angry. She just mostly blew me off. She said a few things like 'good riddance' a couple of times maybe, but she mostly wanted to change the subject. So now that I think about it, it's possible she was a little shifty. It was like most of the things I asked her growing up. I never got straight answers from her. You've met her, and you've seen what she's like."

"Yes, I have. She's pretty sneaky. I think we need to find Jameson Harvey, and if we can't, we need to hire someone who can."

"Weston, this is my problem, and as much as I appreciate your input, I don't want your work to suffer because you're trying to locate this guy for me."

"Don't worry. I promise this will only be something I look into when I have the time. I won't blow off any clients or shortchange them in any way." Then he chuckles. "When I was a kid, I used to pretend I was a spy sometimes, so this is sort of a hidden talent of mine." He winks at me and kisses my cheek. "Indulge me. Now, let's go eat that salad and the delicious muffins Callum made to go with it."

Over the next several days, I work like a fiend on my manuscript so I can send it off and have a little bit of time to myself to look into my crazy mother and this mystery man Jameson Harvey. Thoughts whirl through my head—some pretty fanciful, I must admit. Sometimes I hope he's my long-lost dad, and other times I decide he's some sugar daddy my mom had. I even wonder if he's my mom's father of whom she's never spoken. But none of the scenarios I come up with make a lot of sense. I try my hardest to drum them out of my head so I can concentrate on my work.

One thing is clear to Weston and me, though. Over the past few weeks Callum has been pulling away from us incrementally, and it's breaking my heart. He's affectionate, especially in bed, but sometimes he looks so sad. We've asked him if something is wrong, and he swears everything is perfect. He just claims to have a lot on his mind. It's deeper than that, though. I wonder if having two lovers is too much for him, or maybe his family actually disapproves of us after all. In my darkest thoughts, I wonder if he's met someone else and wants a more traditional relationship instead of us. In any case, he's keeping quiet about it, no matter what. It's all very un-Callum-like behavior. He's also taken some phone calls out in the backyard where we can't overhear, and he looks so serious.

"Is everyone in your family alright, Callum?" Weston asks as Callum walks back indoors after one of his strange calls.

Callum blinks at him and seems to orient his thinking

before answering. "Oh, yeah, everyone's fine. I'll have dinner ready in about twenty minutes." And he goes about preparing another of his amazing meals for us.

Thirty

CALLUM

I DON'T KNOW WHAT TO DO. THE IDEA OF LEAVING PETRA AND Weston is killing me, but I entered into this relationship with trepidation, knowing that I have to focus on my career. I love them. That's absolutely clear to me, and I've told them so, but Petra is struggling so hard with her mother's betrayal, I can't stomach the idea of adding to her grief right now. And I am not exactly sure what I want to do anyway. Do I stay where I know I'm loved and cherished by the two most delightful people I've ever met, or do I leave and try to follow a dream I've had for years? I can tell they want me to open up more, but what do I tell them? That I'm considering leaving? They'll think I've been using them or just playing with their emotions when all along I've been growing deeply in love with them. I need to talk to someone. Hah! That's a laugh. Weston is a psychologist, and he would be the best person to speak to, but I can't. I just can't.

Finally, I decide to take some action—maybe somewhat evasive—so sue me. At breakfast on Friday, I tell them, "You guys are going to be on your own for dinner tonight. I'm going to go to my parents' house straight from work, and I'll probably be back late." I don't like the looks on their faces, so I blunder along, no doubt making things worse. "I didn't have time to make anything for you, so maybe you can indulge in some take-out pizza while I'm gone. That should be fun, right?"

They look at me with questions in their eyes, but I've shut them down so often, they don't seem to want to ask. I can't blame them.

Finally, Weston asks, "Callum, you'd tell us if there was something we could do to make things better, right?"

Petra looks on the verge of tears.

I clear my throat. "Yes, I would. I promise you, there is nothing you're doing that's bothering me. I just need to go see my mom and dad for a while and maybe get my head on straight. I have a lot on my mind. Some of it is good and some of it is kind of difficult."

Petra stands and wraps her arms around me, squeezing in as closely as she can. "Callum, you are so precious to us. If you're struggling with something, we need to know. Maybe we can help in some way you haven't thought of."

I take a deep breath and say, "I'm off this weekend, so we can talk then, okay? I just don't have a lot of things figured out right now."

Weston furrows his brow and looks deeply into my eyes. Those soulful brown eyes of his are penetrating, and I get the feeling he sees right through me sometimes. But all he says is, "Drive carefully. It's supposed to rain tonight." And then he adds, "We'll miss you until you get back."

"Look, I'm only going to be gone for the evening. It's not like I'm getting deployed or anything." I try for a choked laugh at my dumb joke, but the idea that I'm leading them to think I'll always be around seems false to my own ears. Before I can make things worse, I'm out the door.

I'm a horrible boyfriend.

On the drive to work, I try to conjure up how I used to see Petra and Weston together and how jealous it made me before we started our relationship. I try to tell myself that they are the ones who are really in love with each other. They won't be too upset if I go away. I'll be the only one who'd be devastated.

Keep telling yourself that, asshole. You're a big, fat liar. You heard them this morning.

♡♡♡

It turns out my parents aren't as much help as I'd hoped. I spill the whole scenario out to them, and they are initially happy for me. But when I add the part about actually leaving Petra and Weston, they look at me with concern.

We talk in circles for hours, and my mom says, "It's your life, Callum. We'll support your decision and love you unconditionally. But no one can make up your mind but you."

My dad adds, "Just weigh the pros and cons and figure out what decision you can live with and have the fewest regrets."

So much for parental advice. I guess they think they've raised me to be an actual adult who can make his own choices.

By the time I get back to Weston's house, it's after one in the morning. The house is dark and quiet, and everyone is apparently sound asleep. I start to go to bed in my own room, but just as I finish undressing, there is a quiet knock on my door. When I open it, I see Petra standing naked in the hallway, with her glorious hair all messed up around her face and shoulders, and sadness in her eyes.

"Sorry, I didn't mean to wake you up," I tell her softly.

She reaches for my hand and says, "I can't sleep without you. Come on." Without another word, she leads me to Weston's bed and gestures for me to climb in. As soon as I do, Weston's arm snakes around my waist, and he kisses my shoulder. Petra slides in on my other side, pressing her warm little body up to mine.

What am I doing?

Thirty-One

WHATEVER CALLUM'S ISSUES ARE, I VOW TO MYSELF TO KEEP an open mind and treat this as though he were one of my clients. No judgment, no emotion, just listening. I can do that, right? I'm a trained professional. I don't know how Petra is going to react, but… I also don't know what Callum is about to tell us. He treated us to an extra special breakfast of eggs Benedict as if he's trying to make us receptive to what he has to say, or maybe he was just stalling. I don't know. He's just been quiet all morning. That's so unlike our Callum.

Once we're done eating and complimenting him on his wonderful cooking once again, we clean up the dishes, then each take a mug of coffee and sit back down at the breakfast table. My stomach is in knots—despite the great breakfast—so I'm trying to stay calm. I have a sneaking suspicion I know what is coming now, but I'll wait and see.

Callum takes a sip of coffee and looks at Petra. I can see love in his expression. Then he shifts his gaze to me, and the same warmth emanates from his dazzling hazel eyes. I reach across the table for his hand. He puts down his mug and extends both hands, taking mine as well as Petra's. His smile is a sad one, though, and I feel a coldness creep into me.

Fear.

"I love both of you. Don't ever doubt that," he begins.

I sense a "but" coming a mile away.

"But," (there it is) "I have to tell you about something that I've been considering for a while and need to make a decision about pretty soon."

Petra grabs my free hand. She doesn't say a word, but I can feel her trembling.

Callum continues, "Petra, I know you've been dealing with a lot, and I don't want to add to your discomfort in any way. But I've had an offer to help start up a café and cooking school from a woman I know."

"Congratulations," I say, and I mean it.

Petra says nothing. She simply stares at Callum and swallows hard.

"The problem is—or the good thing, depending on your point of view—she recently inherited a big old Victorian house down in Madison, Indiana that's zoned for commercial and residential use, and that's where she wants to do this."

"How do you know she's… ah… legitimate?" I ask. I sure don't want Callum to give up his job and move away only to realize he's been taken for a ride. Most people in Indiana are aware that Madison is known for its restaurants and culture. It's a picturesque, historic city on the Ohio River in southern Indiana—and definitely too far away from Carmel for a daily commute. But what do we know about this woman? Is she interested in Callum for other reasons? I don't want to ask him that because it would look as if I were distrusting her intentions and intimating that he's more of a pretty face than an excellent chef and cooking teacher.

"She's on the faculty at Vincennes where I studied culinary arts, and I've taken a couple of her classes. She found out where I was cooking and teaching in Carmel, so she's been scoping me out. I guess I passed her inspection."

"When would you need to be down there?" Petra asked quietly with a hitch in her voice.

"Sometime in January, I think. She's having the kitchen renovated to get it up to code for commercial cooking, and the ground floor needs some remodeling. Her idea is to serve breakfast and lunch and then offer cooking classes in the afternoons. I mean, it sounds like a good idea, but I… don't know. She's promised me an attractive starting salary. And she even said I could use the upper floor to live in if I wanted." He looks at us pleadingly. "I just don't think I can leave the two of you to do this, and I'm not even sure I'm ready for a bigger responsibility than I have at my current job. I think it sounds like a great opportunity, and it's quite flattering, but…" He trails off and looks down. "It's scary. Maybe I'll give up everything, and the place will be a flop. Restaurants come and go all the time down there because it's such a touristy place. And maybe the people who frequent the restaurants won't want to take classes. When I went to work at my current job, it was an established business that had been successful already for several years. Maybe this woman has terrible taste."

"How badly do you want to advance your career, Callum?" I ask.

"Of course, I want to advance, but I'm not in a terrible rush to do something chancy."

"How badly do you want to leave us?" Petra asks softly as a tear rolls down her face. She hastily lets go of my hand to swipe it away and then grabs me again.

"I don't want to leave you two at all! I just don't know how many times this kind of opportunity will come along, and will I end up having to leave town eventually anyway?" Callum's voice breaks, and he looks like his heart is breaking with it.

With her chin jutting out, Petra asks, "What if we all moved to Madison so we could stay together?" She looks at me pleadingly.

Callum shakes his head sadly. "I can't ask you to do that.

This is Weston's house that he grew up in. I'm sure it means something to him." He looks at me. "Right?"

I shrug a little. "It does, but houses aren't as important as people. Petra and I have portable jobs. I just don't know how it would work financially. We'd have to look into it. Maybe we could all buy a house together…"

"I'm not exactly rolling in dough right now," Petra says with a glum look. "Thanks to my so-called mother."

Taking a deep breath, Callum tells me, "I don't have much yet in the way of savings either, but it's very kind and generous of you to even consider it, Weston. Here's the thing, though. I read the other day that sixty percent of all restaurants fail in the first year, and in the first five years, eighty percent fail. It's not promising odds. If the new restaurant fails, then you'd be stuck in Madison, and you'd have sold your house for nothing."

"You're not nothing," I protest. "And this isn't just a restaurant. It's a cooking school too. So if we did this it would be more like making an investment in you. But maybe you need to do some more research into the woman who's asked you to join her. Does she have any business experience? Is she a hard worker? Trustworthy? Also, what are taxes and living expenses like in Madison compared to Carmel? Where is your salary coming from? Will it be based on the immediate profits from the business, or does she have money set aside already? And… ah, what did your parents say?"

"Not much. They basically said to decide on what I could

live with when I make my decision." He sighs. "Maybe I could just come back here on my days off to be with you." No one says anything to that, so he goes on to say, "That sounds awful."

I think for a moment and then ask, "Would you consider asking her to come up here to meet with us? Maybe if Petra and I can talk to her along with you, it will help you form an opinion you can live with. Does she know you're in a serious relationship? If she's any kind of person at all, she ought to be sensitive to the feelings of your partners as well as to yours. I know we're unconventional, but maybe she also needs to know that." I let that sink in a moment and then ask, "What's her name, anyway? I don't like referring to her as 'that woman' all the time."

"Her name is Professor Bates. I think her first name is Marsha."

"Well, ask Marsha to join us for brunch next weekend. Or, if she doesn't want to drive all the way up here, which is understandable, maybe we can meet her down in Bloomington or something and split the difference. That's about halfway. Or —I have an even better idea! We could make a trip all the way to Madison and see the property with you. I assume you haven't taken that trip yet, right?" Callum shakes his head, so I look at him with a satisfied grin. "Callum, you can't make an informed decision without seeing what you're getting into. We can stay overnight down there and make it a mini-vacation.

Why don't you call her right now and set it up? Is that okay with you, Petra?"

"It makes sense to me. Call her, Callum, and I'll go figure out what to do with the dogs for one night. I think they'd be happier playing with other pooches instead of taking a long car ride."

"And I'll find us a place to stay," I tell them with conviction. I wish I were happier about this, but at least we'll be helping Callum make a momentous decision. Then I tell them both, "Let's not worry or be sad about this until we know more, alright? This might be a great opportunity for all of us. You never know." Then I look at Callum and tell him, "I love you," and I give his hand a squeeze. "You've got this."

Petra and I head out of the kitchen to find our laptops, leaving Callum staring at his phone like it's going to bite his hand off. I'm proud of our man, but I don't envy the decision he needs to make.

Thirty-Two

I SCROLL THROUGH MY CONTACTS UNTIL I FIND PROFESSOR Bates, but I don't hit the call button right away. At the moment, I'm feeling fairly negative about her proposal, and I don't want to project that in my voice. I'm almost ready to call when another thought goes through my head. Professor Bates is an attractive woman in a somewhat overblown way, but she's given me a flirty vibe a few times that has me on alert. There is no way in hell I want to get involved with her, and I'm happily committed to Petra and Weston. But maybe she's just friendly, and I'm overthinking. What would an older woman like that want with me anyway? I didn't tell Petra and

Weston about it because I didn't want to sound silly or egotistical.

So I concentrate on the great opportunity this is offering me and on how much I love cooking, creating recipes, and teaching. Once I feel somewhat buoyed, I poke the button. The call goes instantly to voicemail. Terrific.

"Hi, um, Professor. This is Callum O'Malley. I was just thinking over your offer, and I was wondering if we could come down to Madison next weekend to see the property you're renovating and ask you some questions. I'm off work on Saturday, so I hope you're available then. Please call me and let me know at your earliest convenience. Um, thanks. Bye."

I hope I didn't sound too much like an idiot, and I hope she calls back soon.

She doesn't.

Hours go by, and I hear nothing but crickets. I'm considering calling again, but I don't want to pester her. I guess I'll give her a day or two. She is a busy woman, after all. I look through my old messages and see the photos she sent of the house and realize really all I can see is that there is a white structure of some sort behind some tall trees. There's a big ugly dumpster in the driveway, presumably for the renovation project. All in all, it doesn't exactly scream "restaurant" to me now that I think about it. I pocket my phone and decide to fix dinner. Cooking always helps me focus, and it cheers me up.

♡♡♡

I HAVE TO WAIT FOR HER RESPONSE FOR TWO FULL DAYS. We've made our plans to drive down there, and we've rented an Airbnb for Saturday night. We even made reservations at a highly recommended restaurant. It sounds like a fun weekend, no matter what we discover when we get there or what my ultimate decision is. When her call comes, however, I'm a little confused.

"Hello, Callum. It was… nice to hear from you." She sounds like she's trying to purr instead of speaking professionally, and it gives me the willies.

"Hi, professor. Oh good, you got my message. Are you available on Saturday to discuss the property?"

"I suppose so. I should be able to spare about thirty minutes at two p.m. Don't be late or I'll have to leave."

"Don't worry, we'll be there in plenty of time."

"We? You mentioned 'we' in your message too. Who's 'we'? Are you coming with your parents?" The purr is gone.

"Oh, my…um… roommates."

"What do they have to do with your decision?"

I blink a few times and then sputter, "Their opinions matter to me a lot, and we all decided to make a mini-vacation of driving down there together. We thought it might be fun."

She makes a soft harrumphing kind of noise, rattles off the address, then tells me, "I have *other* candidates who are anxious for the job, Callum, and I doubt they'd need to run this by their little friends. Most people would take this offer sight unseen." She hangs up.

So much for enthusiasm. I very much doubt her assertion that anyone would uproot their life to work with her on this project without knowing all of the particulars. I'm not sure she's going to be a very good employer if this attitude keeps up. And her voice went from vixen to vile in sixty seconds flat. I'm far more anxious now to take a road trip with my partners and eat at a nice restaurant than to speak with Marsha Bates. But… we'll see.

WHEN SATURDAY MORNING ARRIVES, HOWEVER, PETRA WAKES up looking pale and uncomfortable. She is gripping her stomach like it's killing her, and I suddenly hope that my dinner last night didn't disagree with her.

"What's going on, sweetheart? Are you sick?"

"Oh, Callum, I have terrible cramps and the beginning of a migraine. This doesn't happen too often—like maybe once a year—but when it does, it's awful. I know the signs."

"What can we do for you?" Weston asks. His face is full of concern. "I've heard orgasms can help," he adds hope-fully. "Both cramps and headaches. It's scientifically proven."

"Oh, just keep the shades down so it doesn't get too bright in here and go enjoy your weekend. I'm going to have to pass on the trip—and the orgasms—for now." She looks at me. "I'm so sorry Callum."

"No apologies necessary, but I don't want to leave you like this."

"No, it's okay, really. When the headache really sets in, and it will pretty soon, I won't even want to talk. I'll take a pill and sleep as much as I can. By tomorrow, I ought to feel a lot better. It's lucky for me I don't have the kind of migraines that last several days—just one or two for me. And the cramps will subside in a few hours. Please go ahead and drive down to Madison. You need to make up your mind, and I'll be fine. Leave the dogs here, though, so I'll have company."

"Can you take care of them on your own?" Weston asks. "I mean, I'll feed them and let them out a couple of times before we go, but you won't be able to manage much with them if you're sound asleep."

"We'll be okay. It's a comfort having them around, truly. This way you won't have to take the time to drop them off at the kennel either. I can manage a little bit of getting up with them. And if they need me, they'll wake me up."

"Weston, I do like the idea that if Petra's going to be here alone, she'll have the dogs for companionship."

"Well, if you're both sure. I'm still not crazy about leaving," Weston says.

"I need to get this done. If you want to stay with Petra, that would be alright too."

"Weston, please drive down there with Callum. I just need

to close my eyes after I go grab a pill." She gets out of bed gingerly and heads to the other bathroom in the hall while holding her stomach.

I feel awful for her, but having two sisters and a mother who's a nurse, I've heard plenty of stories about female maladies. What a pain for them. Men have it easy.

A little while later, I bring Petra a cup of strong coffee, hoping the caffeine will also help her pain, and I have a bagel and some fruit for her to nibble on. If she feels like it.

"Thanks, Callum," she says, apparently trying not to groan. "This looks great." She looks awful. Her eyes are squinty, so I suspect the headache is settling in.

I set down her tray and kiss her forehead. "Should we call you throughout the day, or will that bother you?"

"Oh, um… how about if I call you in a few hours? If I can manage to get back to sleep, that will be the best thing, so yeah. Waking me up wouldn't be so great."

After showers and breakfast, I let Petra know I've left easy microwavable meals in the refrigerator for her in case she gets hungry. And finally, Weston and I are on our way south. We should be quite early unless there is a traffic jam. And in Indiana, you can usually depend on one of those.

Thirty-Three

I CAN'T IMAGINE WHAT CALLUM IS FEELING. SINCE HE'S driving, I don't want to interrogate him and make him nervous or upset, but he seems to be projecting a steely resolve this morning. I don't know if it means he's planning to ask a bunch of hard questions when we get there, or if he's already decided that leaving us is a forgone conclusion. So on the drive down, we listen to music, and I ask him general questions about his cooking classes. We've never really talked much about what he does in them and what kind of students he has.

"All sorts of people show up. Almost all of them come with a friend or a family member, and that's good because they can work as a team. Once in a while, it's a young couple who want to learn how to cook now that they're married, or some are couples on a date who don't know each other very well, and they can be interesting to watch. The majority of the students are women though, and they're all ages. Usually, they're happy to be there and are ready to have some fun, but I've had a few who are there under duress because they've somehow never gotten the basics of cooking figured out."

"Do they ever hit on you?"

He laughs. "It happens, but I haven't let it go anywhere. I usually try to act oblivious."

"Do you ever have any cooking disasters?"

"Once in a while someone will mess up horribly, but most problems can be fixed somehow. The goof-ups are always good learning experiences."

"Have you ever messed up on a recipe?"

"Moi?!" Callum snickers. "Bite your tongue, Weston."

"So I take it you have."

"Yeah," he sighs. "I got distracted a few weeks ago—probably because I was kind of sleepy after a long night of playing with you and Petra. I burned the white bean chili." He smiles at me and winks, then quickly looks back at the road. "Totally worth it. I was just really careful not to scoop anything off the bottom of the pan when I served it, and I don't think anyone noticed. I wasn't crazy about the flavor though."

I chuckle for a moment, but my smile fades as my thoughts shift back to home. "You think Petra's okay?"

"I sure hope so. If you want to head straight back after we meet up with Professor Bates, that would be okay with me."

"I dunno, Callum, that's an awful lot of driving for you all in one day. Let's have a nice dinner and relax. We can see what she sounds like when she calls us. If she calls us. If we think she needs us, we can always drive back tonight. And if you're too tired, I can drive your car."

An hour later, we've checked into the Airbnb and dropped off our backpacks. We hit a trendy café for a quick bite, and we're heading to the address Callum's former professor gave him. It's on the far end of the commercial district of Madison, but I guess it's still fairly close to other businesses. It's on a pretty street, and the zoning is definitely mixed. The houses and storefronts are all well-maintained and attractive until we get to one that has a burnt-looking, weed-choked lawn and a huge, overflowing dumpster in the front yard. The dumpster smells to high heaven.

Callum parks on the street, and we step out of the car. The smell is ghastly—like a filthy litterbox filled with rotten fish.

"Good lord," I exclaim. "What on earth do you think went on in this house? I hope it's not this bad inside. You might never get the smell out."

Just then a couple of workmen lumber out the front door hauling a stained and tattered rolled-up rug between them. They both have masks on their faces and are wearing heavy gloves. They heave the rug into the dumpster, and we both jump back as a plume of dust flies up and blankets the air. More smell. Oh, ugh.

"Excuse, me," Callum says, "Is Professor Bates here yet? I'm supposed to be meeting her here."

The men eye him. It's hard to see the expressions on their faces because of the masks, but they look a little bit like they're smirking. "She's upstairs in her room," one of them says to us.

Callum looks at me quizzically and mouths, "Her room?" Then he says audibly, "I had no idea she actually lived here. *How* can anyone live here?"

The worker just shrugs and heads back indoors. They leave the door open, so we take it as our cue to enter at will. Jeez… I can't wait. I wish I had a handkerchief or a leftover pandemic mask handy. I hope I don't lose my lunch.

When we get inside, however, we're pleasantly surprised to see that there has been some serious renovation and cleaning done to the property already, and the smell seems to be all located outside in the foul trash bin. Callum looks relieved as he says, "The neighbors must want that dumpster removed in the worst way."

I follow him through some empty rooms toward the back of the house where instinct must be telling him to look for the kitchen. What we see there, I must admit, is not at all what I feared. It's a clean space with a tall ceiling and gleaming new appliances that to my untrained eye appear to be top-of-the-line. Callum silently spins in a slow circle, taking in the counter space, cooktops, and all the accouterments that I don't understand. He looks impressed. And then he casts a worried look my way.

I move closer to him and sling an arm around his shoulders. "It's okay if you like it, Callum. We'll understand."

I give him a squeeze just as we hear footsteps clopping into the kitchen. We turn to see a heavily made-up woman of an indeterminable age marching up to us. Her high heels make a terrible clatter on the hardwood floor. I guess she'd be attractive if she toned everything down about fifty percent. She kind of looks desperate to make an impression this way.

"Hello, Callum. Right on time. That's a good sign."

"Professor," he replies and then doesn't seem to know what else to say.

I've stepped back from Callum to give him space, but I notice that as I do, he decreases the distance by inching closer to me.

Professor Bates eyes Callum with a very cougar-ish look and then turns her eyes to me. I feel immediately as though I've somehow been violated by her thoughts. I don't like it, and I immediately don't like her. But I can't say a thing about it because this isn't my business.

"So this must be your roommate. Didn't you imply that you had more than one?"

"Yes, um, sorry, Professor Bates, this is Dr. Weston Alister, my um *boyfriend*. Our other roommate couldn't make it."

Well, that's something of a new development. I've never

heard Callum refer to me so formally before—or call me his boyfriend, and I have to say I kind of love it. I don't, however, like the look on the professor's face when she hears it.

"Nice to meet you, Dr. Alister," she says without reaching a hand in my direction. Her tone of voice implies that meeting me is actually not at all nice. My extended hand is ignored, so I drop it to my side. With a thinly disguised sneer, she turns to Callum, "I was not aware that you had a *boyfriend*. I've only seen you with a few various young ladies on your arm around campus."

Callum stiffens. "I was not aware that my personal life was in question or had any bearing on my employment, Professor. If it does, then we're done here."

"Don't be so touchy, Callum. All I need you to understand is that the living accommodations upstairs are only suitable for one more person."

"Does that mean you are going to continue to live here after the renovations are completed?"

"That was my original plan, yes."

"And you didn't think it might have been a good idea to give me a heads up that we'd be roommates as well as co-workers?"

"Oh, I have no intention of working here. I'll be commuting twice a week to Vincennes to continue with my classes there. I'll only be here in an advisory capacity."

Finally, I can't stand it any longer and have to ask her, "Why does this property smell so godawful?"

She stabs me with an irritated look. "The previous tenant was a hoarder, and the place was a pigsty when I took it over. The dumpster will be gone by the end of the week. Not that it's any of your business."

"Sorry, *ma'am*. Callum's well-being is definitely my business. You see, we love each other."

The look that crosses her face is priceless. She tries to cover it up, but the disappointment is as obvious as her lip enhancements. She wanted Callum for her boy toy, and her plan has been foiled. I feel rather awful now for Callum as I'm sure he hoped he was asked to work here because of his skills, not his looks. He must be feeling terribly objectified. I scoot even closer to him and rub his arm.

Looking longingly around the kitchen, Callum announces with a sigh, "Too bad. This might be a wonderful kitchen to work in once it's completed, but I'm not interested in the kind of arrangement you seem to have in mind. I hope you find someone to work for you, but I'm sure you know that a person's sexuality is private, and it's illegal to inquire about it as a hiring qualification."

Professor Bates's face goes red, and she blusters at us, "I don't know what you mean by an *arrangement*. That's a terrible thing to accuse me of. Shame on you for thinking it!"

"Wouldn't you only want me here if I weren't queer?" Callum asks with a slight smirk.

"Well, I… um… know your cooking skills are quite commendable, and you have experience teaching, but…"

He interrupts, "They are, and I do. But you didn't answer my question, and your lack of conviction is all I needed to hear. So, I think it's time for Loverboy and me to leave now, and I wish you well. You've made my decision easy as pie, Professor. Thank you from the bottom of my heart." He gives her his best dazzling smile—one that could make angels jealous of its beauty. "Don't worry, I won't bother to sue you over this. It's not worth the aggravation. Good luck." He takes my hand, and we quickly make our way back to the car, holding our breath as we pass the stinking dumpster.

Thirty-Four

WOW, THAT WAS EYE-OPENING. I'M SO EMBARRASSED, BUT it's great to have Weston's support and not have him tease me or give me a hard time about things. At least it's a pretty fall day, and the trees are all magnificent, so it was a nice drive.

"Look, Weston, I'm sorry I dragged you down here to witness that. Something tells me you're not as surprised as I was, however."

Weston sighs. "I can't say that Professor Bates has much going for her, but I have to admit I understand her attraction to you, Callum. I was blown away by you the moment I laid eyes on you."

"You were?"

"Absolutely. And then I got to know you—something *Marsha* hasn't even tried to do—and that's why I'm hopelessly in love with you."

"Aw. You say the sweetest things." I can't help snorting a little when I say this. Probably ruined the message a little. "She's a real piece of work, isn't she?"

"That she is. I wonder if you asked around if you'd find out that she's been a bit predatory among the male students."

"Ugh." I look over at Weston, who seems lighter and less worried than he did on the way down. "When we get back to the Airbnb, do you want to contact Petra?"

"Yeah. I hope she doesn't mind."

"Hopefully, when I tell her I'm not leaving, she'll at least cheer up."

"Yes, there's that. I certainly feel like the weight of the world is off my shoulders right now. You must be relieved too, even though it's also a disappointment for you."

"It's not as disappointing as you'd think. The right thing will come along. I still worry that someday I may have to make the decision to go somewhere else or ask you both to uproot your lives."

"We'll see. No reason to fret about it now. Hey, there's a good parking place right in front. We're lucky again."

I park the car, and I can't help grabbing Weston's hand as we walk into the cottage we rented.

Once we get inside, I send Petra a text:

Callum: How are you feeling?

Petra: About the same. How's it going down there?

Callum: Could have been lots better. But the good news is, I'm not taking a job here.

Petra: Yay! I'm so relieved, but I'm sorry it wasn't better news for you. What are you doing now?

Callum: We've talked about heading over to Clifty Falls State Park for a hike, then we'll have dinner. Can we call you after?

Petra: OK. I hear CFSP is pretty. Take some photos.

Callum: Will do. Miss you.

Petra: Me too. TTYL xo

Callum: Feel better xo

♡♡♡

AND THAT IS JUST WHAT WE DO. THE PARK IS GORGEOUS THIS time of year, so we find a promising trail to follow and snap photos of anything that looks like something Petra might enjoy. Plenty of hamming it up for the camera and lots of muscle flexing ensues, so we end up laughing our way through the park. It's a great stress reliever.

"I feel so light and unburdened now that the job situation

is resolved. Thank you, Weston, for not badgering me to make a decision and letting it all work itself out."

"Like I told Professor Cougar, your happiness is vitally important to me, Callum. If we need to make some ah… hard decisions in the future, Petra and I will be there for you. You mean the world to us."

"You and Petra mean the world to me as well. It's amazing how all of this worked out for us, isn't it? Who'd have expected that answering an ad for a roommate would end up like this for us? We were incredibly lucky."

Weston slings an arm around me and squeezes. "Lucky indeed. Are you about ready to go find that restaurant? I'm starving."

DESPITE THE GREAT REVIEWS, WE FIND THE RESTAURANT'S décor too fussy for our taste, and the menu is overpriced and pretentious with plenty of oddball pairings. The wine list too is overblown with ridiculous claims about the flavor of the featured wines. Weston looks up at me with an amused expression and asks, "Does wine *ever* just taste like it comes from grapes?" I can't hide my snort, and that makes us both laugh harder. "This one 'suggests notes of cloves and tangerine,' and this one over here 'expresses a whisper of vanilla and nutmeg on a chilly evening.' I don't want to drink a damn Christmas cookie, for crying out loud."

"I guess this makes people feel better about spending a fortune on the stuff." Just then the waiter arrives and asks as he looks down his nose at us whether we've decided on a bottle of wine, so I answer, "I'd prefer a Corona. With a lime, please. And I'll have the duck."

Weston smiles and says, "Corona and lime for me too. And I'd like the prime rib—rare, please."

The waiter gives us both a condescending smile and a nod, saying, "Very good, gentlemen," with an odd accent. Then he gingerly plucks up the wine list as if he didn't want to leave it with a couple of cretins like us one more minute.

I like wine as much as the next guy, but the hoopla over it makes me laugh. Little does the creep know that I'm probably far more educated about wines than he is. Looking at Weston, I ask, "Do you think he realizes we're on the *Ohio* River here and not the Seine? I bet he's at least a fifth-generation Hoosier who's trying to pretend he's European."

Dinner arrives with some rather unfortunate vegetable sides that also make us have to squelch our laughter. Beets and poorly prepared kale seem to be featured in this establishment, whether you like them or not, but the main courses are delicious. At least there's that.

We skip dessert, opting to get back to our place for the night where we can call Petra. I know Weston misses her as badly as I do, judging by how many times he brought her up during dinner.

The cottage is cozy, and we light a fire before we lie next

to each other on the bed to give her a FaceTime call from Weston's laptop. When she answers, I'm thrilled to see her beautiful smile.

"You look good, sweetheart. How do you feel?"

"Oh, so much better. My headache never really developed into a migraine after all. After I slept it off, it finally went away completely a little while ago. I think the stress of worrying about you was making it bad, and then without that stress, I could relax and improve. Anyway, I took a shower, and now I feel pretty human again. I sure miss you guys. And Callum, I hope you're not too disappointed about the job, but I'm so happy you're staying put."

"I'm pretty relieved myself."

"Have the dogs given you any trouble?" Weston asks.

"None at all. They napped with me actually, and it was very cozy. They went out and ran around for a while, and then I fed them, so they're relaxed now. I heated up some of the lobster ravioli you left, Callum, and it was delicious. Thanks!"

"He didn't make you eat kale with it, did he?" Weston asks.

"Not a bit." She laughs and makes a silly grimace.

I chime in, "Kale is highly overrated in my opinion, and it tastes like lawn clippings. There are plenty of delicious ways to eat healthy foods that don't make you get little green particles stuck in your teeth or want to hurl."

"And that is one of the million reasons you are our favorite chef," Weston says softly and kisses the side of my head.

"Do you want to tell me more about what happened today?" Petra asks.

"Not really," I answer. "We can fill you in when we get home. I'd rather enjoy our conversation with you now instead."

"And by enjoying the conversation, do you mean you two might consider putting on a little show for me? You know how much I love to watch you."

Weston answers quickly, "We can do that. Shall we do what comes naturally, or do you want to direct the show, sweetheart?"

"Hmm, a little of both maybe. Why don't you guys start by taking off each other's clothes?"

We position the laptop so Petra has a clear view of us, and I reach for Weston's shirt. Our shoes and socks were already kicked off before we climbed onto the bed, so the pants slide down quickly. When we're down to just our boxers, we kneel on the bed and start kissing. Our hands are in constant motion, caressing and enjoying the feel of each other's body.

"Very nice, you guys."

We steal a glance at Petra playing with her own breasts, rubbing and plucking at her nipples through her thin shirt.

"Why don't you also lose some clothes, Lovergirl?" I ask.

Her shirt goes flying off over her head as she grins at us.

"Very nice, yourself," Weston tells her with a grin.

"Take more off," she says.

I slip my hands into Weston's boxers and grab his butt,

yanking him toward me. When he chuckles and I can feel him hardening, I shove his underwear down his thighs. As he climbs out of them, I quickly ditch my own, and immediately we're back to where we were. Our thick shafts rub against each other as I gyrate my hips, and both of us grab handfuls of ass. "Are you up for some fucking?" I ask Weston between kisses.

"Not so fast," Petra orders with a chuckle. "I'd love to see a little sixty-nine action from you first. You don't do that very often."

We both turn to look at her and see that she has reached down into her thong, and she seems to be stroking her clit with one hand while the other continues to play with her pretty nipples. Weston turns to me and wiggles his eyebrows up and down suggestively. His adorable dimples are enough to make me swoon. The man is perfection. Petra is perfection. How could I even remotely have considered giving up on them for one minute? I blurt out, "I love you both so much!" Their smiles are incandescent. "Now let's make our woman happy, Loverboy."

I scooch down on the bed in one direction, and Weston positions himself facing me, going in the other direction as we both reach simultaneously for each other's massive hard-on. As I engulf him with my mouth, I hear Weston's happy intake of breath, and then he too opens for me. The ambrosia of his hot mouth and skillful tongue swamps my senses with delight. I make happy noises around him as I lap and suck, pumping him with one hand while the other slides between his legs and past his balls to caress his taint. Soon his actions match mine, and I'm trying hard to keep it together. I'm overwhelmed with love for this man, but I want this to last. I have this sudden and profound need to fuck him senseless, so I pull back and ask, "Weston, I need to get my dick inside of you pretty soon. That okay with you?"

He nods vigorously as he gives me an incredibly hard pull with his mouth.

"Ahh!" I cry, and then I laugh. "We need to stop this, or I won't be able to." I return the mind-blowing suction, and Weston lets go a stream of hot cum down my throat. I guess he was as turned on as I was. I lick him clean as his chest heaves, and I pull back saying, "I need to grab to lube. Just a sec."

"You guys are so beautiful," Petra sighs. "Make sure I can see the action while you're getting fucked, okay, Weston?"

Weston grabs a pillow to raise his hips and lies down on it facing upward. He looks at me like I'm the most wonderful thing he can think of, and it makes my dick throb with want. "Can you see, Petra?" I ask.

"Yes," she answers as she whips off her thong. Her fingers are really going to town on her juicy little bud now, and her hips are pumping into her hand. "I just hope I can keep my eyes open," she adds.

I lube Weston up quickly and grease up my fingers and my dick for him. He seems more relaxed than usual, so the time it takes to get inside of him is pretty quick. I'm guessing his recent orgasm helped loosen things up a bit. In no time, I'm sliding my weeping shaft into his pretty hole, and I lean down to kiss his lips. Even though he just came minutes before, he's growing hard all over again, so I stroke him as I push into him slowly, deeper and deeper. He's making happy sounds in the back of his throat as I penetrate him. Finally, I'm seated all the way inside, and I feel his body tremble.

I pull back, feeling his tight muscles squeeze me, and I pound back in again. He cries out, "Yes! More! Fuck me, Callum. Do it hard. I *love* it."

His eyes are closed, so I glance over at the laptop where I see Petra's fingers grinding on her sensitive pussy. I wish I could touch her too, but I can't deny that this is fun and definitely a hot way to play for a change. Over and over I plunge into Weston's tight body and stroke his dick with my hand. I see then that Petra has straightened her legs and is squeezing her hand between them as she convulses in spasm after spasm. I chuckle to see that she couldn't manage to keep her eyes open through her orgasm, but I'm glad she seems so satisfied.

And that seems to be the catalyst that takes me over the edge too. I throw back my head and pour out everything I have into Weston with a huge roar of satisfaction. It seems to go on and on, as Weston begins to shake too, splattering his cum all over my hands and his stomach.

It is messy… and glorious.

Thirty-Five

I'M AMAZED AT HOW WELL I SLEPT CONSIDERING THE LONG nap I took yesterday, but knowing that my men are on the way home today put me in a great frame of mind. And Weston was absolutely right—the last vestiges of cramps disappeared after the mind-blowing orgasm I had. I haven't been this relaxed in days. I decide to do some housekeeping until they get home, so after a quick breakfast, I head downstairs to start cleaning. I start with the bathroom and realize my mother left it in a mess with towels on the floor and toothpaste in the sink. How anyone could be so messy in less than one day is beyond me. I guess it serves me right for not cleaning up sooner, though. I should have done this right away. We just haven't been down here much since her so-called visit.

I'm picking the bath towel off the floor when something drops on my foot. *That's odd.* I bend over and pick it up. It's a sturdy-looking single key on a ring with a fob that says, "Wally's Discount Storage" and has a Chicago address and phone number on it. How curious.

I shrug and stuff the key into my pocket, then finish sprucing up the whole basement. By the time I'm done, you'd never know a slob had been in residence. I vacuum the large room and then put fresh towels out and take the dirty ones upstairs to toss into the laundry. I'm just loading the washer when I hear the guys coming into the kitchen. *They're back!*

I zip into the kitchen and jump into Callum's arms, and Weston comes up behind me and squeezes me with his loving embrace. I kiss the daylights out of both of them.

"It feels like you've been gone for so much longer than just one day," I exclaim. "I'm so glad you're back."

"Ow." Weston pulls back and asks, "What on earth do you have in your back pocket?"

I slide out of Callum's arms and pull out the key to show them. "I found this under a heap of towels in the bathroom downstairs. My mom must have dropped it out of her bag when she left in a rush. I've never seen this before, but it's definitely from Chicago."

Callum asks, "Have you called the number or looked them up online?"

"Not yet. I was busy cleaning up. She left a pretty gross mess, and I should have gotten to it sooner. I just never thought about going in there before today to straighten up."

"No problem," Weston says. "Let's see if we can find out anything about them." He whips his laptop out of his backpack and does a search for the business. It comes up immediately. "It appears to be a place where you can rent storage lockers." He looks at me. "Maybe she didn't get rid of as much as she claimed, or she needed a place to stick some of her stuff. You should check it out, Petra. But is there a unit number on the fob or anything?"

I flip the fob over and sure enough, there is a smeared number on the back that was apparently written in felt pen. "Wow, look at that. It's number twenty-eight," I tell him. "I'm going to call them right now."

I dial the number with the phone on speaker, and it rings long enough that I'm considering hanging up, but I'm wondering if I can leave a message when finally a man's voice answers curtly, "This is Wally. Whaddya want?"

"Oh, um, hi Wally. I'm calling from out of state actually, and a relative of mine left a key from your place with me. I was wondering if she has a current locker and if you know what's in it."

"It's none of my business what folks store so long as it ain't explosives." He chuckles at that. "What's the name on the account, though? I can tell you the status."

"Oh, yes, the name is Maggie Feeney."

"That dippy little redhead? I can tell you that locker's about to go up for auction any day now. She ain't paid her bill in six months. I've called her over and over, and she has one excuse after the other. I give up. This place ain't no charity."

"Oh, I'm sorry. How much does she owe you?"

"It's a medium unit, and I gave her a real good deal at eighty bucks a month. Most places'll charge plenty more'n that. I have the auction company coming on Tuesday to inventory it, so if you want it, you gotta pay me before that."

"I see. If I drive up there tomorrow, will that be okay with you? I can have a look around and see if I want anything."

"Oh, no you don't, sister. If you want the crap that's in it, you gotta pay upfront. I have an extra lock on the unit right now, so you won't be able to get in without my permission."

"I see." I look at Callum and Weston with wide, questioning eyes, and they're nodding at me. So I tell Wally, "I'll see you tomorrow then."

"Fine by me. I'm open ten to eight, but I take off an hour for lunch around one. Closed Thursdays and Fridays cuz I'm here on the weekends."

"Thanks. I'll be sure to be there in plenty of time so as not to inconvenience you."

"I don't take no personal checks. Plastic or cash only!"

"I understand. See you tomorrow." I disconnect the phone and look at the guys. "Charming man, don't you think?" While they're snickering, I remember something. "You know... the key was next to the wastebasket in the bathroom. I wonder if what she meant to do was throw it away considering she owes him money."

"We may never know," Weston answers sagely. "Looks like we're taking another road trip."

"You'll go with me?"

"Of course I will. That's a long drive to go alone. It's over three hours each way."

We both look at Callum, who looks sad. "I'm afraid I have a brand-new class starting tomorrow, so I won't be able to take the day off on this short notice, but I can take a break and come home to let the dogs out in the middle of the day."

WE ALL GET UP EARLY THE NEXT MORNING. WESTON AND I figure we'll find a place to stay once we get to Chicago. We may decide to turn right around and come home, although we packed for overnight. I feel sorry for him after his long trip to southern Indiana so recently. He'll be pretty tired of driving after our trip too, and knowing this, I'm terribly grateful for his company.

"Maybe you'll find lots of stuff your mom said she got rid of. You never know," Callum says hopefully. He kisses us both as we climb into Weston's car and says, "Have a safe trip. The dogs and I will be fine 'til you get back."

We make our way over to 65 and head north to Chicagoland. I can't say I'm too anxious to see the place because I didn't enjoy living there very much. Curiosity has me in its grips, however, and a part of me hopes it's a real treasure hunt. My mom can't complain if I take what she's ignored for so long and clearly meant to give up. She can't exactly say I owe her either after the stunt she pulled on me. "I sure hope I'm not wasting your time, Weston," I tell him.

"Not at all. I get to spend time with my girl. And I was able to rearrange my schedule for today, so I'm not messing anything up with work. I do have to take a call tonight at eight though. It was the best I could do."

The drive is mostly just boring until we hit the city, and the traffic is horrible for a while. Finally, we locate Wally's Discount Storage, and it looks like a complete dump. The place needs a decent coat of paint, and the parking lot is full of potholes that could bust an axel. We carefully lock the car behind us and find our way to his office. This is not a nice neighborhood. The rickety door squeaks as Weston shoves on it and holds it open for me. I step inside a dreary space with a man—Wally, I assume—sprawled out in his chair behind a metal desk. His head is thrown back, and he's emitting loud snores that could wake the dead. I clear my throat, and the noise rouses him. He jolts forward and squints at us. The aroma of cheap gin hangs in the air. Wally lets out a long belch and asks, "Can I help you?"

"I'm Petra Feeney, sir. I spoke to you yesterday about my mother's locker." I produce the key. "Number twenty-eight. I know you're owed back rent, and I'm prepared to take care of the debt and determine if any of the contents are worth keeping."

"Oh yeah. The redheaded bimbo's kid. Well, here's the bill." He slaps a piece of paper on the desk, and I scan it.

"This is fifty dollars too much." I glare at him. "You said it was eighty a month, and it's been six months."

"Interest," he drawls and licks his lips.

"If I walk out now, you'll get nothing unless you can sell any of the contents. If I pay you the $480 Maggie owes you, you might still be able to sell what I leave behind. I doubt I want anything. I'm just here to see what she left as much as anything."

"Five hundred and you got a deal. Any less than that—no dice."

"You're a crook."

He shrugs.

I fork over five hundred-dollar bills and glare daggers at him. "Give me the extra key or show me where the unit is. Please."

Wally stuffs the money into his pocket as he stands. "Follow me," he orders as he shuffles out the door and turns right.

He leads us down a long row of doors that look like small garages, and I notice that a number of them have double locks. I nudge Weston as I point to three in a row, and he nods, whispering, "Business must not be too good right now."

Just then we pass by a unit where the door is open, and a

middle-aged couple are arguing loudly and colorfully about the contents. Each seems intent on insulting the other in the foulest language possible, and I find myself blushing. Wally passes by like it's no big deal, but Weston steps around me to be a buffer between me and the arguing couple. He puts his arm around me protectively and skirts away from the opening. We hurry past them and Weston whispers, "I was afraid they might start throwing things."

Finally, after passing row after row of locked doors, some larger and many smaller, we stop at number twenty-eight. Wally inserts his key and removes his padlock, and without a single word, turns back and walks away, leaving us in front of the storage unit. "Thanks, Wally," I call after him, but he doesn't react in any way. I look at Weston, who has an amused expression on his face, and say, "Strange man," as I shake my head.

"He's probably ready for another shot of gin." Weston snorts. "Well, let's see what's in here."

Trying not to let my hand wobble, I shove the key onto the lock and realize it's not going to let go easily. I jiggle it around and pull in and out a few times before the innards of the lock decide to engage. Breathing a sigh of relief, I undo the darn thing from the latch, and Weston heaves the metal door upward. It's fairly dark inside as this is the shady side of the building, but we manage to locate a light switch, and that helps immensely.

"Huh," I say brilliantly as I survey the piles of random

boxes and a few pieces of furniture I recognize from the condo. None of my pretty bedroom set seems to be there, and that makes me a little sad. There are a couple of somewhat nice chairs, an old lamp from my mother's bedroom, and so, so many boxes. I start to pry them open. Box after box is filled with household odds and ends and old clothes—like from when I was a kid. Some have old shoes, some have paperback books, and some look like the contents of wastebaskets—I kid you not. I look questioningly at Weston and ask, "Why would anyone bother to store this kind of junk? I feel so foolish for spending my money to end up with this garbage."

"Oh, let's keep looking. Maybe you'll find the lost diadem of Ravenclaw or something." He chuckles at his own joke.

"Yeah, right."

We spend the next half an hour or so ripping open boxes and sifting through them listlessly until Weston opens one and says, "Ohmygod. Petra? I think you need to take a look at this."

Thirty-Six

Petra is holding up a pair of clunky chartreuse high heels, muttering to herself with a disgusted look on her face. "Who would ever wear these butt-ugly things?"

I guess the tone of my voice jarred her. Her head jerks in my direction and she drops the stupid shoes back into their box. She's right; they are butt-ugly. She stands and rushes over to my side in the back corner of the storage unit.

I have a handful of envelopes in my hand, and the box in front of me has many more of them. They are made of thick, expensive paper stock and addressed with neat handwriting to Petra Feeney at a post office box. Our eyes are riveted to the return address, however. Each of them is from Jameson

Harvey at a Chicago address. Turning them over, we see that they are all unopened.

Petra drops to her knees and begins pawing through the letters, exclaiming, "The postmarks on some of these are almost as old as I am." She looks at me with wide, troubled eyes. "What the heck, Weston? I've never seen these before in my life. Why wouldn't my mom have shown them to me? And who *is* Jameson Harvey? Why would he spend years writing to me?"

"I have no idea, sweetheart. Just add mail theft to another of her crimes. Are you going to open them? Maybe you'll get some answers."

"I'm afraid to." Her hands are shaking.

This has to be one of the biggest shocks of her life, I'm sure, so I think fast. "I have an idea then. We only have about five more boxes to open, so let's take a peek in those and see if there's anything else that's remotely interesting. Then we'll go find a place to stay, grab some lunch, and you can relax in a comfortable room and open them. There's no reason to sit in this unit any longer than we have to. It's awfully chilly in here anyway."

"Yeah, okay. That sounds good. You grab those, and I'll poke around in these." She scoots two boxes toward me.

Within five minutes, we've determined that the remaining boxes are more of the detritus that Maggie Feeney didn't care about. It's a wonder she paid a nickel to store most of this stuff. There is just no understanding that woman. I do a quick search on my phone and find a Hilton that has a restaurant and won't break the bank. I book a room, we lock up the unit, and we head over to the hotel. It's out of the shady neighborhood, and that makes me breathe more easily.

We check into the room, deposit our bags and the box of letters, wash our hands, and head to the restaurant. Petra absentmindedly orders a burger and fries like she can't be bothered to make a weightier decision about what to eat. I'm not even sure she's all that fond of burgers or fries, so I order a grilled salmon salad. When the meals come, she looks at my food with poorly disguised envy, so I trade plates with her. "I thought so," I tell her with a grin.

"Weston, you are the best. And you're like a mind reader. What did I ever do to deserve you and Callum?"

"You're you, and that's enough. Besides, I love burgers. I'll just slide this thick slab of raw onion off of it before I chow down though. I'm hoping to get lucky tonight, and I don't want stinky breath." She giggles softly at my silliness. "Enjoy your salmon."

"Are you sure? You ordered it."

"Absolutely. Let's eat up so we can unravel the truth. You must be curious to know what's in those letters."

"What if they change everything I've ever believed?"

"My guess is they… ah… probably will." I let that sink in for a beat as her eyes widen. "You'll probably be confronted with a new reality, but you'll have Callum and me to help you navigate it. Just remember that *nothing* in those letters reflects on you because you didn't write them, and you also didn't hide them."

Once we get back to the room, I send a text to Callum letting him know the gist of what's going on and that we'll be here overnight. His response is quick, so I assume he's teaching.

> Callum: Wow. Call me later.
> Miss you.

> Weston: Will do. Miss you too.

I look up from my phone to see that Petra is taking photos of the box of letters. Then she arranges a bunch of them on the desk to show that they've never been opened. "Good idea," I tell her.

Petra then sorts the letters into order from the oldest to the newest and takes another photo. We finally get comfortable, and she takes a deep breath. "Here goes nothing."

She borrowed a knife from the restaurant to use as a letter opener and slips it under the flap, making a neat slice in the top of the envelope. The letter inside is the same heavy stock of fine quality paper. It's just a short note, but it comes out with a crisp fifty-dollar bill tucked inside.

Dearest Petra,
I know you're too young to read this, so hopefully
your mommy will read it to you. Happy third birthday,

Sweetie. I wish I could be there on your special day. Just remember your daddy loves you very much, and I miss you terribly. Your mommy is supposed to start a savings account for you, but go ahead and spend a little now on something fun.

Love,

Daddy

PETRA'S EYES FILL WITH TEARS AS SHE STARES AT ME. "Weston," she whispers. "I *have* a father! I want to go see him. The return address is local." She looks pleadingly at me, and it breaks my heart. "Why would my mom keep me from him all this time? Why would he stay away from me? He says he loves me." Her voice breaks with a sob.

I gather her into my arms and let her cry it out. When her breathing goes back to normal and she dries her eyes, I say, "There could be all kinds of reasons. Maybe he's a bad person, or he was in jail, or he has another family." I feel her flinch when I suggest this. "Remember, it's no reflection on you. You were just a toddler when he wrote that."

"She still should have been honest with me. I could have taken it."

"Yes, now you could, but maybe you were too young to understand, and she was protecting you. Then she was so in the habit of not telling you, it just never became an issue for you." I stroke her hair as she leans on my chest. "I'm not trying to make excuses for her, because it's despicable to lie to a person about their parentage, but she may have had her reasons."

Honestly, I'm starting to doubt that Petra's mother would have done anything to protect her daughter—the woman has shown herself to be pretty horrible—but staying positive seems to be calming Petra down.

Petra finally sits up on her own and opens a few more envelopes. The contents, including the cash, are roughly the same for a couple of years' worth of letters. Gradually, however, they change. One of them is dated around the time Petra turned ten years old, and in this one her father becomes a bit stern with his message.

Dear Petra,

I understand your mother has been gone a lot, and you are with a nanny. I would love to come see you, but by the terms of our agreement I cannot.

It would be nice if you would show me some manners, young lady, and acknowledge the letters I've sent. Surely by now you've learned to write.

I hope you are getting these letters, and your greedy mother hasn't absconded with this money too. Maybe it's not your fault. For now, anyway, I'll give you the benefit of the doubt.

I love you, Petra.

Dad

"HE MUST HAVE FELT BAD ABOUT THIS ONE BECAUSE IT HAS A hundred-dollar bill inside." Petra looks me in the eye. "At least he's unwittingly paid me back for that stupid storage locker of junk. The only thing of value was this stuff she tried to hide, and she would have loved to have known this cash was in there. I'm frankly surprised she couldn't smell there was money inside."

The frequency of the letters begins to peter out as Petra gets older, but the amount of money grows exponentially larger in each of them. They are filled with remorse and self-recrimination for something we cannot identify.

One of them nearly breaks Petra's heart.

Dearest Petra,

I am so proud of you. I flew in to watch you graduate from high school today. You're so beautiful, and hearing that you won academic awards and writing awards made my heart feel as if it would burst with pride. I wanted so badly to stand up and cheer and say, "That wonderful girl is my precious daughter!" I'm so sorry I didn't have the courage to do it— and hang the repercussions. The main reason I didn't was because you might suffer embarrassment because of my outburst. I doubt you'd recognize me anymore. You were just a baby the last time I held you in my arms.

Why wasn't your mother at the ceremony? I hope she isn't ill. We may have serious issues, but I do have a soft spot in my heart for her even after all these years. Maybe I ought to know better.

Please write back to me Petra. College will start soon, and maybe I can come see you on campus sometime. Your mother doesn't need to know. She's so rarely in the country anymore anyway. I hope whatever is keeping her away from you is making her happy because from my point of view, she's making some huge mistakes.

Don't worry about tuition. I've taken care of it the same way I did for your private schools all of these past years. Your mother probably told you that anyway, so I guess I didn't even need to bring it up.

I hope you don't hate me for staying out of your life. Is that why you've never written back?

Congratulations dearest one,
Dad

"WESTON, THIS IS KILLING ME. MY MOM TOLD ME SHE HAD money, and that's how we got to live in a nice place with so many privileges. She made me grovel and thank *her* all the time for her supposed generosity like she was doing me a big favor by feeding, clothing, and educating me. When I got older, I just assumed she had wealthy parents—although she never spoke of them. You know how kids are. They don't usually question the why of things—they just accept them as their due. But it's been my dad all along, and she lied about it. I must have seemed like the worst ingrate to him for never speaking up and thanking him for his support. I feel terrible!"

All I can offer is a hug. It's not nearly enough, but it slows down her shaking.

The last letter is postmarked during Petra's freshman year in college, but interestingly, the post office box is a new one close to her college campus in Iowa. It's also stamped with a forwarding address to the original box in Chicago. This one is the worst yet, despite having five thousand dollars stuffed inside.

Petra,

I had a long chat with your mother today. She assured me you've been getting all of these letters, and you've chosen to ignore me. This is unacceptable. I've shown you as much love and understanding as I possibly could from afar, but I know so little about you—only what your mother deems necessary—I don't know how to communicate with you. I've made it clear that your living expenses have been taken care of generously, and I've always included pin money for you to spend on whatever you thought would be fun. It breaks my heart that you have apparently turned into a selfish brat who has no care for the feelings of your own father. I hoped we could finally see one another once you're a legal adult, but I'm washing my hands of you. The terms of your trust fund will end when you turn twenty-five, but if I could stop supporting you prior to that, I would. I've asked you countless times to answer my letters, and yet I've heard not one word from you. I won't stop loving you, but I cannot keep hoping for you to contact me. It hurts too much to carry on these one-sided conversations.

It's time to cut you loose. I wish you well.
Dad

"OH MY GOD, WESTON. WHAT AM I GOING TO DO? WHY DO you think he had to stay away from me? What happened? I'm so confused, and I feel like crap. He says he loves me, but if I were him, I'd hate me!"

"Well, you'll never know unless you go see him. Is there a phone number for him on any of those?"

"No. I looked for it on each one. Nothing. Maybe we can find one online though."

So we spend a frustrating hour using record searches and

come up with nothing. His name comes up in a Google search, however, and he's listed on LinkedIn as a former CEO of a company called JAH, Inc. We've never heard of it, and they oddly don't have a website. Calling them up turns out to be an exercise in futility, however. No one would give us any information about Jameson Harvey. Either they were protecting his privacy or he's been gone too long for the people there to know him. When asked the nature of their business, the only answer given was "investments," and then they disconnected the call.

"Are you brave enough to just show up at his house?" I ask. "Hopefully, he still lives at the same address as what's on the envelopes."

"Yes, I guess so. But not today. I need to relax and think about things. We can go tomorrow. You'll go with me, won't you?"

"Of course. You don't even need to ask, Petra." I think for a minute and ask, "How would you like to go have a quick workout with me in the gym downstairs? After that, we can grab some dinner and then call Callum and fill him in. There's nothing like exercise for clearing your head."

Thirty-Seven

PETRA

AFTER OUR WORKOUT AND A RUN ON THE TREADMILL, WE shower and then go have dinner in a tiny local Italian restaurant. By the time we get back to our room, I'm feeling somewhat normal again—albeit pretty stuffed. Weston is always such good, reassuring company, and I can almost believe that things will go great tomorrow. We'll find my dad, and all will be forgiven. He'll be wonderful. I just know it.

I have a dad!

Weston unpacks his laptop to call Callum and suddenly remembers he has a business call he needs to make. "Oh no!" he exclaims, putting his hands to his face, looking like *The*

Scream by Edvard Munch. "I forgot Chicago is an hour earlier! I'm late for the counseling call. Oh, just shoot me."

While he's frantically setting up for the call, I tell him, "I'm going to head down to the lounge where I can have a drink and call Callum. Your client deserves privacy." I also grab my laptop in case Callum's not available, thinking maybe I can get some writing done until Weston's free. *Yeah, sure... like my head is in a good space for working this evening.*

Breaking into my thoughts, Weston tells me, "I'll be counseling for an hour. Be careful downstairs, sweetheart." He's still looking down and fiddling with his earbuds as he says, "Nancy! I'm *so* sorry to be late. I'm traveling and in a different time zone." He looks up at the screen. "Ah... Nancy, I'm... ah... turning around until you tell me you've put on some clothes. We've talked about this. I don't do... ah... naked therapy sessions, and I don't care how free it makes you feel."

Thankfully, I can't hear Nancy's response through Weston's earbuds. I smile at him and blow him a kiss. He rolls his eyes and shakes his head as I exit the room. As soon as I close the door, I dissolve into giggles. Weston's face was as red as a stop sign. He certainly must have some interesting clients.

I order a glass of wine from the bar and then find a secluded corner to sit in. Then it dawns on me that it would still be fun to chat with Callum via FaceTime. I send him a quick text and then locate my earbuds.

Petra: Calling you via FT from a
public area. Make sure you're
dressed!

Callum: Oops. Give me a second. ;)

I wait a couple of minutes—just in case—and then give Callum a call. He looks so good when he answers, and he has all three of the dogs squished together next to him so they're in the picture too—more or less. The sight immediately warms my heart.

"Aw, hi, guys!"

"Hi, Lovergirl. Where's Loverboy?"

"He's upstairs talking to a client. He almost forgot about her tonight. I can understand why though. It's been a long, emotional day for us. I guess he filled you in a little on what we found."

"All I know is that you found a box of unopened letters from the guy who paid for the condo you lived in. Did you read them?"

"Oh, Callum. I did. It was… amazing and heartbreaking. The letters prove that he's my father!"

"I'm not surprised. Weston and I had a hunch. What all did he say?"

"I'll let you read them all when we get back, but the major issue is that he wrote them to me for years, assuming—because my evil-hearted bitch of a mother told him so—that I'd been reading and ignoring his letters the whole time. What my mother didn't know—because she hid them rather than opening them—is that he also stuffed cash into them. Thousands of dollars' worth."

"Wow. I guess it's a good thing she wasn't nosier about the contents, or you'd never have found them. It's kind of a wonder she saved them, even if she never expected you to locate them."

"Yes, that's one silver lining. I wonder if she thought she could someday use them as leverage for who-knows-what, or maybe she just forgot she had them. He actually hasn't written anything for about seven years. Anyway, I'm sure glad I followed a hunch and looked into the contents of that storage unit. Nothing else was the least bit interesting though." I clear my throat as it begins to close up on me with emotion, and I feel a tear start to roll down my cheek as I tell him, "He sounds like a nice man, Callum. I just can't imagine what went on between my parents that made him stay away for my whole life. He hadn't seen me since I was a baby, but he showed up at my high school graduation—something my own mother didn't bother doing. He just didn't come and introduce himself to me. Why do you think he'd do that?"

Shaking his head slightly, Callum answers, "Hopefully you can find out. Are you going to track him down?"

"If he still lives at the same address, we're going to see him tomorrow. I hope he hasn't moved because he's a hard guy to locate otherwise."

"Well, fingers crossed. I hope it works out for you."

"I hope he doesn't hate me. My mom has lied to him so much. I took photos of the unopened letters I case he doesn't believe me. Originally, I was doing it in case I needed them as proof that my mother's been stealing my mail. At this point, I don't even care about the crap she's been pulling. I just want to get to know him."

"I can't imagine how that would feel. I'm both happy and sad for you."

"I know… me too. Oh, and his letters also mentioned some things that were pretty curious. Apparently, I've had a trust fund all these years that I've known nothing about, and there might be money in an account—somewhere. It sounds like he's been my sole support. It wasn't my mother after all. She's such a *liar!* She led me to believe she had rich parents, though she'd never tell me anything about them or why their money came to her in the first place."

"It sounds like you're going to have a lot of questions for the guy when you see him. I hope he's understanding."

"I do too. So, tell me what you and the guys have been up to? Everything okay on the home front?"

"We're doing fine. My new class is off to a good start. When I got home, the dogs and I ran around in the leaves for about an hour so I could wear them out. I think they miss you and Weston as much as I do though."

We chat about all kinds of things for a while until I'm stifling a yawn when Callum says, "Petra, I know it's not all that late in Chicago, but you guys left at the crack of dawn this morning, and you're obviously dead on your feet. You and Weston need to get a good night's sleep tonight before you tackle meeting your dad."

"You're probably right." I turn and see a familiar face smiling at me as he approaches. "Oh, here's Weston now." He sits down next to me, and I hand him an earbud. For the next half hour or so, we talk until we're all yawning our heads off.

"We'll probably see you tomorrow unless something unforeseen happens," Weston tells Callum. "You never know."

"Best of luck," Callum says. "I love you both."

We echo his endearment and disconnect the call.

BY THE TIME WESTON AND I HIT THE BED, WE'RE BOTH nearly down for the count. We snuggle together and, even though I expected to have a million thoughts running through my head, his warm comfort spreads through me like a tranquilizer. The last thing I remember is his kiss and loving whispers that he's proud of me and loves me. I'm asleep in less than a minute.

Thirty-Eight

WESTON

"Morning, sleepyhead. I guess I didn't get lucky after all last night. Tell me honestly, was it the garlic bread?"

Petra warms my heart with her soft laughter as she answers, "We shared that bread, silly. I'm sorry I passed out."

"No worries. I was right behind you. Are you ready to meet your father this morning?"

"After a shower and at least three cups of strong coffee, yes." She looks thoughtful as she asks, "Do you think we ought to check out of the room or book it for another night?"

"Mm… let's take our stuff since we have so little with us, and if we need to check out and head home, I can do it from my phone. Are you going to tell good old Wally he can have what's in the locker?"

"No. I've been thinking it would be wise to take a second look. I'd hate to miss anything because we were in a rush and getting too cold."

I nod thoughtfully. "Maybe your dad might know something. There was some… ah… funky costume jewelry that I discounted, but maybe I was wrong, and it was stuff that was actually worth something. Perhaps we should hire someone to haul the boxes to the house where we can be more systematic and careful."

"Good idea. It's hard for me to believe she paid to have just a bunch of trash stored. The boxes and furniture won't all fit in your car anyway. It's possible there was more of value than we originally thought. I just wanted to get out of there."

I notice that Petra seems to be fussing with her appearance this morning. She's fiddling with her hair and putting on makeup—something she rarely uses and doesn't need. I'm frankly surprised she had any in her travel bag. So I tell her, "You're incredibly beautiful, sweetheart. Don't worry. If he expects perfect hair and makeup, he's not worth it. You always look perfect to Callum and me."

WE PLUG THE ADDRESS INTO THE GPS AND ARE NOT TERRIBLY surprised when it leads us to one of the nicest neighborhoods in all of Chicago. I pull into the spacious driveway of a mammoth house and look at Petra. She looks… well… petrified. "Are you ready?" I ask needlessly.

Taking a deep breath she asks, "You'll stay right next to me the whole time?"

"Of course. You know that. It's going to be just fine."

I step out of the car and round it to her side, but when I open her door, she seems frozen to the spot. "It's alright. You're going to be great. He'll be happy to see you. Come on, sweetheart." I extend my hand and take hold of her trembling one. Finally, she steps out and silently we head for the massive front door.

After ringing the bell, we hear a deep couple of woofs that sound like a giant dog. Then we wait and wait until we hear quick footsteps approaching. The door swings open, and I feel Petra deflate. There is no way this man is her father. He's an attractive Asian man, probably not much older than us. He has a friendly face, however, and smiles at her. Standing quietly next to him is a gorgeous and stately brindle Great Dane.

"Sorry to bother you, sir, but we're looking for Jameson Harvey. Does he still live here?" she asks in a shaky voice.

"Petra!" he exclaims. "I would know you anywhere. Your father isn't home right now, but come in, and let me get you a refreshment. Coffee? Tea? I'm so sorry Jameson missed you." He opens the door and beckons us in, saying happily, "Don't mind Storm here. He hasn't eaten anyone in weeks. Seriously, he's a giant softy."

Well, this is weird.

"Um, thank you. Coffee would be good. And you are…?"

"I'm Bing—your father's major domo around here as well as his driver and currently his dog sitter. He'll be back next week. Can you stay?" He speaks without the hint of an accent so I'm guessing he's U.S. born, but what do I know? It doesn't matter anyway.

"Oh, I wouldn't want to impose, and Weston and I need to get home, but thank you."

"And home is…?"

"Carmel, Indiana."

Nodding like he knows where Carmel is, Bing leads us into a cavernous room with fantastic furnishings and wonderful paintings and sculptures adorning the area. It's strangely homey for such a large room, probably because of the bright colors and comfortable-looking chairs. Bing seems like the personification of cheerfulness, bouncing along as he walks. "I'll just order that coffee now," he says as he makes a notation on his phone. He types for a moment and asks us, "Please make yourselves comfortable. Who is your charming man, Petra? Your boyfriend? I don't see any rings, so I assume you aren't married."

"Oh, yes, sorry. Bing, this is Weston Alister. One of my roommates."

Well, that's pretty unclear. I try not to be ruffled by my description. I know she's still nervous. I shake Bing's hand telling him, "Pleased to meet you," before taking a seat.

Storm settles on the floor next to Bing, looking aloof and regal. He really is a gorgeous dog.

"The refreshments will be here in a moment," he assures us, and then his cheerfulness seems to fade. "I am curious, Petra, why has it taken you all these years to make contact with your father? He's had a terribly hard time dealing with the rejection."

"*He's* dealing with rejection?" she nearly screeches. "I didn't even know he existed until I found out yesterday by accident!" She breathes deeply and softens her voice before she continues, "Sorry. I grew up feeling abandoned by my father whom I was led to believe rejected *me* from birth!"

I always suspected her assurances that she never missed her "sperm donor" masked some deeper feelings.

Bing's eyes flash in anger. "What are you talking about? Your father was a constant in your life and as involved as their agreement would allow. It broke his heart that you never responded to one word from him."

Petra reaches into her purse and pulls out her phone, saying, "I need to show you what Weston found yesterday in a ratty storage locker my mom rented who-knows-how-long ago." She scrolls through her photos and comes to the ones of the unopened stacks of letters. "I never saw these until yesterday. Not. One. I'm afraid my father and I have been played."

"Oh, my God." Bing breaths. "That insufferable bitch! Sorry, sorry. I know she's your mother, but from what I've heard…"

"All true, I assure you," I tell him. "And probably even *worse* than you've heard."

A lovely young woman brings a tray in and sets it down on the coffee table in front of us. I don't miss the hungry look Bing gives her that probably has nothing to do with her snacks. He winks at her, and she flushes crimson.

The tray is filled with steaming coffee mugs and a platter of delectable pastries that smell like they just came out of the oven. My mouth waters even though I consumed a hearty omelet less than an hour ago. Petra just reaches for her coffee, but I can't resist an almond-encrusted bear claw to go with mine. "Thank you, miss," I tell the retreating woman. She turns and smiles, then quietly takes her leave.

"Bing, my father had to have some idea of what my mother was like or this 'arrangement' or whatever they had wouldn't have happened. Can you explain anything to me? For one, why didn't he arrange to have custody of me if he loved me so much and knew that my mother was gone all the time?"

Bing gives her a thoughtful look, sips his coffee, and finally answers, "Petra, I shouldn't stick my nose in this at all. Your father needs to have a long talk with you when he gets back. He's not even accessible by phone at the moment, but I'll fill him in as soon as possible. It may be difficult, but it's obvious that the two of you have much to learn about each other."

"I guess you're right. I'm not being fair to you by putting

you in the middle. But I do wonder about one thing. How did you know immediately who I was?"

Smiling broadly, Bing stands and says, "Follow me."

Petra stands and looks at me as if to say, "You promised not to leave my side." So I quickly chew my mouthful of the most delectable pastry I've ever encountered and wipe the crumbs off with a linen napkin. I stand, take her hand, and we follow Bing out of the room and into a formal dining room. He gestures, à la Vanna White, to a painting on the wall, and Petra gasps.

"How did he have me painted?"

"He purchased a copy of your college yearbook from the year you graduated and hired an artist. It's a wonderful likeness, don't you think?"

"I guess. Why would he even want me on his wall if he was so disappointed in me?"

"He's never stopped loving you, Petra. I think he figured one day you'd come around, and he was right—here you are. You'll soon discover your father has an infinite capacity for love and a trusting nature that can sometimes be his downfall."

The tears start then, and I have to envelop Petra in my arms. I know she needs me.

With a stern expression, Bing continues, "Break his heart again, and you'll have me to contend with."

"I would never," she says with a gulp. "I never knew I did."

We head back to our seats and after more chit chat and thankfully the rest of my bear claw—okay two bear claws, but who's counting?—Bing pumps Petra for information until we decide it's time to get back to Indiana.

"I can't help noticing you've enjoyed your pastries, Weston. Would you like to take some with you?" Bing asks out of the blue.

"Oh, ah… they're delicious, but I don't want to deprive you and whoever else lives here."

Bing's face lights up and he laughs. "No worries, I can always make more. It's a hobby of mine, and I always make too many."

"You *made* them?" He nods proudly as I say, "In that case, sure, I'd love some. Thank you!"

Petra gives Bing all her contact information and extracts a solemn promise from him to have her father contact her as soon as possible. I cancel the room at the hotel and locate a small moving company to get all the boxes and furniture out of the locker. We drop the key off at their office and let Wally know when they'll be there to empty the locker and return the key. He grunts and answers, "Yeah, whatever." He abruptly hangs up. Charming man.

The last thing I do before we hit the road is send Callum a text saying we're on our way back.

> Weston: We'll be home by dinnertime. All is well, but the dad wasn't home. Lots to tell anyway.

Callum: Anxious to hear. Dinner will be ready at 7. Glad you're coming home.

Thirty-Nine

Petra

I AM A COMPLETE BUNDLE OF NERVES. NOW THAT I KNOW A little more about my dad, I crave hearing everything from him. I must admit I've scoured the internet again looking for information, but all I've found is the reference to his investment business, and nothing personal whatsoever. I even tried looking up Bing, but all I managed to learn is that Bing is a fairly common Chinese name.

And I feel horrible, even though I know none of my dad's or my mutual heartache is on me. What must he have thought of me? That I was just like my mother? Speaking of my mother, nothing has turned up about my prized books, and she hasn't surfaced anywhere that the cops have located. My guess is, she took the money she stole, boarded a plane to who-knows-where, and she's long gone. I know I've lost a lot of money to her, but it doesn't sting anywhere near as much as what she stole from me emotionally—a relationship with my father.

For the next several days, Weston and Callum are the perfect boyfriends. They take care of me—and each other—in many little ways that I love. The sex we share is incredible, and we all pour out our hearts to each other.

Callum's cooking has reached a new pinnacle of delicious-ness. As he puts it, he's trying out his own flavors in hopes that he can one day have a restaurant that demonstrates his personal flair. He told us yesterday, "I'm in no rush to have it happen. Like we talked about before, the failure rate for restaurants is high, so I don't want to barge in and make a million mistakes right off the bat—not that I have the money to do it yet anyway." He isn't at all bitter about his former professor's attitude and deviousness. He decided the whole thing was pretty funny when he stepped back and thought about it.

Weston continues to be our rock. He's so understanding and gentle—the perfect boyfriend for Callum and me. And sexy beyond belief. What can I say? I'm living my dream with these men.

Callum and I are snuggling in bed waiting for Weston and the dogs to come upstairs after their last outing of the night. Giving me a sultry look, Callum asks me, "Is there anything from one of your books that you'd like to try? It can be anything you've written or read."

I have to think about this because while I've certainly read my share of ménage romances, an awful lot of them focus on domination and pain, and I'm not really good with that for myself. "Well…" I hedge. "We could try a different type of double penetration. It sounds a little scary though."

Callum bursts out laughing. "Scary? How could anything involving the three of us be scary?"

"Because it involves both of you sticking your dicks into me in the *same place*."

"Is that even possible?"

"I read about it a few times, and it sounded amazing, but I never knew if that was just a creative writer doing a great job making something up. So, I finally looked it up on a popular porn site and saw videos of it. It's really a thing. Want me to show you?"

"Well, sure. I'm always up for something new."

I grab my laptop and do a quick search. In less than a minute we're sitting up watching two men in the throes of DP-ing a woman's pussy, and I have to say they all look pretty happy about it. Wow. I'm squirming and Callum is as hard as a rock when Weston comes into the bedroom.

"What on earth?" he asks with a laugh. "I heard the moans from halfway up the stairs and thought you two were already getting it on. Loudly. But then I realized there was background music."

Not taking his eyes off the screen, Callum explains, "Petra wants to try something, Loverboy. Are you up for this?"

Callum turns the laptop toward Weston, whose chin drops. He looks rather bug-eyed for a moment and then asks as he begins yanking off his clothes, "Want to try that right now?"

"Grab the lube. We're going to need plenty of it," Callum tells him and looks at me. "Are you sure?"

"I am, but let's go really, really slowly." Is it getting hot in here?

Callum whips off the blanket and buries his face between my legs. I gasp as he prods and strokes with his fingers and his tongue. In no time at all, he has me panting and begging for more of his ministrations as I grab his hair with one hand and pinch my nipple with the other. He chuckles as my first orgasm of the night rips through me like a freight train.

Weston then gently scoots Callum to the side and slides two fingers inside me, latching onto my clit like it's his favorite snack. I'm already so sensitive, I cry out and then shudder with another climax. Callum is sucking a nipple and stroking Weston's dick at the same time. It's already as hot as Hades in here, and we haven't even gotten to the good stuff yet. Weston takes hold of Callum's hand, removing it from his dick, and slides their fingers into my pussy together. I'm so slick from my own juices and their saliva, they slide in effortlessly, but Weston grabs the bottle of lube anyway with his free hand. He squirts a bit onto their hands as they pump in and out of me.

Even if they don't manage to get their dicks inside of me, it's terribly exciting to feel their fingers probing me *together*, but these men are determined. I can't stop the greedy noises that keep erupting from me. I'm starting to sound like the porn lady, and I have to stifle a giggle at that thought.

Weston asks as he looks at Callum, "Want to be the bottom or the top?"

"I'll be the bottom." We grease up Callum's erection nice and slick before I raise up and slide down onto him. He rolls onto his back, and Weston helps me sit on him, facing outward.

"Ohhh, so good." I purr.

Callum lets out a moan. "You feel perfect. Hot and tight. Now let's get our man in there with me. I can't wait to feel you both at the same time. Lube up, Loverboy. It's showtime."

Weston's erection seems to be pulsating, he's so hard, and my heart is pounding—I'm beyond excited. This is the scary part though. I don't want it to hurt. "Try a finger in there first, okay?"

"Sure. Good idea." He squirts some lube on his index finger and strokes up and down on the base of Callum's cock. Slowly he prods his way inside of me little by little. It's a very strange sensation at first, but I kind of love it.

After a minute or so, his finger is all the way inside, rubbing up and down, and Callum is groaning, "That feels incredible! Shove another one in there."

Weston complies, and I'm starting to feel stretched to my

limit. How am I supposed to take both of them? But gradually I relax. Weston pulls out and lubes up his hand again, this time prodding my opening with three fingers. There is a jolt of pain that goes through me, and I cry out a little. His hand goes very still.

"No, keep moving, Weston. I need it. I need you both!"

"This is the best thing I've ever felt," Callum exclaims. "It's like you have a magic pussy with built-in grabbers or something."

"Grabbers?" Weston laughs.

"Wait 'til I try that next time with your dick inside her first. You'll see what I mean. It's amazing. Petra, are you ready for the real thing?"

"Yes, I think so." I try as hard as possible to relax everything as Weston pulls his hand away. I already miss the extra feeling, but not for long. I lean back onto Callum's chest, and Weston probes my opening with his well-lubed shaft. It's thicker than his fingers, and more concentrated, so the stretch feels different. I gasp as he pushes in an inch or so. He lets me relax a moment before checking with me.

"Ready for more?"

"Do it," I tell him. Meanwhile, Callum is making happy noises while he plays with my nipple with one hand and strokes my clit with the other.

"Here goes." He grits his teeth and flexes his hips, pushing into me a few inches this time. I expect to feel my flesh ripping, and I'm suddenly so scared I have to close my eyes.

But much to my delight, he slides in alongside Callum. "Yes!" he cries. "This is… wow. I feel everything. Callum, you feel wonderful rubbing against me, and Petra, you're like a velvet vise around us. This is amazing. Are you ready for us to move even more, sweetheart? Does it hurt?"

My eyes fly open. "It does kind of in a weird way, but I love it. Try moving in and out more."

Weston pulls out a bit and shoves back in, causing Callum to holler, "Fuck, that's good! More!"

"Yes!" I moan. This is like nothing I could have imagined. It's truly all of us loving each other as intimately as possible. I reach for Weston and pull his face to mine so I can kiss him. And I feel Callum kissing my neck from behind me.

Gradually, Weston speeds up and increases the force of his hip flexes. It's complete sensation overload as I cry out with the most massive orgasm I've ever experienced. I'm shaking and jerking as Weston makes the noise we know as his "coming" sound. Callum is right behind with his continued joyful cries peppered with creative profanities.

It's messy and glorious. I'm so glad we tried this.

"You have to promise to write this in a book," Callum tells me breathlessly as Weston chuckles.

"Definitely. Wow," I say. "So when you hear about a famous and very sexy book about a woman named Peta with two dashingly handsome and dazzling lovers named Cullen and Winston… you'll know." I dissolve into giggles as the men slide out of me. We can't let go of each other for a long time, though. We've reached such a deep level of closeness, not one of us wants to break the mood. We lie there wrapped in our sticky cocoon for a long time.

"That's the way to make love." I tell the men in a sleepy voice, and they both agree. We all cling to each other in a group hug.

♡♡♡

UNFORTUNATELY, AS THE WEEK PASSES, I HAVE YET TO HEAR from either my father or Bing. Bing didn't give me my father's contact information—just took mine with a promise to contact me as soon as possible. Nothing but crickets.

As the seventh day after our meeting comes and goes, I begin to have serious doubts that I will ever get to meet Jameson Harvey.

After the ninth day passes, I'm getting pretty angry and hurt. I decide to talk to Callum and Weston about driving up to Chicago again. I want to confront Jameson Harvey myself. They kiss me and hold me and tell me to have patience.

On the tenth day, I reach a new level of sadness I've never felt before.

I've been rejected once again.

I'm feeling horribly down when I hear the doorbell ring. My heart leaps as I momentarily fantasize that this has something to do with my father. Except, adding insult to injury, the man at the door is none other than Randy, who looks at me with a creepy leer and says, "Well, well, here's pretty Petra finally. I've missed you, babe."

Without a second thought, I swing the door wide open and order the dogs, "Get him, boys!"

All three dogs burst outside barking their heads off. Randy's face contorts into a nasty look of anger as he stumbles back. Dave starts jumping up and down, and that's all it takes for Randy to turn tail and sprint back to his car. Dave nips at his heels the whole way.

I holler at him, "Don't ever show your face here again, you loser!" And then I can't help but laugh. "Good dogs, come inside now." They earned a handful of treats for that.

I can't wait to tell the guys about this.

Forty

Callum

Eleven days.

That's how long that fucker took to acknowledge his daughter's extension of an olive branch. I thought our sweet Petra was going to have a nervous breakdown waiting to hear from him. Thank God we have our own resident shrink in case that were to happen. Seriously, I know she couldn't sleep, and she was eating very little. In the past few days, there wasn't much Weston and I could do for her outside of watch her fret and try to reassure her that everything would work out eventually.

Sex is great, but it doesn't solve everything.

Finally, he had his flunky call and tell her they are on their way down here and they'll be here in a about an hour. He couldn't even call himself? And who just says, "We're on our way," like he's the king of the world and Petra didn't have plans for her Saturday? I'm so unimpressed, and I hope there's a good reason for all of this misery. I also feel bad for springing my family on them with not much more notice than this. It's different looking at it from this perspective, I realize.

Naturally, Petra is going crazy trying to make sure the house looks perfect, so she and Weston are vacuuming, mopping, and dusting like house elves while I throw together snacks and something for lunch as quickly as possible. The house looks fine if you ask me. Every so often, I catch Weston's eye and we both roll them at each other. I think he shares my doubts about this guy. About ten minutes before the appointed arrival time, Weston gently tells Petra that she might want to go take a fast shower and put on something a bit nicer.

She looks down at her wrinkled t-shirt and yoga pants and gasps, "Ohmigosh, you're right!" and she barrels up the stairs to pull herself together. In eight minutes, she's back down again looking like a new person, as Weston and I put away the cleaning supplies. Then we both go grab clean shirts.

I kind of liked the yoga pants, actually. They make her cute butt look delectable.

Right on schedule, the three dogs run to the door as we hear a vehicle pull up out front. Since I'm the closest to the foyer and very curious, I open the door. I see a handsome Asian man who must be the guy they called Bing step out of a limousine and open the back door. His expression is one of solicitousness and concern—which puzzles me a bit—as he helps an older gentleman out of the car.

Before I can say or do anything, Petra rushes past me with the dogs hot on her tail. She comes to a halt about a yard away from him as she stares into the face of her father for the first time since she was a baby. I can't see her expression, but Jameson's face beams at her with a glorious smile. He silently opens his arms to her, and she goes to him, snuggling into his chest. His head drops to hers so that his cheek rests on her hair, and his eyes close. No words have been spoken yet, but the scene is so achingly tender, my throat closes. I feel a tear dribble down my face that I quickly dash away.

Weston steps up beside me, slips his arm around my waist, and I hear him sniffle. "She needed this so badly," he whispers. I guess he's as moved as I am by the sight of our beautiful woman finding her long-lost dad at last.

Even the dogs are being polite and sit quietly behind her like three gentlemen. Somehow, they pick up on the intensity of this scene.

Bing turns and faces us, and his eyes sparkle with unshed tears as well. He gently takes Jameson by the elbow and says, "Let's get you into the house now. It's chilly out here."

Petra's face is covered with tears as she turns toward us. She smiles and says excitedly, "Dad, I want you to meet Weston Alister. He's a psychologist and this is his house. And this is Callum O'Malley, who's an incredible chef and cooking instructor. And these guys," she goes on quickly, "are Goliath and Dave—Weston's dogs—and this is Gus, my dog. I bet they'd love to meet Storm sometime."

We all shake hands as Petra's father introduces himself to Weston and he introduces himself and Bing Ma to me. Jameson's voice is a little wobbly, so I have to think he's somewhat shaken by the circumstances.

We all head to the hearth room part of the kitchen where we've lit a cozy fire in the fireplace, and I offer coffee and fresh-baked cookies. I notice that Jameson is looking around with curiosity.

As he takes a seat he asks Petra, "Darling, it's no doubt none of my business, but I'm sort of flabbergasted that you live in this house, as pleasant as it is, with roommates. I'd have thought you'd be living in your own stately home by now."

Petra scowls for an instant before she answers, "I don't make the kind of money quite yet to afford my own house, and I haven't been in the market for a sugar daddy, so I'm not sure what you're implying." Uh oh. Her hackles are rising.

Jameson's face looks horrified, and he quickly explains, "I only mean, what are you saving all of your money for? I've been contributing to your accounts for years, and there is no reason you need to rent a room from someone."

"I have no idea what you're talking about. What accounts? One of your letters mentioned a trust fund I've never heard of, and Bing mentioned an account that I assumed took care of my tuition, but I'm so confused! This is all news to me."

Jameson closes his eyes as if struggling with his emotions. When he opens them again, he looks pained. "Petra, I cannot believe the depths your mother sunk to. I should have known she was capable of such subterfuge, but I always held out hope that she was a better person than current circumstances suggest. Unless she's somehow gotten her hands on your accounts, you should have quite a fortune saved up by now."

She looks stricken, and everyone is silent for a moment, so I decide to comment, "Petra, I think Weston and I need to head downstairs for a while to let you and your dad speak privately." I look at my watch and add, "In fact, Declan's game has been going on for a while already, and if I miss it, I'll be considered the worst brother ever. My family might just ostracize me." I look at Bing and ask, "Are you a football fan?"

Bing stands quickly and answers, "I am now." He turns to Jameson and says, "Let me know if you need anything."

"Thanks, guys," Petra says softly.

We all troop down the stairs with the dogs and leave Petra and Jameson to get acquainted without an audience.

Weston turns on the television while I think about what I just experienced. My feelings about Jameson have gone through several iterations in the past ten or so minutes. I'm no longer angry with him because he so clearly loves his daughter, and that love has nearly broken him. It's as clear as crystal. He's a little older than I expected, having a good twenty years on Maggie, so their relationship is a puzzle. But even if he's possibly approaching seventy, he looks to be in somewhat ill health rather than exhibiting advanced age. Bing's solicitousness to him underscores that. He's a good-looking man, and Petra has his same facial bone structure and eyes. I thought she looked like Maggie, but the resemblance is much stronger with Jameson.

"They're going to have a lot to work out, aren't they?" I ask Bing.

"Oh, you have no idea," he answers. "It's not my place to talk about it, but I will say that I'm sorry for Petra that he took so long to come down here to see her. He didn't think it was fair to make her travel up to Chicago again so soon to see him, but he was out of town longer than expected, and then he had to meet with his lawyer, and that took a few days. He was pretty exhausted this morning, so I let him sleep most of the way here. He planned to call ahead, but he conked out before he had the chance."

"Why did he want to meet with his lawyer?"

"He's settling his estate."

Somehow that statement had an ominous ring to it, so I change the subject and ask, "Bing, Weston tells me you like to bake in your spare time. He generously shared one of the bear claws you sent him home with. It was delicious!" And that prompts a lively discussion about cooking that we carry on as we watch the game. I get the sense that Bing definitely knows his way around a kitchen.

Bing Ma seems like a great guy. I have to think that Jameson is lucky to have him working for him. I wonder absently how they got together as boss/employee, but before I can ask, Declan throws a bullet of a pass for forty-seven yards, his nearly surrounded receiver jumps up, snatches the ball out of the air with one hand and runs it in for a touchdown. I'm suddenly engrossed in football. Go Buckeyes!

My phone chimes, and I look down, unsurprised to see a text from my sister.

Gracie: Did you just see that?!!

Callum: Wow! What a play!

Forty-One

I have so many questions for my father, but he seems tired, and there is a tinge of sadness behind the happiness and energy he tries to project. I can't put my finger on it, so I decide to ignore the feeling that all is not well. He doesn't seem to have any trouble asking me questions about my life, though. In fact, he peppers me with questions about my career and what I've been writing. He seems pleased that I've never confined myself to a particular genre and have done non-fiction, business documents, marketing campaigns, and trade manuals as well as fiction. Finally, his curiosity seems satisfied, and I decide it's time for some answers from him.

I try for easy questions first, but right away it's clear that the "easy" ones don't necessarily have easy answers.

"How did you meet my mom?"

See? That seems straightforward enough until he tells me, "I found her."

"Huh?" Always with the eloquent answers here.

He takes a shaky breath and begins. "I used to walk to work for exercise whenever the weather was nice, and a few times I saw this exquisite young woman sitting on a bench as I'd pass by. I guess I thought she was waiting for a bus or something, but I couldn't help noticing her beauty. I began to smile as I passed, and she would look away as if she were shy. More and more I wanted to get her attention, so I stopped driving to work at all.

"One morning I headed out, and it started to rain quite unexpectedly. She was still there—sitting in a downpour. I wished I'd had an umbrella to offer her because she was trying to cover up with a sweater that I realized was inadequate. She then darted away into the opening of a building, but the doorman shooed her away like she was a piece of trash. I went up to her, hoping to assist. As I approached, I also realized that she was terribly thin and had a bruise on her chin. She was shaking like a leaf, even though it wasn't all that cold yet.

"When I asked if I could help, she shook her head and told me something to the effect that no one could help, but I was armored and mounted on my white steed then, and I was ready to rescue the damsel in distress. 'Have you had breakfast yet?' I asked her and then made up some cock-and-bull story about being so hungry, I needed a Belgian waffle before starting my workday. That poor thing's eyes looked so miserable and starved, I took her by the arm and led her to the nearest café. I sent a text to my assistant to let her know I'd be late and proceeded to order enough food for an army."

"Um. Wow. And that was my mother?"

"Yes, Petra. She was so far down on her luck, she'd been on the streets for weeks, barely scraping by. She lived in a shelter at night at least where she got a small meal, but during the day she couldn't stay there. We got to talking, and I realized she was quite bright, so I offered her a job at my company, effective immediately. She was so appreciative, it warmed my egotistical heart, and I felt on top of the world. Foolishly, I also told her she could move out of the shelter and into my guest room, and I'd see to it that she had some proper clothes. Winter was coming, and I hated the idea that she might freeze."

I don't know what to make of this story, so I ask, "Can I get you some more coffee?"

"No, thank you, but I would like some water if it's no trouble."

When I return with the water, he continues, "I won't go into all of the details of what happened over the next couple of years, but suffice it to say that I was smitten, and she had me wrapped around her little finger. I bulldozed her into a job on the custodial staff because the HR department refused to give her anything else without experience or a background check. But I insisted. She seemed so shy and reticent at first, but later I came to realize that was all part of an act. I fell for her hook, line, and sinker and soon she was sharing my bed rather than using the guest room. It was the happiest I'd ever been, and when she told me she was carrying my child, I tried to rush her to City Hall to marry her. But she didn't have a birth certificate. We were never legally married because although I tried and tried to locate her birth records, I never could. She had given me the wrong city, wrong state, and the wrong year of her supposed birth, so I came up with nothing."

This brings up one of my biggest questions. "Why isn't your name on my birth certificate?"

"It is, dear one. Why would you ask that?"

"Because my mother told me... Oh crap. Another one of her lies? I guess I never saw my real birth certificate."

"I assure you I have a copy of it in my safe. Your mother must have doctored the one you saw. And, by the way, on the original one your legal name is Petra Feeney Harvey, but she seemed to see fit to obliterate Harvey from your identity. From what I gather, she went to some pretty ruthless lengths to erase me from your life."

"Why would she do that?"

"Selfishness and greed, Petra. After you were born, and I

didn't expect her to keep working, she became bored and developed a serious gambling problem. She racked up debts all over the place and didn't want to spend time with you at all. I hired the best nannies I could find and spent as much time with you as work would allow, but I had employees to worry about and this company to run." He shakes his head. "I made some stupid mistakes."

"I'm sure you were doing your best." I feel the need to wipe the look of defeat off his handsome face. The more I've studied him, the more I realize I look like him, and I find that comforting.

"Thank you for your faith. Around the time you turned two, she was in so deep with debts to some terrible people, and I swore to her that was the last straw. I wanted full custody, and I would buy her a house somewhere far away. I was thinking Las Vegas might be her speed. I offered her a large yearly stipend. That seemed like a generous offer since she hadn't exhibited any maternal instincts whatsoever. But..." he pauses. "She suddenly turned as possessive as a wild animal. She wanted full custody herself and swore she'd expose me as a child molester and ruin my reputation if I challenged her. She somehow produced her long-lost birth certificate proving that she was only *sixteen years old* when I took her in. Naturally, she'd told me that she was twenty-two, and I'd believed her. From what you tell me about the doctored certificate she showed you, however, the one she produced for herself was probably a clever fake.

"Anyway, so now I had to worry that I'd have to register as a sex offender and my company would collapse. Or worse, I'd end up in jail. I'd had a baby with someone who was still a teenager.

"I paid her debts to make her happy and bargained with her. She was to avoid certain illegal gambling establishments, and she would move out of my house and into a property I would pay for because by then I couldn't stand her. And yet I still craved her. I am a weak man, apparently." He hangs his head for a moment.

"She did not want to move out of my house, but when I said that wasn't an option, she insisted on staying in Chicago where she claimed to have friends. I never met any of them though. I put the condo I bought in your name, but as a minor you needed it in the name of your custodial parent as well. I now understand that she sold the property and absconded with those funds a couple of years ago.

"She seemed like such a hideous influence on you. I continued to hire nannies who loved you, but only barely tolerated your mother, which meant they didn't tend to stick around for long. I enrolled you in the best schools, but your mother's vindictive nature continued. It was as if she needed revenge for me booting her out, and you were her pawn. Each time I demanded to see you, she would threaten to expose my sins all over again, and her stories would grow in magnitude about how I supposedly forced her into becoming my sex slave and repeatedly raped her in vicious ways. I assure you,

Petra, I never raised a hand to her and treated her with utmost respect while we were living together. You were conceived in love. But the shame and fear of her grotesque stories and what they could do to me ate at me daily. I was afraid to get a court order to see you for fear of the lies she would spew to keep it from happening. I'd created my company from nothing with hard work and had loyal employees who depended on me to keep it afloat. I couldn't let her ruin all of us.

"Finally, I made the ultimate heartbreaking bargain with her that I would stay away from you as she wished and pay for all your expenses, so long as she got herself a job and made some contribution to your upbringing as well. She readily agreed to that and then promptly started leaving the country for extended trips. When I tried to see you at boarding school, I discovered she'd left explicit instructions that I was a terrible man who could not be trusted in your presence. I was not permitted access to you. She had them snowed, and I was not allowed on campus—even though they were all too happy to cash my checks. I'd have removed you and put you somewhere else if I could have gotten to you. Plus—I didn't want to disrupt your life any more than necessary. The school assured me that you were happy and had friends there.

"It was a foolhardy decision to even show up at your graduation, but I figured they couldn't do much after that."

"I wish you'd shown yourself to me, Dad." I try not to cry. "I wish I'd known."

He sighs. "This probably explains a lot of my dilemma

now. I longed for you, I wanted to be a part of your life, and so I wrote countless letters to you. Letters that went unanswered for so long, they broke my heart. I was sure she'd rubbed off on you and you'd learned to hate me. I should have fought harder to see you; I know that now. But as the letters I wrote went unanswered month after month and year after year while your mother assured me that you were getting them, I began to tell myself you were happier without me in your life.

"Did you know that your first word was da-da? It was one of the happiest times of my life when my precious baby girl called me that."

At this, my father's voice seems to give out, and he takes another gulp of water. I scoot closer to him on the settee and rub his back as he slumps over, looking dejected. His bloodshot eyes look haunted as he regards me and whispers, "I thought I'd lost you forever, and it was all my fault. My priorities were all messed up. I made huge mistakes, and I made a deal with the devil."

"It's over now, Dad. Now we can spend time together and get to know each other better," I say with as cheerful a voice as I can muster.

"That's just it, sweetheart. We don't have much time. I'm dying."

A lump forms in my throat, and it takes me a moment to force out the word, "What?"

"When you were in Chicago and came to the house, I was at a Swiss clinic getting treatment for the cancer I've been dealing with for a year now. Nothing is working, and this was my last chance. I was non-responsive to the treatment."

I hear my father's words and at the same time I hear the guys downstairs cheering about whatever they're watching on TV… oh yeah… football. I'm glad there is some joy in the world because my corner of it looks pretty bleak right at this moment. I finally have a father. He *is* a nice man who loves me after all. And he's dying.

Why is this happening? I can't even see through my tears now.

My dad looks at me and asks, "Will you come back to Chicago with me? I want you to move in and spend what time I have left getting to know me. I need to know you too, Petra."

I feel my face losing all its color as I consider leaving Weston and Callum for an extended period of time, and I frankly don't like it a bit. On the other hand, how can I deny this man? It's like it's his dying wish. I can't come up with a quick response, so I say nothing. I just wipe my face with the back of my hand and gape at him.

"You should also understand, Petra, that as my only heir, you will be inheriting a rather substantial estate. I have provided for Bing and the rest of my personal staff in my will, but the company and real estate will all go to you. I'm glad it's all in your name and it's ironclad now. There is no way your thieving mother can bleed you dry this time. And I'm also glad to see that you seem to be someone who's worth it. Bing told me a lot about his meeting with you, and I can see that you're intelligent and kind. Will you come home with me?"

Now the tears start pouring down in earnest. "Dad, I… Yes, I'll come up to stay with you, but not all at once. Can I come up for a couple of days a week? I can take the shuttle or fly, and it won't be too bad, but I just don't feel right leaving Callum and Weston for an extended amount of time. We've discovered that we are all a lot happier when we're together. We don't like being separated."

"You have a rather unique relationship then with your landlord and fellow roomer. What's this all about? You'd prefer roommates over me after what I've just told you about making bad choices?"

"Oh, um. No. You need to understand about us. We're not just three roommates. We're in a serious relationship. I'm not choosing them over you, I'm trying to compromise."

"You're in a relationship with *two* men simultaneously?" His expression is skeptical.

I stiffen my spine and say, "Yes. I am in love with both of them, and they are as committed to each other as they are to me. Some people call this a throuple or a triad. I'm not particularly fond of labels, so I just call this us."

"Well. That's… something." He stares at me a moment as if concentrating. "Do they treat you with respect?"

"Tremendous respect. And they demonstrate their love all the time in many ways."

"Huh."

He sounds like me!

"Well, perhaps we can all talk about this together then, if you promise me this isn't some kind of experiment or a wild-oats fling you're having." I shake my head vehemently at him, and he continues. "You said one of them is a chef and the other is a psychologist, yeah?"

"That's right," I say, but I can't imagine where he's going with this. "They are both brilliant and talented."

"Do you know what kind of company I run?"

"Just that it's some kind of investing and that you don't have a website. Frankly, in this day and age, I find that pretty odd, but…"

"I don't need one, Petra. We have a very short list of extremely exclusive clients, and they know us without having to refer to a website."

"Oh?"

"I invest in a few select companies that build exclusive restaurants all over the world. Some are at destination resorts, and some are private clubs, but the one thing that is common is that they are completely top-drawer."

"Oh!" Suddenly, I feel my hopes rising.

"We may just have a place in the company for a talented writer who can deal with publicity and training manuals, not to mention hundreds of other applications, a psychologist who can evaluate the wants and needs of the prospective customers so we can advise accordingly, and a talented chef who can create wonderfully unique menus. Do you know three people like that?" He grins at me conspiratorially.

"You could find us positions to work in our own fields together in your company? That's amazing!"

"It's going to take some hard work and dedication, but the company will eventually become yours anyway. You may as well figure out how to run it."

"And you would trust me with that responsibility?"

"I hardly have a choice, Petra. I won't be around much longer. It will be up to you and your men to see to the future of the company. I'll guide you and give you the best opportunities to learn what you need, and I have managers already in place who will assist you, but this infusion of talent might be just what the company needs. We've stalled out a bit over the past year due to my health, I'm sorry to say."

"How would we do this?"

"First, you'll need to come to Chicago and meet with the various divisions of the company. Your psychologist friend…"

"Weston."

"Yes, Weston. He'll have to meet with the division that evaluates the customer experience possibilities. They've been looking for a psychologist to take onboard for a while actually." He stops then as we hear the sound of the TV turning off downstairs and the voices of the guys sounding like they might be coming up. "Sweetheart, let's table this discussion for a little later. I'd like to get to know these men a little more before we go on, alright?"

"Sounds good, Dad." I grab his hand. This is such a bittersweet moment. I have tremendous hope and terrible grief all rolled into one big ball in my stomach. I don't want to go to Chicago just to watch my dad die bit by bit, but he needs me with him. And this could be the best opportunity—not just for Callum and his future plans—but a way for Weston and me to be involved in a meaningful way as well. I can't wait to hear what they have to say about it.

Forty-Two

It's halftime in the football game, and Bing seems nervous. He's checked his phone a few times and asked us if we thought Petra was okay. I don't really get the sense he's worried about Petra as much as something else, however, so finally I ask, "Do you want to go up and check on them?"

It's as if I've just given him permission the way he jumps up and heads up the stairs. I decide to follow and tell the dogs to follow me so they can go out. Obviously, I could have let them out the back door on this level, but Bing's worry has me on edge, and I need an excuse to check on Petra too.

Callum is in a group text session with his family who are all gloating over the score that Ohio State has racked up over

Purdue at this point. He's grinning and laughing at their comments, so I don't want to make him a nervous wreck too. The irony of it strikes me as funny that they are rooting against an Indiana team because his brother Declan was recruited out of state to play football. Blood is thicker than water, as they say.

When I get to the kitchen, I see that the conversation has taken an emotional toll on both Jameson and Petra. Their eyes are red, and they are gripping each other's hands like a lifeline. If people could somehow manage to look both happy and sad at the same time, Petra and her dad have that covered. I'll let Petra fill us in later as she sees fit. There is no reason to pump either of them for information.

As soon as I register this, Callum bounds into the room all smiles and announces, "I can have lunch ready in ten minutes." He heads for the refrigerator and starts pulling out containers of whatever he has in his mind to fix for us.

"Can I help?" Bing asks. Petra and I get out the cutlery and plates and arrange drinks for everyone.

Within minutes, the dining room table is nearly sagging under the weight of several delicious dishes for us to sample. I'm once again amazed at Callum's ability to rise to the occasion and feed us like royalty. The fare is varied and probably not originally meant to all go together, but with two extra mouths to feed, Callum needed to punt.

For the first few minutes of the meal, we all confine our comments to flattering Callum for his creative cooking.

Jameson isn't eating a whole lot, but he is definitely sampling everything and asking lots of questions. He acts like he's giving a final exam the way he's probing Callum about the sources of his ideas and his experience in culinary school. Callum loves to talk about his cooking, so he dives in, answering each question with zeal. He seems to have forgotten that halftime is over, and the football game is back on by now. I hope his family understands that he's missing it for Petra's sake.

But then, strangely, Jameson turns his eagle focus onto me and starts to ask questions about my psychology degrees. He seems quite happy to hear that I have a Ph.D. and that I not only have private clients whom I counsel, I also consult with businesses and work closely with corporate HR departments. He narrows his eyes at me and nods, looking especially pleased.

"I understand you're both in love with my daughter," Jameson announces, startling us with his blunt statement.

"I… ah… yes sir. That's true," I say with as much sincerity as I can muster.

Callum just blinks at him until Jameson also stares him down, and he answers, "Yes, we are." He sits up straighter and continues, "and also with each other."

I steel myself for a challenge, but Jameson's reply catches me off guard. "Good. Then perhaps you will all consent to coming up to Chicago. You can all live in my house—permanently if you choose, and your dogs are welcome. You know there is plenty of room, and your privacy will be ensured. I'd like for you all to learn the ropes of my company because soon it will become Petra's responsibility, and I'd love to know that she has your full support. There are jobs waiting for all of you to start as soon as possible. You, Callum, can exercise your culinary skills by creating menus for some of the top restaurants in the world and training chefs at the same time. Weston, you can be in charge of creating the right atmosphere and work climate for both employees and patrons of those restaurants, and Petra will use her writing skills in countless ways as she works with marketing and prepares technical documents and training manuals. All of these aspects of the business will come together to create restaurants that have the right feel to become a destinations worthy of diners who expect the finest. I see the three of you as the dream team with your creativity and brains. We need a shot in the arm from brilliant, creative young minds."

My jaw probably drops a foot, and I'm speechless, but Callum is a little more together and asks, "Thank you for your faith in us, but may I ask what's the rush? We have responsibilities and lives here in Indiana." He looks at me and then Petra. "Or—at least I have responsibilities here. The others are more portable, I guess."

Petra quickly looks down at her lap and sniffles softly as her father studies Callum and then me and answers, "The cold, hard truth is that I don't have much time left. I desperately want to see my company in the right hands, and I think that

Petra and you young men have what it takes to do the job. I won't be leaving you alone with this task; I have loyal employees in place who will serve to advise you. But the unfortunate truth is, I have an incurable cancer that won't leave me alone, and I'm out of options." He clears his throat. "I am not so selfish that I want to take Petra away from the two of you so that I can subject her to watching me die. I want to spend the time getting to know each other and building something positive for your futures. If you both love Petra as you claim, I hope you mean to *have* a future with her, and this isn't just some game you're playing temporarily."

"Wow," I say. "Of course we expect to have a future with each other. But now I completely understand the mixed emotions we saw on your faces when we came upstairs. This is… ah… hard to take in. It's exciting, and the possibilities for a what you are proposing are endless, but to realize that after all these years, you two are together again just to essentially say goodbye is rather… ah… heartbreaking. I'm flattered and so, so sorry, Jameson."

"I couldn't say it better myself," Callum agrees. "Thank you for considering us for something so important."

"I've learned the hard way," Jameson answers, "that nothing is more important to me than my daughter and her happiness and well-being. My priorities have not always been set in the right order, but there is nothing like facing your mortality to give you the kick in the ass you need to get it all straightened out." He looks exhausted suddenly and asks, "Do you think you could show me somewhere that I could lie down for a bit of a nap for a while? I think Callum has a football game to get back to, and I'm beat. We can resume this conversation later."

"Thank you. I'll take you up to my room," Callum tells him. With Bing's watchful help, they head for the stairs.

Petra stops them suddenly when she asks, "Oh hey, Dad, did you happen to give me a wonderful set of first edition Winnie the Pooh books in a beautiful box when I was little?"

Jameson turns with a happy smile on his face and says, "I did. You always loved stories, and they seemed just right for you. Aren't they something?"

With her shoulders drooping, she answers, "Thank you so much for the thoughtful gift, Dad. They were my prized possessions until my mother stole them. I'm trying to find them now, but so far, I'm having no luck."

All of the air seems to whoosh out of Jameson as he says, "Oh, sweetheart, I'm so sorry. I'll see what I can do too." He turns back around shaking his head muttering what sounds like some rather creative obscenities.

What a day. My head is spinning.

Forty-Three

CALLUM

WELL, THAT WAS A SURPRISE. MY HEAD IS SUDDENLY FILLED with notions of producing magnificent dishes and overseeing menus for fancy restaurants. Could this be for real? It sounds like the best of everything. I would get to create and advise without the repetitious, stress-filled work and late-night hours.

Bing and I get Jameson settled—the poor guy could barely make it up the stairs. I briefly considered offering him the living room couch when I saw how labored his walking had become, but I sensed he wanted some privacy as well as a rest. He made it up just fine in the end. I have to hand it to him. He has a very strong will. Petra must get her backbone from him.

Thank God she's nothing like her thieving disgrace of a mother.

As we head back down to the football game, I ask Bing, "How long have you worked for Jameson?"

"Oh, gosh. About ten years now, I guess."

"Wow. So you know him really well?"

"I do. I take care of his household and drive for him, plus I'm his personal assistant outside of the office. He has an assistant at his company who does that side of his life, but my duties are more home-based."

"You live there with him?"

"Yes."

"If you don't mind me asking, how did you score a job like that?"

Bing chuckles and says, "By becoming part of his collection."

I can't help but frown and look at him questioningly. "Collection of what?"

"People. I'll explain. I was originally hired to work in the lunchroom at the company. It was an easy job I could do while I went to night school to get my degree. The meals are catered in-house every day, and I'd been acting as a busboy and sometimes dishwasher. One day Jameson's phone must have fallen out of his pocket because I found it under the chair where he'd been sitting. Immediately, I told my boss that I had to take it up to his office because I knew he wouldn't want to be without it for a minute. When I barged into his office all red-faced and breathing hard from running, he told me to sit down and have a glass of ice water with him. We got to talking and hit it off like crazy. Long story short… he ended up helping me get my degree in business with the stipulation that I would move out of the dumpy, unsafe boarding house I was living in and come work for him personally. I was skeptical at first that I was some kind of charity case for him until I discovered my job entailed long hours and plenty of hard work. The position has shifted some over the years as our needs have evolved, but I can honestly say that he's not only my employer, he's my best friend."

I sense there is a lot more to this story and wonder why he was living in a bad place, but I've probably pumped him for enough information. If we end up living in the same—albeit huge—house together, I'll have plenty of time to get to know him better. And anyway, it's time to get back to Declan's game. I see from my messages that they've scored another touchdown and conversion already.

Huh. Look at me, already assuming we'll all be moving to Chicago to work at Jameson's company. I have to remember—this isn't just my decision alone. It certainly is tempting though.

While I'm watching the game, I'm also jotting down a list of groceries I need to have delivered before I can fix dinner. I fill out the form quickly and get back into the text group with my crazy family. We all love to gloat about Declan's talents. It's too bad Gracie's games don't end up on national TV.

Weston and Petra have finished cleaning up the kitchen, and they join us to watch the end of the game. That's when Bing chooses to import some welcome information.

"In case you were wondering, JAH, Inc. doesn't have anything in their bylaws that prevents employees from fraternizing with one another." He chuckles. "If they had, Petra may never have been born. Anyway, there are a few couples of various configurations amongst the ranks. It's a friendly company."

We all smile and nod, and Petra snuggles closer to me, while Weston throws an arm around her shoulders and gently strokes my neck. He loves to maintain our connection. I truly have hope now that we'll be able to continue what we've created, and my heart feels so full. I just wish it weren't simultaneously breaking for Petra and Jameson. Still… a thought begins to percolate in my brain, and I make a mental note to discuss it with Weston as soon as possible.

After a sumptuous meal, Bing and Jameson retire to their suite at a local hotel. The three of us have a necessary conversation about our possibilities.

"Well, I for one am extremely excited about my personal possibilities with Jameson's company. I have always wondered how a busy chef runs a restaurant and has time for a family. As much as I love to develop recipes and fix meals on a relatively small scale, that's always been a worry of mine. So, Petra, I'm devastated about your father's illness and feel terrible that you're having to get to know him under these conditions, but for myself, I certainly want to embrace the possibilities he's offering me." I look at Weston. "How do you feel about this, Loverboy?"

Weston is quiet for a moment and then speaks. "I… ah… agree with you, Callum. This offer to work with Jameson is the best and worst possible scenario all rolled into one giant ball of emotion for me. I wouldn't mind leaving Carmel—even though I like it here and it's always been my home. I will no doubt miss some things, but I can certainly see doing corporate consulting rather than having personal clients who frankly… ah… wear me down mentally. I think for my own mental health, this would be a terrific change, and I want to support Petra and you in everything you both do. I like Jameson and Bing a lot, so moving up there sounds interesting to me." He looks at Petra. "It's really your decision to make, Petra. I'll go where you want to go. And Callum already seems ready to do it. I'm thinking we'll all have to pass some kind of interview process once we're there, however. The last word is Jameson's, but there are other people's opinions he'll want to take into consideration, I assume."

"You're no doubt right about that," she says. "Thank you both for being incredible about this. I know my dad has presented great opportunities for each of us. I also understand that we're all going to be walking into an emotional minefield. I guess I have to make sure you're ready to watch me fall apart when I ultimately lose the man I've dreamed of knowing my entire life—whether I admitted that or not." She looks a bit sheepish and continues, "I know it's going to be horrible in one way, but I also know I can't turn him down. He needs me, and in getting me, he is also getting you and your talents. It seems like the best way to make a good thing out of a terrible situation. My vote is to go up there one at a time and see how things feel to each of us so we can make the decision as a united front."

♡♡♡

The next day, Petra leaves with Bing and her father to spend a couple of days in Chicago, and Weston and I have the opportunity to start devising a scheme we're both happy with.

Petra's plan is to get the lay of the land as the heir-apparent to the company, so Jameson wants her to meet with several of his top employees. He doesn't want any jealousies to plague her from people who might see her as an interloper, so he wants to make this transition very carefully.

"After all," he tells us, "Petra may realize her talents are in other areas and won't ultimately want to be the CEO. That doesn't mean she can't own the company though." He chuckles at his own observation. "Or we may want to completely restructure the company. The possibilities are endless."

After Petra's successful trip north, it's Weston's turn. And he also gets to spend a lot of time evaluating the company as they evaluate him. All goes well, and he comes back ready to take on the challenge.

It feels odd for Petra and me to be here without him, but we have the opportunity to fall more deeply in love the way Weston and I did while she was gone.

And then finally, it's my turn to travel to Chicago on my own, and I leave plenty of meals for Weston and Petra to heat up while I'm gone. When I meet with the staff of people in charge of advising the prospective restauranteurs, they are skeptical of me at first. I talk a good game, but I can tell I'm not convincing anyone that I'm old enough or know enough to handle such a responsibility. No one seems ready to accept me until I throw down the gauntlet. I tell them all to meet in the lunchroom the next night for dinner and bring their significant other. I promise to wow the socks off of them with an original and nutritious dinner that will seem as sophisticated as anything they've ever tried. I get plenty of snorts, and "Sure, kid" types of answers, but no one wants to turn down the possibility of an exquisite meal or, conversely, the means for bashing the boss's possible new addition to his "collection."

Anyway, I barely sleep that night because of all the plans I have to pull together on short notice. Jameson kindly offered Bing as my new temporary assistant, and Bing rises to the occasion masterfully.

The upshot? It works. They rave. I'm in.

Forty-Four

Weston

I am so excited about this employment venture. I hadn't actually realized how down I often felt after a client session when someone was terribly depressed until I stopped having to do it over and over. So now I've farmed those clients out to my colleagues, and hopefully everyone will be happier and better matched—most of all me. Working on building something new and great is so much more personally rewarding. I hope that doesn't sound selfish, but helping to create a place to relax and enjoy Callum's masterpieces is a wonderful plan. I'm so proud of him, and I'm thankful to Petra's dad for creating this opportunity.

And speaking of Jameson, we've all been living in Chicago now for a month. I thought we'd have to watch the poor man get worse and worse. He's such a great guy, the idea of that gave me more than one sleepless night, believe me. But he doesn't seem to be feeling any worse at all. In fact, his color is better, and he hasn't been napping several times a day like he did the first few days we were here. I am afraid to mention this to Petra because she's grown so fond of him. We all have. He's definitely filling in as a father figure for me, and I don't mind admitting that. I guess I needed one more than I realized.

Moving into the mansion was a trip. The three of us have our own wing. It's gorgeous, but it's going to take us a while to put our own stamp on the look of our quarters. Right now, it's kind of old fashioned, and I sort of miss the basement and movie nights at my house. That couch provided us with some fond memories. But the sitting room is nice, and the bedroom has a new Alaska king bed that Jameson kindly installed for us. It's even roomier than what we used to have, even though we still like to sleep in a big mound of intertwined arms and legs. Plus, we have the run of the rest of the house, and it has a wonderful gym and game room. Callum naturally loves the kitchen and spends a lot of time in there tinkering with recipes. He has his own kitchen at the office where he can experiment to his heart's content, and everyone has learned to readily volunteer to be his taste testers. He's become quite popular. Petra and I were happy to see that he had no trouble giving notice at his job in Carmel. He's as excited as can be for this new experience.

Here in Chicago, Dave has a new best friend. He took to Storm like they were meant to be. The retrievers have always had their own bond, and Gus and Goliath certainly enjoy Storm's company, but for whatever reason, Dave won't leave the big guy alone. Storm is sweetly tolerant of the mini Aussie. I was glad to see that the house—mansion—had a huge yard for them to explore and enjoy. Jameson is pleasantly tolerant of having a houseful of dogs. He adores them, actually.

I haven't put the house up for sale, and I'm not sure yet what to do with it. It'll be a great place to use when Callum wants to visit home, or maybe if we just need some time to get away. I may decide to rent it out and make some money that way. We'll see. There's no rush as long as the property is maintained, and the HOA doesn't come down on me for ignoring it. I've been able to hire a caretaker with my new-found affluence. And speaking of affluence... the three of us are happily making huge salaries that we previously only dreamed of. I'm not even sure what to spend it on, and Petra and Callum seem to feel the same way. What a goofy "problem" to have.

Before we left Carmel, we took a space heater out into the garage and went through all of the boxes from the storage unit again and determined that nothing of importance was hidden in the old clothes. Questions to Jameson about the jewelry confirmed that it was as junky as I'd thought. We loaded up our cars and dropped it all off at the charity shop that raises money and provides shelter for abused women.

Callum had an interesting notion that he and I are discussing off and on when we get the chance. We need to figure out timing and logistics. And we need to speak to Jameson.

I love the idea.

Forty-Five

I can hardly believe the changes in our lives. I love living here—not just with Weston and Callum, but also with my dad, of course, and Bing, and all of the household staff. Rather than seeming like an episode of *The Gilded Age* with servants running around staying out of our business, everyone seems more like a big family. Bing and Bess—who brought us coffee and Bing's bear claws on our first visit—live together in another part of the house, and they are as cute together as can be. I'm quickly becoming good friends with Bess, and I must say it's nice to have some female companionship.

Bing seems like the big brother I never had, and I love him for it. The way he cares for my dad is a beautiful sight. He's never bossy or obtrusive, but he watches Dad carefully to see if he's getting enough rest, staying hydrated, and eating. Bing manages countless issues all day long. Dad's comfort is Bing's mission in life, and his affection for the man is as heart-warming as it is heart-breaking. We're all headed for some unbelievable grief.

My dad is such a kind person. He listens to everyone and always has something interesting to contribute to a conversation. He has a brilliant mind for business and knows about each of his employees on a personal level. I've noticed how he seems to be sleeping a lot less lately, and yet he appears to be comfortable. He must be taking fewer pain pills, though I can't imagine why.

"Are you guys ready to head down to dinner?" I ask. It's been about eight weeks now since we've moved in, and it's an adjustment for Callum to let someone else do most of the cooking. He still can't resist puttering in the kitchen and often adds something to our meals, but the day-to-day cooking is done by Bess. He spends his days at work researching and cooking, so you'd think he'd have his fill of it, but he loves it. Bess never minds having him in the huge kitchen, and Bing can be found in there baking as well when he has the time.

"Let's do it," Weston answers. "I'm starved."

"I hope she hasn't over-salted the sauce," Callum grumbles.

I give him a playful pinch in the ribs. "That was *one* time." I smile when I realize he's laughing. He was just kidding. Bess is a talented and proficient cook, even if she's not quite at Callum's level.

When we get to the dining room, my dad's face is incandescent. He looks so happy I wonder what on earth is going on. As soon as we sit down, he raises his wineglass and says, "I need to make an announcement. So, cheers to great news!" This is out of character. I haven't seen him drink anything alcoholic since we arrived, but we all raise our glasses to him questioningly. He takes a sip and sets down his glass, saying, "My, that tastes like ambrosia."

Dad looks at all of our attentive faces and says, "I saw my oncologist this week, and today I heard back from him. Apparently, the treatment I received in Switzerland was a success after all. It was a somewhat delayed reaction, but he feels strongly that less stress and a better attitude contributed greatly to my body's ability to heal itself with the help of their new drug. I am not one hundred percent cancer-free as yet, but the tumor that's left is miniscule, and it's shrinking. If it does not disappear completely, at this point it's small enough to remove surgically without compromising my health."

We all gasp and cheer in delight. Everyone is shouting their congratulations as I jump out of my chair and throw my arms around him. Tears are streaming down both our faces. He pats my back and laughs happily as he cries with me. We're a mess, but a more relaxed one than ever before. I eventually untangle myself from him and return to my seat.

"So, now that I know I have a chance of being around for a

good many more years, I'm wondering if you fine young people might consider filling up the house with more residents."

"Huh?" I ask. He needs *more* people?

"Babies, Petra. You and Bess are obviously hopelessly in love with your partners, and it's time to make some new lives. Make this old man the happiest person in the world and let me watch your beloved children grow up. If you want to get married first, we can arrange that, and I'd love nothing more than to proudly walk you down any kind of an aisle you choose. I know the logistics might take some arranging and need to be worked out, but in these modern times, I think just about anything is possible." He laughs heartily and adds, "This is Chicago. If I have to pay off a judge to marry the three of you, so be it!"

Five sets of eyes are staring at him, and as he waits for a reply, he raises his eyebrows. "Have I overstepped? Oh dear. If so, I'm terribly sorry. I was so excited when I discovered that I actually have a future, I started planning it without consulting anyone else."

As if on some unscripted and silently acknowledged cue, Callum and Weston rise from their chairs and turn to me. Dropping to one knee, they look at me and ask almost in unison, "Petra, will you marry us?" and they look at each other and clasp hands, asking again, "Will you also marry me?"

When all three of us cry out, "Yes!" simultaneously, the table erupts with cheers.

My father toasts to our engagement with a huge grin on his face, and I can't help babbling, "This is the best day of my life! My father is going to be okay, and I'm going to be married to the two most amazing men I've ever met. I never expected any of this, and it's all happening at once!" Thank heaven for linen napkins because I've produced enough happy tears to fill the swimming pool out back.

Bing and Bess seem to be having their own private whispered conversation while we all carry on. Finally, Bing clears his throat and asks, "Jameson, do you think you could do double duty and act as my best man as well as walking Bess down the aisle? You are so important to both of us, and I wouldn't want to deprive her of the honor of your services. You are my true family, and I can't imagine anyone who deserves being called best man more than you."

"I feel the same way, Jameson," Bess says. "You are the best. I would be so pleased if you could do me the honor."

"It would be *my* distinct honor to do that," he says. "And you know I love you both. But I haven't heard of any wedding plans."

"I actually proposed to Bess last night, and we were going to announce it at dinner this evening. We were preempted by your fantastic news, though," Bing says with a laugh. His whole face seems alight with joy, and Bess has never looked more beautiful.

Everyone cheers again and shouts, "Congratulations!"

Bing turns to Bess and bestows on her the kind of passionate kiss you see in movies. Whew! Atta boy, Bing!

"Well, that's settled nicely then," Dad declared in a self-satisfied voice. "I guess you all aren't exactly put off by my declaration of the need for children around here."

"Not at all," Callum answers for all of us. "Actually, Weston and I have been planning to speak to you and ask for Petra's hand the old-fashioned way, and we've been trying to work out how to propose to her in a super romantic way, but… this works too."

"I'll say," I laugh. "That was plenty romantic for me, and I doubt there is anything you could call old-fashioned about this family. We are gloriously… us."

"We should all go ring shopping together," Bing suggests laughing. "Let's do it tomorrow. The jewelry stores won't know what hit them."

I realize I have something to discuss with Callum and Weston—not here at the table, where everyone would probably want to weigh in on it—but maybe tonight. The idea is thrilling. "A June wedding sounds like fun. How *do* three people marry, though?" I ask the table. "And do we want to make this a double wedding?"

Everyone has an opinion, so the dinner passes with a lively conversation and great food. My dad sits at the head of the table looking like the happiest man on earth.

LATER THAT NIGHT, WE'RE IN OUR WING GETTING READY FOR bed. I can't help noticing that Weston and Callum are looking at me with a deeper level of possessiveness and caring than I've ever seen before. They look at each other the same way, and I can relate. I feel this incredible sense of belonging and rightness in the world.

"We're doing this, aren't we?" I ask rhetorically as we slide into our smooth, cool sheets. "We're permanent and it's all real, and it's wonderful." I kiss Weston and then Callum, and they kiss each other. "Do you really want to be fathers?"

"Ah… so much," Weston answers.

"With all my heart," Callum swears.

"I need to ditch my IUD at some point then because I love the idea as well."

"Do it tomorrow," Callum says.

I laugh and counter with, "I thought we were ring shopping tomorrow with Bess and Bing, and I'll need to get an appointment first anyway."

He looks pouty for a moment, then leers at me saying, "Well, then let's practice, even if we can't make babies."

Weston grins and says, "Let's do it Petra's favorite way. Get her used to extra loads of swimmers in there all at once."

"Two in one?" Callum asks.

"Yes, please," I reply.

This time, we take it slowly, bit by bit. There is no rushing to the finish line, just pure sensuality and adoration of one another. Callum, as promised, demonstrates to Weston how it feels to have magic "grabbers" inside of me, and Weston cries out, "Whoa! That's amazing!" After letting us enjoy that for a while, he removes his hand and carefully slides into me alongside Weston.

Callum slowly lets us all relish the feel of loving each other inside my body in such a special way. He strokes in and out with his shaft, pulsating and rubbing against Weston. Weston's eyes nearly roll back in bliss, and he strokes my clit in rhythm with Callum's pumping. Over and over, we groan as we're simultaneously swamped with pleasure. I think about having a lifetime of this type of bliss as my climax overtakes me and floods my senses.

When we're all spent and relaxed, I whisper to them, "I'm so lucky. I get to love more, feel more, do more. This is the life. I love you both so much."

Epilogue

PETRA

I NEVER DID GET MY PRIZED POOH BOOKS BACK, BUT LIFE HAS given me many more treasures than trinkets, so the sting of my mother's betrayal barely hurts anymore. When thoughts about her surface, I do my best to banish them.

My greatest treasure is my family. I have two amazing husbands and two handsome, delightful little boys. My father is healthy, and he enjoys his life immensely. Bess has had two girls, so the testosterone levels in this house are somewhat balanced by that.

I can't say everything has always been smooth sailing. Two years ago, we noticed that Dad was experiencing bouts of severe pain, and we were all silently convinced the cancer had returned. It was a sad time and quite frightening. I was pregnant with my second baby, and my blood pressure wouldn't behave under the stress, so I was sent to bed for a couple of weeks. My father had a full physical, and it turned out, thank God, that he had gallbladder trouble. A quick surgery had him feeling fine again. What a relief.

The other issue has been that even though he loves everyone here, Weston has had a harder time adjusting to constantly living around so many people. His upbringing was a lot more solitary than Callum's, and I was used to multiple roommates, so it wasn't so crazy for us. But Weston needed to find some alone time for himself now and then. Our solution was to designate the mansion's library as a quiet space for anyone who needed a respite from the cacophony of so many residents and babies under one roof. Weston doesn't retire to the library that often, but when he has something important to think about—or his ears get tired—he certainly uses the option. So do I once in a while when it's all too much. About the only one who never uses it is my dad. He thrives on the activity and noise. If he wants something from the library, he'll take it out to a more well-used area of the house.

Weston finally decided to sell the Carmel house when we all agreed that there was no going back to it. He took a few mementos out of the house and then sold it furnished to a couple being transferred from another country. They were thrilled to have it ready for them to move their family in. Callum and I wondered if Weston felt sad about losing the house, but his reply was, "It's just a building. You two are my home." Then he warmed our hearts when he took every penny he made from the sale and donated it to a mental health foundation. Oh, that man.

Dad officially turned over the company to me last year, and I was recently featured in *Forbes Magazine* as one of the youngest female billionaires in the country. I'm right up there with Kim Kardashian and Rhianna. Wow. Me? Petra Alister-O'Malley? People are probably wondering, "Who the heck is she?"

I love the work of running the company—and I do have a wonderful support system in place as Dad promised. Obviously, I had to give up ghostwriting to make time for work and child-rearing, but I have started writing my own novel that I may take years to finish. It doesn't matter. I embrace the challenge, and I've come up with a nifty pen name.

Regarding my mother, I honestly pity her. She had someone willing to love and cherish her. A man who'd have given her the moon. For her own warped reasons that I'll never understand, she tried to grab it all for herself, and in doing so she alienated everyone who could have loved her. Her priorities are so messed up. Weston says she's a sociopath. She certainly is a sad excuse for a human being. Some days I worry she'll show up at the door demanding her share of whatever she's determined she's owed, but the reality is, we're far too covered in security for that to ever happen. I hope. Though I don't honestly give her a lot of real estate in my brain, I've wondered now and then if she saw the *Forbes* article. I fantasize that she is sitting in a seedy bar somewhere like Amsterdam and sees a familiar face on the cover of the magazine that was left by a patron, and she grabs it and starts to plot how to get to me and cash in.

Eh! Probably not.

But… today is a beautiful spring Sunday afternoon. The sun is warm, and the flowers are blooming, so we're planning to take the children outside to play. We have toys and snacks and lots of love to share.

The dogs will love it too.

It's going to be amazing.

The End

Interested in more MMF stories?
Check out Books by Ariella Talix after the acknowledgments.

Acknowledgments

I read a lot. And lately, I've even been reading more than usual. I've read some fantastic books, some good books, a couple of real duds, and some that were almost great except for something that made me think "huh?" here and there. But in all cases, I studied them and tried to learn something, even though I do not expect every book that is written to be exactly to my taste. So I sincerely want to thank all of the romance writers out there who toil over a computer day in and day out for our collective reading pleasure. It's largely a thankless job, frankly. With book piracy on the rise and cuts in royalties, most writers honestly make diddly-squat. I'm proud and excited by the fact that *all* of my books continue to be read, especially considering the competition. Each and every time a book sells or pages are read, it's like a gift to the author, and we love you for it.

If you're familiar with my books, you probably noticed a distinct change of style with this one in that I switched from third-person, omniscient narrator, and past tense into alternating POVs in first-person, present tense. It was basically an experiment to see if I felt I could tap into the characters' emotions better. I welcome your comments and observations no matter whether you loved it, hated it, or felt indifferent. My next project is another historical romance in the "Hearts of Gold" series in the early California days, so I will not continue this style for that one, but for future contemporary books, I'd love to know how people reacted. ariella@ariellatalix.com Whether I hear from you or not (though I hope I do), thank you for reading this book and for continuing to download and purchase my stories. Without the support of readers, it would all be for nothing. Thank you from the bottom of my heart.

Thank you to all of the bloggers and ARC readers who leave early reviews. Those make a big difference in the success of a new release. I appreciate each and every review.

Always worthy of high praise, my editing and creative team rocks…

It starts with my extraordinarily talented cover artist, Dar Albert of Wicked Smart Designs. She is wicked smart and wildly talented—often coming up with exactly what was in my imagination only *way* better. I think the cover of this book is nothing short of genius, and it helped me write the book. I love this cover so much; I want to give it a hug.

Next in line is my delightful beta reader Susan whom I *finally* got to meet in person after several years of friendship online. I'm thrilled to say that Susan is just as sweet, funny, and beautiful in person as I'd expected. She is the first one to set me straight when I've made an error, need to expand a scene, or make no sense. Hey—it happens! ;) Thank you to Susan for finding plot holes and general weak spots. And thank you for being awesome.

Then Amy Maranville of Kraken Communications takes over when I send her what I'm always sure is a perfect manuscript. Oh, the ego of an author! Amy has wonderful ideas and gently sets me straight, making the process fun.

And then the person with the last-but-not-least input is Mattie Davenport of Davenport Edits who does the final proofreading and weighing in with her insightful opinions. I love working with Mattie. It may take a village to raise a child, but an author also needs their own village of helpers to launch a book. My most sincere thanks to these fine people. I would be lost without them.

Two other people I need to thank for their helpful promotional work are Colleen Noyes and Anne Victory. They both work tirelessly and diligently to get their jobs done, and they have made a huge difference in the success of my books.

I've met so many wonderful authors over the past years, and they are full of encouragement and advice for one another. It's a terrific community actually. But at the very top of my list are my author besties Ava Cuvay and Sutton Bishop. They are always ready for a night out for dinner and a few adult beverages while we discuss "business." I don't know how we all got so lucky to be living in the same small town. There must be something in the water that promotes creativity.

Group Hug was going to be my first true standalone book,

and I planned to keep it that way until I realized there were many subplots that can turn into more stories. Bing Ma might start to keep me up at night begging to have his fascinating story told. Also, I'm writing part of an anthology with the Kentuckiana Authors that will raise money for pancreatic cancer research, and my novella not-so-surprisingly became a spin-off from *Group Hug*. The anthology will be released in November 2024 and is called *Wild Cards*. My novella is *Jack of Hearts*.

My earlier book *Just Curious* was also going to be a complete standalone until I had to make them friends with the characters in *Compelling Urges*. Sometimes these pesky players know best, and they boss us authors around until their stories are made public.

It was fun to bring the setting for *Group Hug* back to Indiana after wandering through Kentucky and California for a while.

One of my dear friends tasked her fifth-grade class to come up with a name for a friendly golden retriever for my book. The names spanned from the sublime to the ridiculous, but the kids threw themselves into the project with their whole hearts, and I love them for it. Obviously, that is where the name Gus came from. As soon as I read that one, he was named. Maybe someday when they are adults, the kids will read the book and remember the project, but for now, it was done under the cloak of invisibility from them. They didn't seem to mind.

Dave and Goliath's names were simply products of my weird sense of humor, and Storm was the sweet brindle Great Dane I grew up with. I hope you enjoyed the inclusion of the dogs in the story as much as I enjoyed fitting them in. I have the greatest affections for dogs, as you might gather, and I want to acknowledge all of them that I have and have had for showing me the purest devotion in the world. It's not unusual for me to have one on my lap and the other squeezed as close as possible next to me. My girls are both large dogs (Gordon setters), and they love to maintain contact.

In case anyone wonders about the section on gift-giving, all of those scenarios except for the anti-vampire candle were true. "Nana" in the story was based on my own grandmother. I have won every "bad gift" discussion I've ever had. I'll never understand her thinking, but she was certainly entertaining.

Finally, I need to thank my family. They understand and encourage my need to create things out of thin air. My husband and son are also two wildly creative people, and my husband is the best person in the world to bounce ideas around with. We may have different opinions, but the discussions are always productive.

Thank *you* from the bottom of my heart, dearest reader, for reading my book.

Books by Ariella Talix

Every book is a standalone story with no cliffhanger.

Each series is more fun when read in order, however. Often characters show up again.

<u>Contemporary Romance</u>

The Drummonds:

<u>Porter the Importer</u>

Make Believe

The Artist

Lovers in Louisville (Spin-off from The Drummonds):

Save Her

Saving Him

Savor This

<u>Contemporary MMF Romance</u>

The Perfect Number (Spin-off from Savor This):

The Rule of 3

The Passion of 3

Living the Fantasy:

Just Curious

Compelling Urges

Standalone:

Group Hug

<u>Historical MMF Romance</u>

Hearts of Gold:

The Golden Rush

Fiddle and Fire

Book #3 coming in 2024